what
we see

ALSO BY CHARLENE CARR

A New Start Series
Skinny Me
Where There Is Life
By What We Love
Forever In My Heart
Whispers of Hope

Behind Our Lives Trilogy
Behind Our Lives

Standalone
Beneath the Silence
Before I Knew You

What
We See

A Tale of Life and Love in
Three Parts

BOOK TWO OF THE BEHIND OUR
LIVES TRILOGY

CHARLENE CARR

Published in Canada by Coastal Lines
www.coastallines.ca

Library and Archives Canada Cataloguing in Publication

Carr, Charlene, author
What We See / Charlene Carr.

Book Two of the Behind Our Lives Trilogy

(What We See, Paperback)
ISBN: 978-1-988232-08-9

This novel is a work of fiction. Names, characters, places, and incidents either are the product of the author's imagination or are used fictitiously. Any resemblance to actual events, locales, organizations, or persons living or dead is entirely coincidental and beyond the intent of the author.

Typography by Charlene Carr
Cover Design by Charlene Carr

First Edition, June 2017

This work is also available in electronic format:
What We See
ISBN: 978-1-988232-07-2

For more information and a chance to join the author's Reader's Group visit:
www.charlenecarr.com

For Sylvia,

A beautiful woman whose words and heart contributed to some of my favourite moments within this story.

.

All these things we hold onto will one day be tossed away: the framed pictures, the old bottles of hotel shampoos, the little scraps of writings—of thoughts and ideas captured tenuously—will pass onto other hands or pollute landfills, just as we'll pollute the earth, leaving our medicated and genetically modified cells to leach out of us.

And yet we hold on.

We hold onto it all, as if by doing so we hold onto ourselves.

We tell ourselves a story: We matter. This matters.

What uselessness.

What beauty.

CHAPTER ONE

Kali put her hand out and felt for the alarm. One smooth motion to the left and the sound of smooth jazz evaporated from the room. She took a deep breath, aware of the air swooshing through her nostrils then escaping the same way. Roll to the side, right foot, left foot, stand. She shifted her head to scan the space—to the right, where light from the window crept around the curtains, the darkness had a red tinge to it. To the left, all was black, empty. Back to the right and the slight sounds of the outside world became clearer: cars driving by, a dog barking. She tilted her head. Her upstairs neighbour, awake before her, shuffling around. She suspected he was wearing slippers. Rubber-bottomed slippers.

Kali shivered. The early fall made its way into the room. She turned, arm out. One, two, five steps and she was at the closet. Her favourite house sweater felt different than the others. Soft, smooth. She pulled it from the hanger and threaded her arms, letting the warmth wrap around her.

There. Not so hard.

She smiled and took another breath, turned. From here,

four steps to the door. She was sure of this but kept her arm out anyway. Not that she should even need to count steps by now. She should just know. One, two, her hand hit the door. Four steps when the door was closed. Two and a bit when opened, which further explained the chill. She'd left the bedroom door open last night in case Theo needed her again.

Kali made her way down the hall, her fingertips trailing against the wall. At Theo's room, she yearned to look in on him, see him lying there curled up, chest rising and falling like waves against the shore. Instead she listened, hearing nothing. She stepped into the room, softly, and there it was, the barely audible sound of his breath. Her shoulders relaxed and she crept back into the hall.

In the living room the light hit Kali, promising a day of sunshine. She turned to the brightness and let the rays caress her face, savouring it. Would she have even noticed before? And was it worth it, this small moment of awareness?

Kali's stomach clenched. Her brow furrowed. She spun from the light toward the kitchen.

"Ahh!"

Pain radiated through her shin. She clamped a hand over her mouth and clenched her eyes shut. What had she hit? The coffee table? The leg of a chair. She was going too fast. Blind people can't move fast. The lack of vision should be enough to remind her, but old habits die hard.

It was too much; she wanted the game to stop. But she wouldn't give up. Not yet. It wasn't a game. It was a war, and this, her living room, the uncertain path to her kitchen, was the battlefield.

She'd show the tumour who was boss. Show it there was no defeating her. She'd be smarter than it. Faster than it. Use the same brain it was trying to invade to show the monster it couldn't shred her to pieces.

Kali opened the cupboard and pulled out a loaf of bread. Two slices in the toaster. Next came the bowls. Simple. She shuffled two cupboards over. Her cereal was on the left and Theo's on the right. Her throat tightened. She couldn't very well hold both boxes of cereal and get back to the counter without knocking something over. So, one at a time. No big deal. She'd be delayed twenty seconds.

This was the furthest she'd made it without her eyes flashing open, without admitting defeat.

Based on the pattering sound, some of Theo's cereal had missed the bowl. Big deal. She maneuvered to the fridge.

Her grip on her chest increased. Milk or orange juice. She felt the cartons. Lifted one than the other, trying to remember which held more. They had milk every morning. Theo drank some before bed. But could she rely on that? She needed to do better. Needed to have them in specific places, like with the cereal.

Kali grabbed the lighter carton and returned to the counter. Carton in one hand, bowl in the other, she held the carton over the bowl. Held it. Held it. Her arm shook. Her teeth clenched. *Pour the damn thing!*

A trail of sweat worked its way down her neck. *Pour, Kali, just—*

A tug on her shirt and Kali's eyes snapped open. She set down the carton of orange juice and surveyed the array of Cap'N Crunch cereal bits littering the counter. She looked into Theo's confused eyes. How had she not heard his steps? He wasn't supposed to see this. Didn't need to know—not yet.

"Oh, wow." Kali laughed. "Mommy must need some more

sleep."

Theo stared at her. He sneaked his fingers into the top of his cast, a useless attempt to scratch an unreachable itch.

"Or maybe you want orange juice in your cereal?"

His nose scrunched and he shook his head.

"So, milk then?"

Theo nodded and Kali turned from him, her heart pounding against her chest. Milk carton in hand, she filled both bowls and set them on the table. Next came toast. Peanut butter spread evenly, edge to edge, just as Theo liked it.

She took another breath, willing her heart to slow. The experiment was over, with only a bruised shin and some cereal pieces on the counter. No big deal.

For today, she could see.

Kali smiled at Theo. "How'd you sleep?"

He shrugged and scooped a spoonful of cereal, his gaze away from her.

"Good dreams."

No response.

"It's getting colder. The leaves will probably change soon."

He picked up his toast.

"Do you remember last year when the leaves changed colour? You loved it." Kali stared at him as he took another bite.

"Theo."

Her hand clenched on the table as she spoke through her teeth. "Theo, honey." Kali took a deep breath then counted to ten. "Look at Mommy."

Another bite, his head turned away.

"Theo!"

He turned, a scowl on his face.

"Sweetie, what's wrong?"

He stared.

"Can you tell Mommy what's wrong? Is it the orange juice?"

The stare continued.

Kali looked at the clock and sighed. She slumped into her chair. "Eat up. We don't want to be late."

BREAKFAST OVER, KALI mentally reset herself. She wasn't blind. She hadn't lost her job or her license or her ability to run her own life. Yet. And in this life she still led, there was no time for wallowing. She pulled on her scrubs, then checked and double checked her and Theo's bags. Lunch. Juice for Theo. Water bottle for her. Change of clothes for him. She slid on her watch. Four minutes to catch the bus.

"You ready?" she called.

Theo appeared before her, sullen.

Kali put on a smile. "What do you think Miss Parker will have you do today?" A pointless question, of course. Though sometimes he mimed his responses, he wouldn't today. No way. Theo sat to pull on his sneakers. "Here, let Mommy—" A glare.

Kali stood back, another glance at her watch. She should be driving. Driving into that nice, large employee parking lot. Not catching the bus. Not racing for the bus that got her to work almost a half hour early. Her bus days were supposed to be behind her.

Theo struggled with his straps. He never struggled with his straps.

"Honey, come on."

He glared again and Kali held her breath. This hold-up was intentional. This hold-up was a slap in the face. But he was three: confused and angry. Clearly, he knew something was wrong and was deciding to take Kali's refusal to explain it to him as a betrayal.

So, she'd do the best she could. Kali put on another smile. "Race you to the elevator?"

He looked away. Kali scooped him up and ran down the hall anyway. He squirmed, his little body vibrating with the injustice of having his power taken away.

She understood his rage, but he'd get his power back. Her? Each day it was being stripped. Even the fact that they were late was a sign. Yes, it was her doctor who recommended pretending. But it was also the little things. Looking for something on the counter or bedside table, baffled as to where it went, then turning her head to have it magically reappear. She figured she'd get used to it eventually, this need to compensate.

That was her life now—an effort in compensation. She checked and double checked every drug she administered at work, every report she wrote. She kept her ears focused, so people didn't shock her as they walked up beside her. She did whatever she could to avoid a mistake, to avoid questions. She couldn't have questions. She'd had one slip-up, thankfully unreported, but she was still on probation. Another slip-up could mean letting her go even before her initial three probationary months at Westwood were up. If she made it that long. She needed to make it that long.

Kali took a deep breath. More than that, a slip-up could mean someone's life.

The elevator doors finally opened and Kali rushed through

her building's foyer and down to the street. She stopped at the curb, remembering to not just glance but turn her body both ways to look for oncoming traffic. Clear. She bolted across the street and down the hill to see her bus clearing the corner ... the next corner.

"Damn." She yelled, setting Theo to the pavement. "F—" She closed her eyes. "Fudge."

Theo looked up at her, eyes wide.

Kali pasted on a smile. "Guess we're calling a cab. Yippee."

She grasped Theo's hand and walked back up to the building's entrance. Fifteen bucks. Not the end of the world, but it felt like it.

CHAPTER TWO

In the cab, Kali let herself reset. It was a normal day. Just a normal day. The type of day she may have if her car was in the shop. So, her son was angry at her. Sulking. Good. That was normal. That was a three-year-old's prerogative.

Kali reached down and ruffled Theo's dreads. He slinked away from her and leaned against the opposite door. No problem. He'd get over it. Probably by the time she picked him up from day care tonight they'd be best friends. If not, today he was finally seeing Dr. Richards again. With rescheduling their appointments from day to evening, and the doc being away, it'd been three weeks. Theo would be happy. Thrilled. He loved it there—loved the toys and the attention.

Kali relaxed into the seat and went over her caseload for the day. She had a woman with Alzheimer's, a man with multiple sclerosis, and another who was simply old—no specific diagnosis given. Up until last week, she'd also had a woman with late stage cancer. A sweet woman. A woman whose family didn't visit enough. It was part of the job, of course. But that didn't make it easier. Or much easier. Kali had read to the woman on her breaks, or when there'd been a lull, and the woman would smile, a look of contentment on her face as if the words rubbed away her pain and fear. Not that she seemed that afraid. Kali asked the woman about it once, and she'd smiled. Shook her head and smiled. 'I have my gems,' she said. 'One day, if you pay attention, you'll find yours, and death won't seem such a horrific thing.'

Kali had smiled back, nodded, but death was horrific. Not necessarily for the ones going—though often it was—but for the ones remaining, to see nothing where once a life existed. It was always horrific.

Kali shifted her gaze to the window, soaking in the world that passed by. A single leaf was starting to turn on a tree across from the stoplight. Fall. Kali wanted to see the fall. All of it.

She might not.

Four millimetres in two weeks, Dr. Manning had said. Not insane. Not ridiculous. But based on her last appointment, on the continued loss of her vision, the tumour was growing fast. She'd yet to see the radiation oncologist but would soon. It was the end of summer, when the medical world slowed down. Once she saw him, she'd have answers. Hope given or stripped away or wavering, uncertain.

Kali could have searched for her own hope: poured through medical journals and looked up statistics—but she knew enough not to travel that road.

The cab pulled up in front of Westwood; Kali walked alongside Theo, who refused to hold her hand. She kissed his forehead before handing him over to the day care worker. For that woman, Theo was all smiles. For Kali, he wiped the spot her lips had brushed. The woman, no older than Kali, tilted her head sympathetically.

Another glance at her watch told Kali she was still ten minutes early. Not bad, even with the wait for the cab.

In the staff room, Kali jumped at a hand on her shoulder.

"Lost in thought?"

Kali turned and smiled at Dianne, her mind racing. Was that normal? Odd? Should she have seen Dianne approaching? It was a problem, trying to hide a diagnosis while surrounded by people whose job it was to watch for signs, to note the little abnormalities others would miss. "Yeah. I guess so." Kali closed her locker. "Shift end early?"

"Just starting. I'm on days this month."

"Oh?" Great. Dianne on days. Dianne, who was one of the sharpest nurses on the wing, who analyzed everything and everyone. Not unkindly ... but still. "That's nice."

"Yeah." Dianne seemed to study Kali. "So, something weighing on you?"

"Oh," Kali slipped into her pristine white sneakers. "Mmm, Theo's seeing the psychologist again today. And he's moody."

"Ahh. He's three, right?"

"Mmhmm."

"Well, it's practically his responsibility to have moody days then."

"You're probably right."

"Better than the twos, though."

"Mmm."

Dianne leaned against a locker. "Anything else?"

"No." Kali put on her best smile.

"Well, one of the other nurses told me Mr. Jamieson had a rough night."

Kali's attention piqued. "Pain?"

Dianne nodded. "You up for it?"

"Always."

And she was. Whether she felt it or not, whether the world around her was collapsing or not, Kali could slip into the zone with the ease of flipping a coin. It was after, when her shift ended, when she slipped off her scrubs, that the fatigue would hit, the sorrow too. She loved what she did. Cherished it. It mattered. But more and more it was wearing on her. Seeing these people's slow demise, she found herself incapable of not wondering what her own would be like.

During lunch, Kali tapped two nausea pills into her hand and swallowed quickly. The pills for her head pain helped, but they made her slower, foggier. She had enough brain fog as it was. They could wait until the night. She could deal with the pain.

She rolled her shoulders and stood. Focus on the job. Focus on Theo—and whatever Dr. Richards would have to say. It'd been almost two weeks since Theo first spoke to Lincoln, and not a word since.

But he spoke. That was good. It was wonderful. Amazing. He spoke and had seen that the world hadn't crumbled to pieces around him.

Kali rubbed her head. Focus on Theo. Focus on the job. Not the pain. The pounding, pressing, expanding pain.

LINCOLN HAULED A HEWN log over to the base of the tree, his muscles aching. Three days and no word. He thought back to that last night, the way she'd looked up at him—hope, fear, affection. The affection was what he clung to. She hadn't been looking at him as a chauffeur, or a necessary means to an end. Of that he was certain.

Lincoln flipped the log into his makeshift pulley and heaved. Again and again, he pulled the rope until the log was level with the tree house's porch. He tied off the rope and wiped his brow.

He wouldn't call her. Not yet. Tuesday was his scheduled day with Theo. So he'd see her then. Them, then. Lincoln scrambled up the ladder and pulled the log over. It was foolish, perhaps, working on this outer wall when the main outer structure was already built. He should be focusing on the inside: setting up the solar heating, tinkering with his methods to store energy, finishing the plumbing ... if you could call the rudimentary system he had in place plumbing. He'd improve it later.

That work took thought, analysis, contemplation. This work took strength. Mindless effort. Physical exertion that captured so much of his focus he could almost forget Kali had cancer. Forget she was losing her vision. Forget he'd promised to be there, whatever that meant, for however long that meant.

He reached out, making sure he was steady on the platform, pulled the log over, removed it from the pulley, and piled it beside the others.

Sweat poured off of him. Lincoln kneeled as the forest's silence surrounded him. He hated and loved this silence. With Romper, barking at the base of the tree, eager for Lincoln to come down and ruffle the spot between his ears, it'd been welcome. Without the dog ...

Lincoln walked to the other side of the house and stared at the smooth water of the lake. Not a ripple. And no rustle of the leaves in the trees. Just silence.

Had he done the right thing? Letting Romper go, letting Kali and Theo in? He'd had no choice. Not about the dog. Not about the mother and her child.

He could almost feel again, the way Kali's hand had squeezed his, the lingering of her fingers before she pulled away. He had no choice. In whatever way she needed him, he'd be there. In a mind whirling with uncertainties, of that he was sure.

CHAPTER THREE

D r. Richards breezed into her office, her smile stretched wide. She glided around her desk and lighted in the chair, smile still strong. "Myrna said you wanted to see me first today."

"Yes." Kali's mouth went dry. Fear covered her. Had she handled this all wrong? Should she have called the office the moment she learned Theo spoke? Would the doctor look at her with judgment, disapproval, disdain? What if Kali had derailed all Theo's progress by focusing on her own problems rather than her son's? "Ummm."

Dr. Richards leaned forward, her smile softer—the counselling smile, the you-can-trust-me smile, the I'm-not-your-mother-but-you-need-one-so-here-we-go smile.

"Theo spoke."

"That's wonderful!" The smile brightened, became more natural. "Tell me."

Kali swallowed. "Well, I wasn't there. It was with Lincoln."

"Lincoln?"

"The man we moved in with. But it was after we moved

out."

"Okay." Dr. Richards pushed up her glasses.

"He said a few sentences. And then nothing since."

Dr. Richards nodded. "Are you happy about this?"

"Of course!" Kali licked her lips. "I'm just worried that it only happened once, and then not again. What do you think that means?"

"It could mean many things. How long ago did he speak?"

"A couple of weeks," Kali spoke quickly, "but we had to deal with the appointment time changing and then you were away and it didn't seem like a good idea to bring him in to see another psychologist, someone who was a stranger."

Another nod. "I can see why you'd think that. I will remind you though, that for big moments like that, breakthroughs, you're always welcome to call in—to get advice, have a quick chat."

Kali's throat constricted. She'd messed up. She fought the welling of liquid pressure building behind her eyes.

Dr. Richards spoke softly. "Could you tell me about the situation?"

"The—?"

"As much as you know, about when he talked. What he said, where he was, what was happening."

Kali swallowed. "I was late." She stopped. "Well, no, I wasn't. But they thought I was. It was a misunderstanding."

"Okay."

"I had actually come early to pick Theo up but they weren't home so I put a note on the door, but then they waited on the stoop, so they never saw the note."

A nod.

"And Theo talked."

"Do you know what he said?"

Kali's chest rose and fell. "He asked if I was coming back."

"So you were late, and he was concerned."

"I suppose." Kali rubbed her hands together.

"And was this in a normal voice? Whispering? Did he speak in proper sentences?"

"Whispering. I didn't ask about the rest."

"It'd be great if you did. Was that all he said?"

Kali looked at her hands. "He said I was sad, that I cried and cried. He wanted to know if it was because he didn't talk."

"I see." The counsellor smile was back, but tighter this time. "And is that true?"

"Is it relevant?"

"It's relevant whether you actually were crying or not. You don't have to talk about why—"

"I was going through a rough time." Kali glanced at the psychologist before returning her gaze to her hands. "Outside of Theo's issues."

"And what did Lincoln say?"

"He said I was coming back. He said he was sure Theo wasn't the reason I was crying."

"Good." Dr. Richards picked up a pen and tapped it against the desk. "And have you talked to Theo about it since? Asked him about the fact that he spoke?"

"I wasn't sure if it was the right thing to do."

"That's understandable." The doctor pressed her lips together. "I imagine the fear of you leaving, of deserting him, overpowered his fear that his speech has destructive power, and he linked a connection between your sadness and his lack of speech, something he knows you're concerned about."

"I didn't want to press it." Kali hated the tone of defence in her voice. She didn't need to defend herself. She was doing the best she could. She blew out a strong burst of air. "He seems to think I'm betraying him when I press him to talk."

"Yes. You've mentioned that before." The pen wobbled between Dr. Richards' fingers, looking like it had become rubber. "Children his age can be very narcissistic, simply because they haven't fully grasped the concept of a world that exists outside of their own scope. It makes sense he would connect you crying and being late to his inability to use his words."

Inability. Kali felt her shoulders relax. This is why she'd pursued treatment with Dr. Richards. Inability, not refusal. Not disability.

"And Theo's mutism is atypical. Generally, it results from severe social anxiety. He has intense anxiety, but not socially. Socially, he's fairly well adjusted."

"The workers at his new day care say he's very sociable."

"That's wonderful." Dr. Richards paused. "I've said it before but I want to reiterate that you did the right thing bringing Theo in so early. Given his age, and the age when this began, many parents would have just waited, said he was delayed. But you know as much as I do that Theo isn't delayed. He's hurting. He's scared. But he has every chance of a normal life. And him speaking—reaching outside his fear—is a very good sign."

The doctor folded her hands on the desk. "I think it's time to introduce stimulus fading."

Kali raised an eyebrow.

"It's a common technique. It's all about setting goals of increasing difficulty for the child to meet. Theo has spoken once, and the world didn't crumble around him. So we have that precedent. *He* has that precedent."

"Yes?"

"So the next step is to encourage him to whisper, which is what he did a couple of weeks ago?"

"Lincoln said it was barely audible."

"Okay. Good. So we start with whispers, then gradually work up to full volume. And each time he does, lavish him with praise. In a genuine way."

"In a—?"

"This Lincoln, is he around? A regular part of your lives?"

"I wouldn't say regular."

"But he could spend time with Theo? Would he be willing to participate in—"

"I can talk to Theo. I can encourage him."

"Of course you can." The doctor's tone was patient. "But so far your efforts haven't been very successful."

Kali opened her mouth to speak but Dr. Richards raised her hand.

"You are Theo's world, or you have been for a long time. It's wonderful that he's built a connection to this man, to some of the children at his day care, which makes this the perfect scenario. I'm not saying you shouldn't try, but Theo talking to Lincoln, it was a lower risk situation. It shows he trusts Lincoln, but doesn't have the same intense bond with him as he does with you. He doesn't rely on him. If something awful were to happen from his speech, he wouldn't be endangering the person he loves and needs most." Dr. Richards looked toward the corner of the room. "You mentioned that your mother, Theo's secondary caregiver, had been practicing words with him almost constantly in the days before she passed?"

"Yes." Kali sighed. "So you think Theo has more fear speaking around me ... in case something bad happens."

"It's certainly possible. Him talking to Lincoln, when he did, shows a high degree of empathy. He was fearful, yes, but his concern for you, along with the fear that something had happened to make you go away, is what prompted him to speak. So presumably, with Lincoln, the fear may be less intense."

"He loves Lincoln."

Dr. Richards smiled. "That's wonderful. But Lincoln is not his mother. His constant. You try too, to help him speak, but if you can, enlist Lincoln. Whispering is good. Working slowly is good. You don't want to scare him."

"Or anger."

"He may get angry and that's okay. I'll work with him here too."

"Should I address the fact that last time he spoke nothing happened?"

Dr. Richards rubbed her finger and thumb against her chin. "I think not. Theo hasn't necessarily made these connections on a conscious level. And, of course, it is possible our assumptions are wrong. We don't want to give him any scary ideas. Rather, let him know it's okay to talk. It's safe. It can be fun ... don't reference the negative."

Kali nodded. This she could do. This made sense. It meant enlisting Lincoln, but it would be for Theo, not her, not because she couldn't handle her own life.

"And as much as possible, try to have a relaxed, joyous atmosphere at home."

Kali tensed. Relaxed? Joyous? More like Fearful. Stressed.

Ominous.

Dr. Richards paused. "You mentioned you've been having a rough time ... is it ongoing?"

Kali swallowed.

"Something you want to talk about?"

"You're Theo's doctor."

The famous nod. "I could refer you to—"

"I'm fine. Everything will be fine."

"You seem stressed. Tight. Tired. Have you been sleeping, Kali?"

Kali clenched her hands.

"Single motherhood is hard. Single motherhood with a child who's struggling—"

"I do just fine with Theo."

"You do wonderfully."

Kali looked away. Why was she so defensive? Why the need to keep the cause of her tears quiet? She had a disease. It was nothing to be ashamed of. Kali looked back at the doctor. But the more people who knew, the more real it seemed. It was already real enough. Kali smiled. "Joyous and relaxed. Will do, Dr. Richards."

Dr. Richards smoothed back her hair. "Well, I guess it's time for me to see our boy."

Kali bristled. Theo was her boy. She smiled and stood. Her boy. Not this woman's.

CHAPTER FOUR

The white walls of the waiting room were pristine. Amazing, with the number of kids coming in and out every day. Dr. Richards would care about something like that—clean walls. She cared about her patients. She cared about Theo. But what was she saying to him right now? Would it help or hinder?

He'd been happier when she picked him up at day care than when she'd dropped him off. Happy, in fact, until she picked him up. She'd watched him, silently laughing with the other children. Chasing a little girl with pigtails then lighting up when he caught her, and turning to run as she chased him.

Then he'd seen Kali and his running stopped. No burst of joy. No rushing into her arms. His shoulders drooped and he walked to his cubby without being asked. Was it just the orange juice? She hadn't even poured it. She'd tried to hide her tears, her tension, as best she could, these past weeks. She'd tried to be his mom, just like always—making meals, taking him to the park, reading stories. But she'd been shorter with him, she knew that. Frustrated with the time it took to decipher his mimes and figure out what he wanted. She'd stopped asking questions for the most part and made decisions for him.

When he motioned for her to watch him on the slide or the climbing bars she looked in his general direction but barely saw. When she read to him or stared at him across the width of the table, it was what she may lose that was on her mind—not what was right in front of her.

Again the pressure welled behind Kali's eyes. Was she so scared she wouldn't see him in future years that she'd stopped seeing him now? Could he tell? Or was he angry at her sadness? Angry his existence wasn't enough to make her happy? Could he even process thoughts like that?

He was three. Three going on four and testy. Maybe his moods were normal.

And now, in addition to figuring out some way to not let her own thoughts and fears pour out on Theo, she had a professional's recommendation to invite the strange man who'd inundated himself into her and her son's life into his recovery as well. Kali's muscles tensed just thinking about it. Letting Lincoln drive her to and from appointments was one thing. Letting him take Theo to the park or toss the ball around was another—that she was hesitant enough about. But asking him to be an integral part of Theo's treatment? What if Theo opened up to Lincoln, started talking to Lincoln, and Lincoln walked away?

Lincoln had changed in the short months she'd known him, yes—he looked less like a homeless person. He'd shown consistency with them. But he still wanted to live in the woods. He was unemployed. As far as Kali knew, with the exception of one party he'd barely attended, he had extracted himself from the lives of everyone he used to know and love and had no intention of changing that.

Yet for some reason, he wanted her and Theo in his life. She hadn't pried before, but if he was going to become the person Theo trusted with his words, if she was going to let him become that, she needed to know more. He could be an ex-con—homeless and jobless because he'd spent the past year in prison. He could be mentally unstable. Or simply unreliable ... with her and Theo nothing more than a passing whim, or some kind of twisted conquest.

She swallowed, old feelings of anger bubbled up. It was clinical, probably, textbook. Little girl is abandoned by father. Little girl's mother parades a stream of unreliable, cheating, untrustworthy men through their lives. Little girl becomes almost-woman. Almost-woman falls in love with man. Man jumps into the ocean with no care or concern for almost-woman forced to be woman too fast and their unborn child. Forced-into-adulthood-woman is abandoned once more. Inability to trust, to have faith, abounds. Now-full-grown-woman decides the only person she can ever rely on is herself and everyone else, men especially, are suspect.

Kali sighed to herself. Well, maybe the whole jumping into the ocean as the means of abandonment wasn't textbook. But the rest certainly was.

"Miss Johnson?"

Kali jumped in her seat. Myrna, Dr. Richards' assistant, stood before Kali, Theo's hand in hers, smiling brightly. "We're all done for the day."

Kali stood and reached her hand to Theo. He took it with a slight smile, and a little piece of Kali felt put back together.

"Thank you, Myrna."

Myrna nodded, smile radiating. And Kali wondered what

her story was. How she could always seem so happy.

Outside the clinic, Kali savoured the feeling of Theo's warm palm against her own. They walked in silence to the bus stop.

"Did you have fun?"

Theo tilted his head back and forth then gave a little nod.

"That's good. I told Dr. Richards you talked to Lincoln."

Theo looked away.

"Did she talk to you about that?"

He glanced up, a shy smile flitting across his face.

"She said she was so proud of you."

The smile grew.

"Was it scary? Talking?"

He looked away.

"I'm really proud of you, too."

A bus pulled up and Theo pointed.

Kali stepped back and shook her head at the driver. "I think probably I should have told you that a long time ago. How proud I was that you talked to Lincoln. How happy it made me."

Theo looked to Kali.

"Happier than a birthday cake even."

His lip twitched.

"With a dozen candles."

The corners of his mouth rose.

"And race cars on top."

He covered his mouth with a hand and gave a silent giggle.

Kali crouched beside him. "I know I've been really sad lately and I haven't been paying attention to you the way I should." She paused. What to say? How much? "Sometimes grown-ups have things that happen in their lives. Big things, and they don't know how to act because of them. They get scared."

His eyebrows rose.

"Mommy has a big thing right now. And it's scaring her. But it's not because of you. It's not your fault. Not at all." She squeezed his fingers. They looked so tiny with the large cast around it. "You're the best thing in my life. The very best thing." She stood. "And I'm so happy Lincoln heard your voice." Kali squeezed Theo's hand. "I hope I hear it someday. That would make me so proud and happy I could burst." She winked. "In a good way. Like confetti sprinkling all over us."

Theo looked away, his brow furrowed. Another bus drove toward them. He pointed.

Kali squeezed his hand. "That's the one."

A LOW RINGING BROKE through the sound of metal slicing into wood. Lincoln almost jumped at the sound. He set down his axe and reached for his phone. He took a deep breath, then another, easing the puffing his work had caused.

Only one person had this number. He stood tall, and a smile pushed its way onto his face, pushing away the exhaustion he'd felt just moments before. "Kali?"

"Hi." Her voice was soft. Hesitant.

"How are you?"

"Oh, fine. Just fine."

The unspoken truth hung between them. "Good. I'm glad."

"And you?"

"Working hard."

Kali's voice fell. "Oh, you at the lot?"

"Yes." Lincoln waited. "Why?"

"I was just—" She sighed. This was the Kali Lincoln rarely saw. The vulnerable Kali, the uncertain Kali.

"What is it?"

"It's nothing. I was just hoping maybe you could come over for a bit. I was thinking pop over for dinner. But I have to feed Theo soon."

"I could come by. Maybe not in time for dinner, but—"

"No. It's fine. Another day. Maybe tomorrow. Or this weekend."

"Is everything okay?"

Silence again. "I saw the psychologist today. At last."

Lincoln's chest filled. "I'll come tonight. I'll be there in an hour."

"It's not like it's an emergency or anything. I just wanted to talk to you." A pause. "Tomorrow will be fine. Why don't you just come tomorrow?"

"See you soon." Lincoln hung up before Kali could tell him not to come. Then he remembered what he'd been doing for the past ten hours. Sweat and dirt coated him like a second layer of skin. He stripped off his clothes and ran to the lake. A soap-free dousing would have to do. Lincoln gasped as the frigid water hit him. He scrubbed himself down as best he could, noticing the way his arms and torso felt more like they'd used to—hard, defined, unlike the softness his months of misery after leaving Montreal had produced. He stepped out of the lake and shook the droplets off of him, feeling like an animal. A strong, eager, excited animal. Kali had called.

Kali needed him. Maybe just as an ear to talk, maybe for Theo. But she needed him.

CHAPTER FIVE

When the door opened Kali was wearing an embarrassed smile. She stepped out of the way to let Lincoln in.

He smiled back. "Sorry I took so long. Realized I needed a wash."

"No problem." Kali waved a hand, dismissing his words, not looking at him. Had her sight worsened?

"Are you okay?"

"Fine." A glance up. Eye contact.

Lincoln's chest released. "Good, so—" They stood awkwardly, a foot apart in the small foyer. "What'd the psychologist have to say?"

Her gaze kept to the floor. One breath, two. Her chin rose—this was the confident Kali now. The determined Kali. "Come in."

Lincoln followed her to the living room where she sat on the armchair, leaving the couch for him.

"Dr. Richards thinks Theo's progress would be best served if you joined in. She believes he's likely to be more comfortable exploring his voice with you than with me."

A puff of air escaped Lincoln.

Kali's eyebrow rose. "This is funny?"

"No, no." Lincoln was the one to wave his hands now. "I just thought ... I don't know what I thought, but you seemed so serious. Did you think I'd have a problem letting Theo, uhh, explore his voice with me?"

"No." Kali's chin stayed raised. Her throat convulsed. "I may have a problem with it."

Not this again. When would the woman trust him? Lincoln pushed out a closed-lip smile. "Okay."

She crossed one leg over the other and leaned toward him. "I don't know you, Lincoln."

"You know I'm here. You know I come when you call," a laugh, "in a completely non-puppy-dog way, of course."

Kali didn't grin. "You have to admit you're not a typical ... well ..." her expression flickered. She pulled back her shoulders. "It's weird. The way you live, the way you present yourself to the world."

Lincoln clenched his jaw but smiled. "Some of the most successful, interesting people throughout history were weird too."

"And not well-adjusted. Not reliable."

"I'm reliable."

"And if you're not? If Theo starts relying on you? Starts having progress with you, and you flake out on him?"

Lincoln turned from her and shook his head. He got that she was nervous, got that this was her son in the balance, but—"Haven't we had this conversation before?"

Kali gave a quick nod. "That night you said you felt shackled, digging your grave ... But it had to be more than that. I need to know more. I need to know what happened to make you the way you are. I need to assess the likelihood of it happening a—"

"My life fell apart."

"What?"

"My girlfriend, Lucy, she left me. For my brother. For my brother who's been the closest thing I've had to a father for the last decade. The same brother I worked for." Lincoln's words came out clipped, fast. "They'd been sleeping together behind my back for almost three years. And her unborn child who I stupidly, rashly suggested she should abort, died the same day of the leaving, the same day I found out the baby likely wasn't mine."

Her throat convulsed again.

Lincoln shrugged. "I was wrecked. Losing it all like that, losing the two people who—" he stopped. "Feeling the fool and still trapped in a life I hardly even remembered choosing. They, the two of them, just ushered me into the life—into the clothes, and the expectations, and the meetings ... And I couldn't figure out why. Why keep their cheating a secret all those years? Why lie about it all?

"I lost ... it, the desire to live, to try. And the questions, the anger, the ... hurt. It made me a mess. There was this massive client meeting. I arrived twenty minutes late, fucked up my presentation." Lincoln raised his hand, thumb and forefinger barely touching. "As a result, we came this close to losing a multi-million dollar client and the axe had to fall somewhere to keep them. So my brother, my brother who'd cuckolded me, even though he could have had almost any other woman he wanted, brought that axe down on my head."

Kali's brow furrowed.

Lincoln stared at her as he breathed, waiting. "That

enough explanation for you?"

She shook her head, the movement barely detectable. "I'm sorry."

Lincoln looked away, his chest tightening, his eyes burning.

"You wanted to abort the baby?"

Lincoln whipped his head back toward Kali. This is what she clung to? Her chin was still high, her shoulders back, but her face had softened, a little 'v' resting between her brows, her eyes trained on him. Of course it was what she clung to.

"Only at first."

"Because you thought it might be your brother's baby?"

Lincoln shook his head. "No. I only found out about that after. We had a plan. I was just getting where Lucy wanted me to be in the company. She wanted to move into a bigger place, travel more. I was logical and practical back then. Having a baby didn't seem to be either of those things."

Kali gave a slight nod.

"I changed my mind almost immediately; when I realized what the baby meant to her. When I realized what it meant to me."

An eyebrow rose.

"There was a precedent." A precedent. Lincoln tried not to think about that precedent. Had pushed it away. But from the day he'd jumped in front of that car to save Theo, it'd been in his mind. Not always, but there, floating, making him wonder. He was fairly certain it was the reason he'd jumped.

Lincoln turned to the window, feeling again the shock, the confusion, the way Ginny had stared at him all those years ago—half like the words she delivered were an afterthought, half as if she were daring him to say otherwise. "The woman I was with before Lucy."

Kali shifted. "There was a baby?"

"I didn't have a choice with that one. She told me after the fact that she'd aborted it. She stared at me like it was nothing. Said having a baby didn't make sense. She was younger than me. She still had a year left of undergrad and I didn't know what I wanted to do with my life. I thought maybe architecture. I thought exploring. She said we had no business bringing a baby into the lives we were living."

But he'd wanted that baby. Had loved it even after it ceased to be. Had spent night after night wondering what his life could have been if she'd given him a say. Because back then he knew what his say would have been: Have the baby. And if she didn't want it, he'd want it. He'd raise it. He'd figure it out.

"The child would have been about the same age as Theo. A little older."

"Oh." Kali breathed the word.

The sky was a deep navy blue, wisps of gold threaded through the clouds. Lincoln clung to the colours, not wanting to see Kali's face, what she was thinking of him.

If Ginny hadn't made that choice on her own, if he'd had a say, every moment since would have been different. He'd never have been with Lucy. And Joseph, would he have convinced him to join the company? Maybe. Either way, they wouldn't be estranged. No second unborn life would have been taken away. He'd have a different life. A better life, maybe.

"If it meant so much to you," Kali's voice was quiet, cautious, "why would you have told this other woman, Lucy, to abort—"

"I had to tell myself it made sense. Tell myself Ginny had done the right thing. The smart thing. The wise thing. That babies should be planned, wanted, or they'd derail their parents' lives, which would derail theirs in the process.

"It took me a while to come to that decision. Ginny left me a few weeks after the abortion. I don't know, maybe she wasn't as okay with it as she thought and just looking at me brought back the memory, made her wonder. That's how I felt every time I looked at her.

"I saw the baby that wasn't there, I imagined the way her stomach would have started to expand. But I was too weak to leave her. Too in love." Lincoln could see it like it was yesterday, feel it, the way they'd avoided each other's gazes, each other's presence. The way he'd wanted to yell, shout, but had kept silent. "I was angry too. Livid. Hate and love— they can be very intermingled."

Kali took a deep breath. "I know."

Lincoln turned his gaze to her.

"This is about you. Go on."

Lincoln took a breath. "I'm not sure what else there is to say. When Lucy told me she was pregnant, it seemed a bad time. I was just about to score this multi-million dollar deal for the company that would place me in a much more involved position. More hours than I was putting in already in order to finalize it. Maybe after, too.

"Lucy had big things going on at work as well. And I thought she was the one. I didn't want anything to ruin our plan." He let out a stilted laugh. "She was the perfect complement to the life she had me chasing. And I chased it. More than her. I wanted it more than her—though I didn't realize that at the time. She created a monster. One we both ended up hating."

"You think she hated you?"

Tiredness seemed to push on Lincoln. "I don't know. I never really asked why she ... well ..."

Kali sat silent. "So then you lost it all and decided to become a pseudo-homeless person, build a cabin in the woods."

"Tree house."

A brief grin crossed her face. "Tree house."

"Yeah, pretty much." They stared at each other. "So, does that answer your question? Is it what you wanted to know? Am I safe or too high a risk?"

Kali opened her mouth then closed it. "I don't know." She pressed her lips together. "Do you think it's a good sign or bad that your interest in Theo may partly stem from making you wonder about your unborn child?"

Lincoln raised his eyebrows. How was he supposed to answer that?

"And how likely do you think it is you'll have a meltdown again?"

Lincoln put his head in his hands and shrugged. "Generally meltdowns aren't planned."

He could hear the slightest smile in her voice. "Well, I have to ask."

"I've given you the information. Maybe you need to figure that out yourself." He raised his gaze to hers. "Or take a chance."

She bit her lip and Lincoln's focus wavered. What would it be like, to feel that lip between his own?

Kali nodded. "Dr. Richards was talking about stimulus fading. Slowly showing Theo it's okay to speak. Prompting whispers. Praising them. Letting him know it's safe."

Lincoln sat straighter.

"She thought you'd have more success than me. Initially."
Kali took a breath. "Will you help?"

CHAPTER SIX

A warm autumn breeze wrapped around Kali, swirling a flurry of fiery coloured leaves around her. She'd woken without a headache. Woken to Lincoln, who had spent the night on the couch, cooking her breakfast. Woken to Theo, practically bouncing in his seat at the sight of this unusual man who'd entered their lives.

Theo, all smiles. Smiles for her too. When Kali told him Lincoln was going to pick him up after day care, the smiles increased. He mimed tossing a ball then catching it. Lincoln nodded. And when Lincoln dropped them off at Westwood and she walked Theo into day care, he'd wrapped his arms around her.

The difference a day could make.

Now, several hours later, Kali nodded at the bus driver who pulled up to the curb, her stomach clenching. None of her patients had any major issues. The medication seemed to be keeping Kali's nausea at bay. Another clench. She'd left work early knowing she'd managed to do more in today's six hours than many would get done in a full day's work.

But she knew a good day could turn into a bad one in just

moments.

DR. MANNING, KALI'S NEURO-opthalmologist, smoothed back her hair, sat, then swivelled her chair so it was in front of Kali's. She seemed so calm. She smiled. But *seemed* was the operative word. Kali's stomach roiled. The visual field felt different than last time. Less. Despite her growing fear, Kali hadn't asked questions.

"How's the nausea?"

"Not too bad." Kali swallowed. Think of Theo's smile. Think of those beautiful leaves. The fall colours she could still see.

Dr. Manning passed Kali what looked like a flat plastic mask with a hole for only one eye: an occluder, if Kali remembered correctly. "Cover your left eye for me, please."

Kali sat as the doctor performed the examination, answering questions when asked and following directions.

"Switch to cover your right eye, please."

Kali did, and the room all but disappeared. Her heart raced. She hadn't done this, hadn't tested her own sight since the last appointment. But her first reaction was false. The room hadn't disappeared. It was here. Blurred. But here. She could make out Dr. Manning's head, body, the wall behind, the desk. The doctor's features were difficult. But if she focused, really focused—

"Relax."

Kali's chest rose and fell. She answered Dr. Manning's questions as she held up her fingers. Kali wanted to ask how many she got right. If she got any right.

"Okay. All done" Dr. Manning shifted the chair over and held out her hand for the mask.

Everything came back into focus. Clear, wonderful focus. The racing of Kali's heart slowed. Lots of people lived through life with one eye. Lived normal lives. One was all she needed.

A sad smile. A tilt of Dr. Manning's head. "We've reached that point."

"What point?" Kali sat straighter.

"Your visual field is less than 120 degrees. It's just over 90, actually."

Kali's shoulders drooped. Almost as fast she straightened them again. "What do you mean? I can see. I can see fine." She read the chart on the far wall.

"Shift your head to the left."

The chart disappeared. Kali's hands shook. Bile rose in the back of her throat. "So I turn my head back, voila. No big deal."

"Kali." Dr. Manning wore the delivering-bad-news face. Kali had seen it countless times, but it was different, having it directed at her. Usually Kali stood back, watching as the doctors spoke the words a patient dreaded most. "Your acuity in your right eye is still good, but with the decreased vision in your left eye, which affected your visual field results, and—"

Kali stopped hearing the words. It had happened. She was blind. There was no figuring this thing out. There was no getting ahead of it. The tumour was winning. Cancer was winning.

"Kali."

Kali struggled to catch her breath. The room seemed to spin. Her throat felt raw. When had she last had a drink? She needed a drink. Kali scanned the room. A sink. No cups. But she could put her head under the tap. That would work.

"Kali."

First, she needed to breathe. Why couldn't she breathe?

"Kali." A hand landed on Kali's knee. Kali stared at it, wondering where it came from, then looked up into Dr. Manning's face. "Kali, are you okay?"

Was she? She was blind. But she could still see. Some. She could see some. But was she okay? Okay enough to nod. Kali's chest shook as she exhaled a shaky breath. Okay enough to answer. "Yeah. Sure." She paused. "So you're saying I'm blind? Legally blind?"

"No." Dr. Manning spouted the word. "I'm sorry, I ... I'm not used to having these discussions with someone I know. Someone I consider a colleague." She smiled. "I started wrong. You have quite a ways to being declared legally blind. Your vision is impaired, which we already knew. It's now impaired enough that I need to contact the Registry of Motor Vehicles to suspend your license."

"Oh." Kali felt her chest deflate.

"This is hard news."

Kali nodded, trying to calm the tremors that still rippled through her.

"But it's not a death sentence. And hopefully, with treatment, your vision will get better. Not worse."

Another nod.

"You received the date for your appointment?" Dr. Manning shifted out of view. She appeared again with what was meant to be an assuring smile. "You're seeing Dr. Jones in Oncology on Tuesday."

"Yes."

"Wonderful. He just transferred here from Montreal. From what I hear, it was a fight to get him. But, apparently, he's from here originally, so that swayed his decision."

"But my license. You mean my driving license, not my nurses'—"

"Yes. Your driver's license."

That wasn't so bad. It was bad, but—"So, what, you take it today, or ..."

"I'll write a letter to the Registry of Motor Vehicles, outlining your visual field and results. They'll send you a letter—through Purolator usually—notifying you your license has been suspended. You'll send or take it in."

"Okay."

"But you should stop driving now."

"All right." Kali stared past Dr. Manning's shoulder. The painting on the far wall blurred into an array of colours that would make any abstract artist proud. She blinked, and the image became a brilliant garden scene once again. "Can I have some water?"

Kali brought her gaze back to Dr. Manning's concerned face. Her brow furrowed, then smoothed. She put on a large smile. "Just a moment."

While the doctor was gone, Kali looked around the room. She laid a hand on her chest. So her license was gone. Big deal. She wasn't driving anyway. Not unless it was an emergency. She lived in the city. The bus system was good. It's what she used most of the time. She could still get to work. Work. Kali shook with a cold tremor of fear. Is that why Dr. Manning hadn't dismissed her, why she was coming back when the appointment should have been over? Could Kali still—?

"Here we go." Dr. Manning appeared as if out of nowhere with a bottle of water. Kali opened it and let the cool liquid flow down her throat.

"Was there something else you wanted to talk to me about?"

"Your nursing license."

This was it.

"I know you take pride in your work." Dr. Manning paused. "And you've already told me about one instance where your symptoms got in the way with your ability to do your job well."

Fear and pride pulsed through Kali. She nodded.

"Have you talked to your supervisor about your condition yet?"

"Not yet."

"You may want to consider that." Dr. Manning pushed out another smile. She reached out of Kali's field of vision, her body disappearing in a way Kali knew wasn't normal. "I did some research though. Technological advancements and assisted technology have come a long way. Many nurses with visual impairment are still able to practice."

Kali couldn't imagine it. She needed her eyes in so many ways.

Dr. Manning handed Kali a sheet of paper. Here are some links you may want to check out, but I imagine someone at Westwood would have even more information. You should talk to them. Find out your options. But I do believe you've reached the point of having an ethical obligation to let your employers know your situation."

"Right." Kali folded the paper but didn't look at it. A paper meant nothing. 'Options' meant nothing. Westwood prided itself on delivering top-notch care. They hired nothing but the best, and they had believed Kali was one of the best.

"Don't lose hope."

Kali shook her head, smiling. Dr. Manning's eyes told Kali she didn't believe the façade but would play along.

"I probably won't see you again until after your treatment."

"Sure. Okay." Kali wrapped her arms around her middle, her spine tall. "That's fine."

"But if you want to see me, or have a question, you can always call."

"Great. Wonderful."

Dr. Manning's hand rested on Kali's arm. "You're going to get through this."

Through this without being able to drive herself to appointments. Maybe without a job. Probably without a job. Without any secure hope of regaining the vision she'd lost and no guarantee that she wouldn't lose more. Kali stood. "Thanks. I hope so too."

CHAPTER SEVEN

Lincoln pulled his truck into the parking lot at Westwood. It was different, actually parking, rather than just dropping Kali and Theo off or picking them up. He wasn't sure he could do it, get out of his vehicle and walk through those doors. He'd only walked through them a handful of times. Years ago. The thought sickened him. He froze, his gaze locked on the doors, remembering the last time...

But that wasn't why he was here today. And when he walked through those doors he would turn in a completely opposite direction than he ever had before. A safe direction. Lincoln looked at the clock on the dash and turned off the ignition. He glanced to the entry and, seeing no one he recognized, crossed the parking lot.

Inside, the light was bright and inviting, not the sterile, hospital style light he'd expected when he first visited Westwood. He knew the child care centre was to the right and followed the corridor to the sound of children's shouts and laughter.

Windows half the height of the wall revealed a collection

of children in bright coloured clothing with smiling faces. They played on an indoor slide, sat at low tables, their hands coloured in paint, or clustered on a mat in front of a woman reading a story, the book turned toward rapt faces.

"Which one's yours?"

Lincoln jumped at the voice. He turned. The voice's owner was wearing polka dot scrubs and sneakers, her hair pulled back in a neat ponytail. She could know Kali, could know Theo, who sat among the children on the floor, his eyes wide. But how to explain? Would this woman want a lengthy explanation or a simple answer?

"The boy with the dreads and the cast."

"Oh?" The woman shifted her head, an eyebrow raised, then looked toward the glass. "He's precious."

"Yeah." Lincoln returned his gaze to Theo. "He is."

"The quiet one."

Lincoln looked at her again, no judgement sat on her face, just a statement of fact. "Yours?" he asked.

She grinned then pointed to a girl with pigtails in her hair, bright bursts of red and orange paint splattered on a smock, and a look of pure delight on her face as she smeared colours on a large piece of paper. "Mine," she glanced back at Lincoln, "is anything but quiet. She's a terror."

"But you love her."

The woman chuckled, her gaze on Lincoln again, this time with amused curiosity. "More than life."

Lincoln nodded. "Well, I better—"

The woman stuck her hand out. "I'm Cynthia."

"Hi, uh," he met her grasp, "Lincoln."

The woman held laughter in her eyes; Lincoln held back the urge to squirm. She kept his hand a moment more than seemed necessary, then smiled. "It's nice to see you, Lincoln. I'm sure I will again."

"Maybe ... or ... I don't know." Was she challenging him? Questioning why he was picking up Theo? Maybe she did know Kali. Maybe she thought he was sketchy, questionable.

Her smile grew. "Well, I hope so."

Cynthia walked past Lincoln with a backwards glance and another smile. A second thought occurred. Not suspicion, but attraction? It'd been so long since a woman had looked at him like that he'd forgotten what it was. Inside the room, the woman waved to the little girl, who threw her arms in the air, her lips moving like a movie on fast-forward.

Lincoln assessed himself. He hadn't worked at the lot today, instead researching childhood mutism and stimulus fading at the new library. After, he'd stopped by the Brunswick Street apartment to change into his best clothes, the ones he'd bought for his mother's party. He'd been too lost in his thoughts to notice if people on the street had been averting their gazes. But maybe they hadn't, and maybe, without realizing it, he'd taken his first step back toward integrating himself into accepted society.

Lincoln kept his gaze on the woman, who oversaw her daughter at the sink then invited the child to leap into her arms once she was paint free. He didn't know what he felt about her smile and attention. He had gotten used to invisibility. It felt safe. But if he were to help Kali the way she'd need help, he'd need to take more steps. She could lose her job. And there was no way of knowing when she'd find another, or how good it would be.

Not that he needed to think about that. Not yet.

The story ended and a flock of children fled from the mat.

Theo caught sight of Lincoln, his firecracker smile erupting. The boy waved to Lincoln, arm held straight in the air and flapping wildly. Lincoln waved back.

Lincoln sought out the woman who had been reading the story. Would she just hand Theo over? Did Lincoln have to sign him out? Would—

"Hi."

"Hi, there." The day care worker looked up from a little girl who stamped her foot then walked away.

"I'm here for Theo?"

"You're not sure?"

Lincoln stepped back. "I ... uh ..."

"I'm just teasing. Lincoln, right?"

"Yes." Lincoln slipped his hands into his pockets.

"Kali told me you'd be picking Theo up today, and I saw Theo waving at you."

"So ..." A small hand slid inside Lincoln's. He stared into Theo's smiling face. "Do I ...?

"You're good to go."

"Right. Good. Well ... he have homework or anything I should know about?"

The woman held back a laugh, her lips pressed tightly together. "Nope. No homework, tonight. Though tomorrow they'll have some algebra, so be prepared for that."

"Right. Yeah." Lincoln choked on a laugh. "He's three."

"He's three." Another smile. "You two have a nice night." She bent down to Theo and cupped the side of his face. "And I'll see you tomorrow."

Theo released Lincoln's hand and flung himself at the day care worker, arms wide. She caught his hug and returned it, then stood and waved at the two. Theo's hand slid back into

Lincoln's. Lincoln gave it an uncertain squeeze. It felt uncomfortably intimate, picking Theo up at day care, taking his hand like it was normal. It shouldn't. The kid had grabbed his hand a dozen times before. But not like this, in a place where kids reached for their parents' hands. Where to all eyes watching, Lincoln was assumed to be the child's father—or soon to be.

They entered the hall in silence and the discomfort that washed over Lincoln when he'd pulled into Westwood's parking lot returned with a vengeance. He focused on the sensation of Theo's hand in his, on the sound of their feet hitting the linoleum, as he walked past the foyer, eyes down to avoid the chance of seeing anyone who'd call his name.

Outside, he released his breath. Lincoln crossed the parking lot quickly and lifted Theo onto the step of the truck. "You have fun at day care?"

Theo nodded as he climbed into his booster seat.

"What'd you do?"

Theo tilted his head back and forth then held his hands out like a book.

"Stories. I saw that. What else?"

He pumped his arms as if running, then climbing, then let his arm fall in a whooshing motion.

"The playground? And the slide?"

A huge nod.

"And?"

Theo's head tilted again, his dreads swishing. He shrugged.

"Something it's hard to show?

No response.

"Or you don't remember?"

Theo bit his lip. Should this be the moment? The books suggested success may be more likely when the child was active—something about having the body engaged lowering the brain's inhibitions.

Lincoln decided to let the question go. He closed the door and walked around to the driver's side. According to Kali, the psychologist believed Theo had a fear of his own voice, of the power, and that perhaps whispering would lessen that fear. Lessen the power.

An idea formed in Lincoln's mind. He pulled into traffic with a grin. He'd already picked up some new dinky cars—the books talked about reinforcing speech through positive rewards. He'd just figured out how he'd use them.

CHAPTER EIGHT

Kali stood outside the hospital, her arms wrapped around her body. It didn't seem possible how much life could change in just a few months: from bad to worse to actually looking up, actually looking wonderful, then back again to a level of 'worse' she could hardly fathom.

You'll get through this, the doctor had said with an encouraging smile. But they were empty words. Dr. Manning had no idea. Kali willed herself to walk to the bus stop, half-smiling at an old co-worker who passed by.

She would go back if she could. Go back to shift work, to not enough shifts, to the rats. It was better than this. She was a nurse. It wasn't just what she did, it was who she was. When she was taking care of someone she could let go of herself, of the fear, the anger. It was what she was good at.

No matter the bad choices and the crappy facts of life that were out of her control, this one thing was good. She'd made the right choice. Not everyone could say that about their job.

Kali stepped into the bus and nodded at the driver. She made her way to the back and slid into a corner seat, her body turned to the window.

There was hope, the doctor had said. Hope she'd get some of her vision back, but not all. Hope things wouldn't get worse. But Kali had seen when hope failed, when a patient clung to hope then watched it be obliterated by the truth.

Would she get financial support? What kind of job would she qualify for if she could no longer be a nurse? How would she and her son survive?

Kali slipped her headphones on, laid her head against the window, and wondered what she was missing out of the absent parts of her vision. How much of the world did she no longer see? She shifted her head and caught sight of a familiar cart. In the next moment Marvin came into view, his brow furrowed and lips pressed tight as he maneuvered all of his worldly belongings up and over a curb.

Kali straightened. How much of this was Marvin's fault? Not the tumour, certainly, but its massive potentially stress-based growth? If he hadn't been such a crap father, if he'd pulled himself together, supported his sons instead of emotionally abandoning them so he could sit with his own misery, maybe things would have turned out differently. If Derek hadn't felt such a desire to be saved himself, maybe he wouldn't have had such a strong urge to save others. Maybe he'd be here, and maybe none of this would have happened.

But that was ridiculous.

None of this was Marvin's fault. Not the tumour, not Derek's decision to jump into the ocean, not all that came after it …

The bus rounded a corner and Kali turned from the window. She laid her head against the backrest, her teeth clenched.

She reached for her phone and pressed play on the music

app, letting the words of Jean Valjean seep into her as he bemoaned his miserable life. When the track transitioned to a chorus singing, "At the End of the Day," Kali thought about next steps. That's what she needed to focus on, how she'd make life work. And the more she knew, the better she could prepare.

She'd done her job today and done it well. The doctor's words didn't change that, so why should they change it for tomorrow? Still, Kali had an obligation. She looked at her watch. Her supervisor should be at work for at least another hour. Kali would see her, lay out the truth, and hope. Her chest tightened. She'd hope.

THE WESTWOOD OFFICE was bright and inviting with large, calming paintings and plush chairs, nothing like the plain, cramped offices Kali was used to over at the ER. Her supervisor, a woman in her mid-forties, wore a relaxed, helpful looking smile rather than the exhausted, pained one Kali was used to from management.

Alison waved Kali in and motioned for her to sit. "I thought you took this afternoon off."

"I did." Kali kept her back straight and held her hands on her lap so they wouldn't tremble.

"I haven't had a chance to mention it, but from everything I hear you're doing wonderfully, Kali. And the clients adore you."

The corners of Kali's lips rose slightly. "I love it here."

Alison leaned forward and rested her hands on the desk. "What can I do for you today?"

Kali nodded, not sure what else to do.

"Kali?"

"I've been having some trouble."

"The workload too much? It can be overwhelming at first."

"No, no." Kali waved a hand. "It's relaxing compared to the ER."

"Right. Of course." Alison let out a little laugh. "So?"

"With my vision. I've been having some trouble with my vision. I mean I can see you just fine. Perfectly. But ... well ... it's my visual field."

"Your—"

"I have a tumour. A brain tumour. Well," Kali hesitated, "it's on my optic nerve and chiasm. A weird positioning. A rare one."

"Oh." Alison leaned back. "I'm sorry, Kali. Is it—?"

Kali waved a hand. "There's almost no chance it will kill me. Not for years, if ever. And I'll be going in for treatment soon, which is likely to be a huge help. It may even reverse the damage." Kali paused. "But the damage is there and I've had my license taken away. My driver's license. And my doctor thought I had a moral obligation to let you know, considering the type of work I do." She bit her lip. "I thought so too."

"Yes. Of course." Alison nodded, her expression constricted. "Has it affected your on the job performance thus far?"

"No. Well, not that I know." Kali looked at her hands. "Once I almost administered the wrong medication, but that wasn't, well, I was tired and in pain and nauseated, which made my vision blur. It wasn't the loss of vision I'm talking about. And I'm on medication now for the nausea and the pain ... when I need it."

"I see."

Did she? From the look on Alison's face, she saw a

56

liability. She saw a mistake that could tarnish Westwood's reputation for years.

"I appreciate you coming to me about this."

Kali sucked in a breath of air. "Of course."

"We may have to do our own assessments. Determine how much this will affect your on the job performance."

Kali swallowed.

Alison reached for a pen and a pad and wrote something down. There are some people I'll need to speak with. Could you tell me the exact name of your condition?" Kali did. "And the treatment?"

"I'm not sure. My GP mentioned something about radio-surgery. But he wasn't sure either."

Alison made another scribble. She looked at Kali. "Cancer therapy, radiation of any kind ... it can take weeks."

"Yes."

"And there are often a number of symptoms, medication to alleviate those symptoms, which bring their own problems. It can be a rough go."

Kali knew little about the radiation oncology department or what they did there. At times cancer patients came into the ER, but the long-term treatment wasn't something Kali oversaw. She hadn't researched her own treatment options. When it came to what she'd go through, she didn't want to know. Not until she had to.

Alison tilted her head, her smile so concerned, so caring, Kali had to fight to keep her composure. "How are you doing with all this?"

"I'm making due." Kali put on what she hoped was a brave face, and not a furious one. "There are worse things." She gestured to the door. "We see that every day."

"You're right. We do." Alison nodded. "But that doesn't make it any less scary when it happens to you."

"No."

They stared at each other.

"Well." Alison's expression returned to one more representative of a business woman. "We'll get that assessment done as soon as possible. By next week at the latest. Until then, I think it'd be best if you took some time off."

"Time—"

Alison tapped a hand to her chin. "You're new. You don't have any vacation built up."

"No." Kali's heart raced. She wiped the moisture off of her palms.

"We'll list them as sick days. During your treatment, I think it would probably be best to take a medical leave of absence."

"Is that—" Kali's voice caught.

"We have a good plan. But you're still on probationary terms. So—"

"So it's unpaid."

"Unfortunately, yes." Alison shook her head. "It's bad timing."

"I guess I should have scheduled my tumour for a few months down the road."

Alison's lips pursed.

"I'm sorry, I—" Kali fought the anger rising in her. But it wasn't anger at Alison. Life. Just life.

"You'll be able to apply for sickness benefits through employment insurance."

"Right. Of course." Kali squeezed her hands together.

She'd never been on E.I., and hoped she'd never have to be. "And after treatment?"

"Another assessment. Hopefully you'll come back to work."

"Right." Kali stood. Hope. And by the time her treatment was over, her three-month probationary period would be too. What would that mean?

Her legs felt like rubber. Her entire future hung on hope and uncertainties. The room spun. Her throat tightened. She cleared it. "Thank you for seeing me, Alison. And on such short notice."

"No need to thank—"

"I'm sorry I'll be leaving you short-handed." Kali slipped out from around the chair, hating the way her hands trembled, the way her vision blurred.

Alison opened her mouth but Kali spoke before any sound came out.

"You'll let me know when that assessment is?"

"Absolutely."

"Wonderful." Kali backed out of the office. She was out of a job. She was going blind. She held back the urge to scream.

CHAPTER NINE

Back at Kali's apartment, Lincoln waved Theo over. "You want to play a game?"

One large nod.

"Great. And this game has prizes."

Theo's eyes widened.

Lincoln pulled out the pack of five cars. "A good prize?"

The boy smiled, and Lincoln took a deep breath, his own smile wavering. He'd seen Theo's eyes when Kali prompted him to speak. The look of betrayal.

Theo stared at him, waiting, then tilted his head when Lincoln kept silent.

"Okay." Lincoln rubbed his hands together. "The game is called ... lead me on."

Theo stood, waiting.

"What's going to happen is I'll put on a blindfold, so I can't see you. Then I'm going to give you the cars—"

Theo's smile burst.

"Wait." Lincoln held up a hand. "I'm going to give you the cars *but* you don't get to keep them yet. You have to hide them."

Theo scrunched his nose.

"They can't all be in this room. You need to hide them throughout the apartment. And I'll cover my ears, too, so it's hard for me to hear where you're going." Lincoln paused. Was this too complicated? Did it even make sense? "And then you'll come back to me and you'll have to guide me to find the cars."

A nose scrunch and head tilt.

The boy was confused. Of course he was confused. Lincoln leaned forward and spoke just above a whisper. "You'll have to lead me with little tiny words. Whispered words."

Theo snapped away from Lincoln, his head shaking.

"No, wait. Little words, whispered words, aren't like regular big, loud words." He hesitated. "They're special. Safe."

Theo's head shook again.

"Does it make you scared? Talking?"

Theo crossed his arms over his chest.

"I get that. I'm scared sometimes."

Theo's brow knitted together to make a series of v's in the centre of his forehead.

"Remember that day you and your Mommy were outside your old apartment with the rats and I came and talked to you?"

The littlest nod.

"Well, I was *really* scared to come up and talk to you. Your mom can actually be a little scary sometimes."

Theo gave a silent giggle then quickly returned to the frown.

"But I walked over there anyway, and the words just came

out of my mouth. I invited you to live with me. And I was so scared about that. But it was the best thing I could have done because it meant I got to know you, and we got to have so many fun times."

Theo twisted his lips.

A bead of sweat slid down Lincoln's back. "So what I'm saying is that sometimes when we do things that scare us, really good things happen. You've seen it, too. You remember when you were scared to catch a softball?"

Theo nodded, his frown firm.

"But you tried anyway, and now you love it and it's super fun and you're super good at it." Lincoln rubbed a hand along his jaw. "I think it's going to be like that for you with talking too. You're really scared because you don't know what will happen. But just like I knew that catching the ball was going to be a good thing for you, I know that talking will be good too."

Lincoln put a hand on Theo's shoulder. "I get that it's hard for you to believe. So we can start small. Little, quiet words. Like a test. So little and so quiet. And we'll see if you can help me find the cars."

Theo's brow smoothed, but his arms remained crossed.

"You don't have to. And if you really can't we can play with the cars anyway. But if you could trust me with this I think you'll see how brave you are. And how when you talk really good things can happen."

Theo stared at Lincoln, and he could almost see the thoughts swirling through the boy's mind. At last he nodded, a move so small Lincoln wasn't positive it had happened. "You'll do it?"

Another nod.

"Okay. So little words. Tiny ones, like 'two steps,' or 'turn right,' or 'kneel down.' Got it?"

Theo didn't look excited, but he nodded. Lincoln tore open the package of cars then reached into his bag for a t-shirt. "I'm going to tie this around my head so I can't see. Then you take the cars and go hide them. When you come back I'll stand and do a few spins, and we can start."

Lincoln folded the t-shirt lengthwise until it was just wide enough to cover his eyes. He brought the fabric to his face and secured it tightly. "Okay. You take the cars and hide them around the apartment ... they don't need to be tricky spots because I can't see."

Silence.

"Theo?"

Plastic crinkled. A clatter. One or two cars hitting the coffee table. Feet padding down the hall.

Lincoln sat with his hands on his knees in the dark. After a few moments, he could feel the pulse of the blood pumping through his body—in his ears, his throat, his heart. Eventually, he became aware of the pulse in his arms and hands. Footsteps padded back. Lincoln waited. "Theo?"

Nothing.

"You there?"

A finger poked Lincoln's knee.

Lincoln stood, spun several times, slightly off balance, and imagined Theo raising his hand to his mouth in a silent giggle. He hoped Theo was smiling. "All right. I'm ready."

Silence.

"Just little words. Like, if you want me to go forward, say 'Five steps,' or 'Two steps.'"

Lincoln thought he heard something but couldn't be sure.

He adjusted the t-shirt so more of his ears were exposed and bent down. "Did you say—"

"Turn right."

A happiness Lincoln didn't realize existed flooded through him. He turned.

"Four steps." Theo's voice was audible, but barely. Lincoln stayed crouched and took four hesitant steps.

"Four."

Lincoln moved.

"Two."

Silence. "The—"

"Left."

Another pause, but Lincoln waited.

"Ten."

Lincoln shuffled forward, his excitement growing. He was in the hall, most definitely, heading toward the bedrooms.

"Down."

Lincoln crouched.

"Down!" The word was louder this time, more insistent. Lincoln bent onto his hands and knees. "Reach."

Lincoln reached out.

A giggle.

Lincoln splayed his hands before him, searching until his hand hit one of the cars. Clapping sounded beside his ear and he grinned. "Good job!" Lincoln laughed and put the car in his pocket. "All right, next one."

"Stand up." Still a whisper, but Lincoln could feel Theo's confidence growing. He guided Lincoln to his bedroom, the bathroom, and Kali's room. Next, Lincoln was ushered back down the hall with, "Ten steps," and "Ten more." They ended in the kitchen, where the final car rested on the chair

Lincoln had made for Theo. Lincoln whipped off his blindfold when his hand touched it and grinned at Theo, who was grinning right back.

"That was amazing, buddy."

Theo raised his hands in the air and pumped them in victory.

"So amazing!" Lincoln picked Theo up and swung him then pulled him in for a hug. He pulled his head back, Theo still in his arms. "You did so good. And your mommy's going to be so proud. I'm so proud! Was it fun?"

Theo nodded.

Lincoln wanted words, wanted him to speak again, but he wasn't about to push. Not now. "Want to go play with the cars?"

A huge nod.

Lincoln set Theo down and crossed to the hall as Theo ran toward his room. The front door flung open. "Kali! You'll never guess what happ—"

Kali dropped her bag on the floor. "I lost my license." Her eyes were glazed. Red. Her voice was tight and her hands shook. "And I'm going to lose my job."

Lincoln stepped toward her. "Are you sure?"

"No." She brushed past Lincoln to the kitchen and pulled down a prescription bottle from the cupboard. "I'm not sure. But who wants a blind nurse? Who can trust a—"

"You're not blind."

"Yet. I'm not blind yet." Kali popped the pill into her mouth and poured a glass of water. Her words came out half slurred with the pill at the side of her mouth. "But I can't go back to work until they figure out how blind I am. How blind I'm going to be." She let out a caustic laugh. "Maybe one day I could be a nurse with assisted technology. But not today." She threw a hand in the air. "Not until my condition has stabilized. If that ever happens." She downed half of the water and let the glass slam on the counter.

Theo ran into the room, the cars cradled against his chest with one arm. He waved to Kali.

"I trained for five years to be a nurse. I worked shitty shifts. I lived with rats." She crossed her arms. "And I finally get the dream job. Life finally starts to look up."

Theo tugged on Kali's shirt.

"I'm not in the mood to play right now." Her gaze returned to Lincoln. "And now this. Now this!"

Another tug.

"Not now!" Kali snapped.

Theo's face fell. Lincoln's heart constricted. The boy turned to Lincoln, accusation in his eyes, then ran from the room.

Lincoln let out a half sigh, half groan. "He talked."

"What?" Kali turned to Lincoln.

"I played a game with him, kind of like hide and seek, except we were finding the cars. And he helped me find them with his words. He talked, and he probably wanted to tell you."

"What?" Kali's voice shook. Her expression crumpled. She looked in the direction Theo had run. "Shit." She held a hand to her head and closed her eyes. "Shit."

CHAPTER TEN

Kali sunk onto the couch. Her head throbbed. The drugs worked fast, but not fast enough. "He talked?"

Lincoln nodded.

"And I yelled at him."

"You have a lot going on."

Kali shook her head and stared at Lincoln. Why was he here? She still didn't get it. Theo, she supposed. She got that. How could anyone not love Theo? But having to put up with her as part of the package? It didn't seem a fair deal.

"How was he?" Lincoln gestured to the hall. "When you went in there?"

"I apologized. I said I had a really bad day at work and I had a headache and I didn't mean to yell. I said I was proud of him. That it was awesome. Amazing how he'd led you."

"And?"

"He wouldn't look at me."

"He will."

"Sure." Kali let out a soft laugh. Eventually, Theo would look at her. Eventually, he'd get over it. But she'd screwed up. Big time. She could imagine the way Dr. Richards would purse her lips. Positive reinforcement was the key, she'd said; Kali had practically punished Theo's success.

"Anyway," Lincoln's voice was softer than Kali deserved, "he did great. This is nothing but a minor setback. One day at a time, right? Just like what you're going through."

Kali turned her gaze to Lincoln, one eye raised. She didn't need another pep talk. "Sure, right."

His brow furrowed, and Kali actually saw him for the first time since she'd stepped into the apartment. He looked good. Clean. Normal. Not like the damaged man she'd seen throw himself into the street.

She wanted to tell him to go and was terrified he'd leave.

"He seems to really love that day care." Lincoln paused. "He looked so happy playing with the other kids. And the day care worker. He loved her. I'm sure all of that's going to help, too."

Kali let out a heavy sigh. "Were you not listening?"

"What?"

"I'm not going to go back to work. Not now. Maybe not ever. Which means Theo's not going back to day care."

"But you're still an employee, right? So—"

"I'm an unpaid employee. I can't pay to have someone else take care of my son when I'm not getting paid."

"Right. Sorry." Lincoln looked toward the window. "I guess I didn't put that together."

Kali waved a hand. It wasn't his fault. Just like it wasn't his fault she wouldn't be able to pay for Dr. Richards anymore either. Those bills were hard enough with a job. Kali closed her eyes, feeling how easy it would be to slip into darkness, to slip out of her life. The way Lincoln had. To let go, hide away.

It was a luxury she didn't have.

She opened her eyes and pushed out a smile. Maybe she didn't need the psychologist anyway, not anymore. Lincoln had more success with Theo than Dr. Richards ever had. She looked to the hall. "I'll have to tell him about day care. Won't I be his favourite person."

"He'll understand."

Or have more reason to hate her. Kali wanted to speak the words out loud. But how much misery could Lincoln handle? She brought her gaze back to him. "Thank you for picking him up. For coming up with that amazing idea."

A slow smile grew on Lincoln's face. "It was fun. Exciting."

"I bet." Kali matched his smile. "What's his voice sound like?"

"He was whispering. But it was sweet. Hesitant. Near the end, as he got excited and spoke a bit louder, I don't know ... it sounded like Theo."

Kali sighed. "I'd like to hear that."

"You will." Lincoln stood. "What do you say we all go out to dinner? My treat. Maybe it'll help to soften the blow." He reached a hand out to Kali. She didn't want to take his money. She still owed him money. But she did want to get out of the apartment, do something normal, pretend her life wasn't a pit of despair. She nodded and took Lincoln's hand. It felt strong and warm, and she let him pull her up.

THEO REFUSED TO LOOK at Kali when she came into the room to tell him they were going to dinner. He sat in the corner, cars in his arms, shoulders hunched over. Kali crouched beside him and apologized again. He turned away.

Don't get angry. Kali put a hand on his shoulder. "We're going somewhere fun. Really fun. With fish and toys and you can order whatever you want."

Nothing.

"And we need to eat."

Silence.

He was hurting. He was scared. Disappointed. Kali felt the anger rising. Not at him, but at her. Anger at her fading vision, her focus on herself. Anger that she'd let her rage and impatience with it all slip out onto Theo.

But how could she not focus on herself, today of all days? Wouldn't anyone?

Her mother had. More often than not. They'd had their good moments throughout Kali's life, but it wasn't until Theo came along that they'd grown really close, that Kali felt like she had the kind of mother she'd always wanted. Most of the time, her mother's concerns came first. Kali came second. It wasn't the type of mother she wanted to be.

"Lincoln's coming. He's taking us."

Theo's head rose slightly.

"We wouldn't want him to have to go all by himself, would we?"

A slight shake.

"He'd be lonely."

Theo shifted around, his face slick with tears. A vice clamped down on Kali's heart. She wanted to turn back the clock, greet Theo with open arms, tell him how amazing he was.

She stood. "Coming?"

Theo nodded and shuffled toward her.

AT THE RESTAURANT Theo started to loosen up, with Lincoln at least. Kali got the occasional smile. But no words. Not one.

Kali could hardly taste her food. Theo loved that day care. Loved his new friends. Would he understand? Could she explain the reason why he wouldn't be going back there without explaining her vision loss ... and was she ready for that? Was he?

"I thought we'd go to the beach tomorrow."

Theo turned to Kali.

What was she doing? Thinking? She couldn't drive. And she wouldn't rope Lincoln into their plans without asking. She didn't want him there anyway. She needed time alone with her boy. "The Banook Lake beach." Only a walk away, not her first thought, but it'd have to do. "We can pack a picnic."

Theo stared her down, a slight look of confusion on his face. He wrapped his arms around his middle and shook gently.

"The water might be too cold. But we can be brave. Besides, it won't be as cold as the ocean usually is."

He tilted his head.

"But we don't have to go swimming, anyway. We can build a sandcastle. No, a whole sand village. With a castle and houses and moat. We can make a great moat."

Theo's smile twitched, then landed on his face fully grown.

"Sound good?"

He nodded.

"And maybe the next day we can go to The Common park. You like that one, don't you?"

A huge nod.

"Then after we can visit Mrs. Martin and Cherie, and maybe see Cheryl at the library!"

Theo's smile faded. He put a finger to his chin, the thinking pose that always made Kali feel as if she were about to burst with love. He put his arms out then dropped them. He looked from Kali to Lincoln, who wore a slight grimace—was he judging her?—then back at Kali. Theo was smart. Kali knew what he was trying to ask, but she couldn't bring herself to help him along. At last he mimed reading, painting, going down a slide.

She could ignore it, pretend she didn't understand, pretend reading and painting and going down the slide were nothing more than things they could do together. Just the way she'd pretended away her vision problems, pretended away his lack of a father. All the hard things. All the things she didn't know how to say.

Kali swallowed and pushed a smile onto her face. "You won't be going back to day care for a while."

Theo's brow furrowed.

"And Mommy's not going to be going back to work either."

He spread his hands and tilted his head, his standard 'why' pose without its usual sweet smile.

Kali opened her mouth then closed it. She opened it again. "Which means we're going to have so much time to spend together. It's going to be so much fun!"

Theo looked from Lincoln back to Kali. He shook his head then shook his hands in front of him. He mimed reading and painting again, offered a smile. Gave two thumbs up.

Kali bit her lip. She pasted on a smile. "I know you like day care. But you go to day care because Mommy goes to work. If I'm not at work, you don't need to go to day care."

Theo scrunched up his face. He pointed at Kali, then put his hands together as if in prayer, tilted them to the side, and rested his head on them. He pointed to himself and did his day care mimes again.

Kali's tension grew. She hated this. Hated herself. "You can't go to day care if I'm not going to work."

Theo swung his hands in a jerky, forceful motion, as if he were shooing Kali away ... or directing her to work. To go to work.

"I can't. They don't want me back."

Theo's hands fell. He glared at Kali, then picked up his glass and threw it at the divider separating them from a family in the booth beside them.

"Theo." Kali hissed.

Theo picked up his fork and threw it.

"Stop that."

His plate and all its remaining food hit the divider then bounced onto the table in a mess of fries and ketchup and the remnants of a bun.

Kali's face heated. She slid out of the booth and grabbed Theo by the shoulders. "You can't do that." She whispered into his face, her teeth clenched. "That's not okay."

Theo lunged across the table for Kali's glass.

"No." Kali cut off his reach and pulled his arm back to his side.

Theo silently growled. Kali's heartbeat thrummed in her ears. This was not her son. Her sweet, happy son.

"Stop it."

He tried to squirm from her grasp but she held on tight. He twisted, a look of anger on his face Kali had never seen.

"We're going home."

Lincoln stood and gestured to a waiter, making a signing-the-bill motion as Kali fought to get Theo off the bench. He swatted and kicked at her silently. Kali gritted her teeth, the hits from the arm with the cast hit hard. She scooped Theo into her arms and held him against her as he twisted and bucked his body. She held onto that silence as tightly as she held onto him. He wasn't yelling. He wasn't screaming. He still loved her. He was still scared of his own power to hurt her and wouldn't risk it, even now.

Kali kept her head down, not wanting to see the judgmental stares of the other patrons. She weaved her way through the tables then pushed open the door. Outside, she clung to Theo as he thrashed in her arms, willing Lincoln to pay the bill and get out now, now, now.

CHAPTER ELEVEN

Hands gripping the wheel, Lincoln glanced at Kali. She hadn't said a word since they'd left the restaurant. Theo hadn't either, of course, and every time Lincoln glanced into the rear view mirror all he saw was crossed arms, a furrowed brow, and clenched fists.

Lincoln pulled the truck into a visitor's spot in front of Kali's apartment and cut the ignition. Kali drew a long breath. Lincoln hopped out of the cab and went around to the passenger's side where Kali was standing in front of Theo, hand out. The kid's face turned from him, his arms still crossed, his fists still clenched.

Kali looked to Lincoln and shook her head. She looked tired, beaten. He could reach out, smooth his thumb against her cheek, let her know she wasn't alone ... instead, he extended a hand to Theo. "Come on, bud. Time to head up."

Theo undid the buckle on his booster seat and took Lincoln's hand. Once his feet were on the pavement he released Lincoln's grasp and crossed both arms across his belly again.

Lincoln kept a hand on Theo's shoulder as they crossed

the drop off lane. In the foyer, he turned to Kali. "Do you want me to—?"

"Want Lincoln to read your story?"

Theo kept his gaze away from Kali but gave a firm nod.

Kali smiled and shrugged at Lincoln. "If you don't mind?" Not just tiredness, but pain swam behind her eyes. Lincoln tried to keep his voice casual. "Sure. Love to." Was it the tumour? The stress of the day? The fact that her son wouldn't look at her?

PERCHED ON THE EDGE OF Theo's bed, Lincoln held the book Theo passed him in both hands and stared at the cover. He turned to Theo. "You need to give your mom a break."

Theo pressed his lips together.

"I know you're mad. I get that. Day care's fun. But your mom isn't doing this to hurt you. She has no choice. And you're hurting her."

Theo's expression remained the same.

Was it stupid, trying to reason with a three-year-old? Lincoln turned his gaze back to the book. It wasn't stupid. Theo was smart. He noticed things. And he was nearly four. If he'd been talking he'd be having full conversations, expressing opinions, *getting* things. He did get things. "I know you know what that means, to hurt her." Lincoln put his hand on the boy's chest. "Here."

Theo pointed to the door then made a pained expression and put both hands against his chest.

"She hurt you? By saying no more day care?"

A nod.

"But she has no choice. If she could still send you to day care she would. You have a choice. You don't have to be mean

76

to her. You don't have to ..." Who was Lincoln to talk? The months-long tantrum he'd thrown after his world imploded was much worse than throwing around a few dishes. He'd deserted his whole life, everyone he loved and who loved him. Lincoln let a long breath stream out. "It sucks. You want to go, I get that. But your mom is going through a really hard time right now. And she messed up today, yelling at you. But she didn't know you had something important to tell her. She had a really hard day. Like one of the hardest days ever. And she said sorry, right?"

Another nod. Brow still furrowed.

"So when someone says sorry, especially when they didn't mean to hurt you, don't you think it's a good idea to forgive them?"

Theo's mouth twisted to the left. Lincoln could almost see it—the sweet boy inside of him battling with the angry, hurt, scared one.

"If you think about it, it's kind of a good thing too. You and your mom will get to spend more time together now that she's not working. And you can paint, and read, and go to the park together."

Theo made moving motions with his hands in front of him then mimed a series of high fives.

"But not with your friends."

A nod.

"Well, there are kids at the park, and I know it's harder to make friends for you, but you did so awesome talking today, I bet once you start talking with the kids at the park you'll make friends with them too."

Theo looked skeptical.

"It's different. I know. You see the kids at day care every

day. But maybe you and your mom could go somewhere else with kids. Like maybe the library has some events or you could take a class."

Theo shrugged.

"I'll ask her about it." Lincoln patted Theo's knee. "You love your mom, right?"

Stillness. Then a slow nod.

"So give her a break, okay? Maybe not tonight. I get it takes time to let go when you're so angry. But tomorrow morning can you do your best to let your mom know you love her? Give her a hug and a smile. Have fun with her at the park. She needs it."

Theo crawled across the bed and leaned against Lincoln's side. He stretched both arms around Lincoln's torso. Lincoln paused then let his arm wrap around Theo.

"Should I take that as a yes?"

The boy's head nodded against Lincoln's chest.

"Story time?" Another nod.

LINCOLN TURNED OUT the light and closed the door all but a crack. At the end of the hall he turned to see Kali sitting in the shadows, feet pulled up underneath her, a blanket covering all but her head, eyes closed. He stepped into the room and her eyes opened.

"You in pain?"

She nodded. "Long day. I took something. Should kick in soon."

Lincoln shifted, foot to foot, then perched on the edge of the chair across from her. "Some show, huh?"

"I've never seen anything like it. At least not from him."

"Who knew he had such verve?"

"Verve?" Kali let out the slightest laugh, then winced. "I guess you could call it that."

"He's okay. He understands ... as much as he can." Lincoln folded his hands in front of him. Tonight had been intense. And he didn't want to run. Theo hadn't been the perfect little boy he'd fallen in love with. Kali was clearly sliding into a dark place it may take work to return from. It was scary, overwhelming, but he didn't want to run. "I can stay again if you—"

"No." Kali leaned forward and waved her hand. "Thank you. So much. You've been incredible. But I think Theo and I need some time, you know?"

"Yeah. Of course." Lincoln patted his hands on his knees then stood. "If you need anything, you know my number."

Kali pushed the blanket off her.

"Don't get up. It's—"

Her arms were around him, her head against his chest. Lincoln stiffened. He wanted to wrap his arms around her. Hold her close. He wanted to—

"Thank you. For Theo, for ... just thank you."

She stepped away before Lincoln had willed his arms to move. He brought a hand to the back of his neck and rubbed it. "Yeah. No problem. It's no—"

"Don't. Don't do that. It's a lot. You've done a lot."

"Okay." Lincoln took a step back, something inside of him shaking. "I guess I'll see you soon?"

Kali smiled, her arms wrapped around her middle the way Theo's had been in his tantrum ... only softer.

"Great. Good." Lincoln took another step back. "Sleep well. I hope tomorrow's better."

Her voice was so soft he could hardly hear it. "Me too."

OUTSIDE THE APARTMENT, Lincoln took in the sky. He grinned, reliving the feel of Kali's arms around him, of the way she leaned into him.

He pulled the smile off of his face. The whole situation was horrible. Kali losing her job, her license, the fear of losing her vision too. Theo, and all the turmoil he was experiencing. It was awful. And he ached for them, felt their pain as if it was his own. But Kali had held him. Not desperately, as she had once before, clinging to him as if she were drowning, holding on the way a person would hold to any floating thing that could save them. No. Today she'd just held him. Softly. Held. HIM. Then looked up with that slight smile.

It was him she wanted for comfort. Him she trusted with her son, herself. And among all the sadness and frustration and fear, it felt better than the first time a girl he liked checked 'yes' on the will you be my valentine note he'd slipped her, better than the first time another girl said yes to be his date for a school dance, better than his first kiss.

Lincoln strolled to the car, a bounce in his step, his keys spinning around his fingers. He felt alive. He felt back. He needed to take it slow, he knew. Not push her. Not scare her away. But Kali, Theo, they could be his life. His family. Having them beside him could give him the courage he needed to step back into his own family.

All those months of misery after leaving Montreal. All the work to create a new dream, pursue it, build something. If it was part of leading him to this moment, it was worth it. And it was part of it, obviously. Because here he was. He grinned.

CHAPTER TWELVE

L incoln directed his truck through a network of streets he could navigate eyes closed. When his muscle memory wanted him to turn left, he went right instead, and after a few more turns was in an area slightly less familiar. Lincoln still had money. Enough money to get him through the winter, maybe even the one after that ... if he was living in the tree house. If he stopped paying rent and utilities. If he foraged and hunted the majority of his own food. But he wasn't going to do that.

Lincoln pulled his car close to the curb and stared at Andrew's truck, a brand new Infiniti Q50 parked beside it.

So, he still lived here. Lincoln hadn't been sure. Andrew was doing well. He could have upgraded but hadn't. Interesting. And based on the two cars in the driveway, he was home.

Lincoln tapped his fingers on the steering wheel. If he stepped out of the truck, walked up the driveway, and knocked on the door he'd be stepping back into a world and a life he'd run from, one he told himself he'd never return to again.

Lincoln eased the cab door open, took a deep breath, then jogged up the steps to place three firm knocks on the front door. Ten seconds. Twenty. Thirty. He raised his hand to knock again when the door swung open to reveal Andrew, a grin on his face.

"If someone had given me one hundred guesses as to who would be standing on my doorstep tonight, you would have been a hundred and one." Andrew stepped aside to let Lincoln in.

"Who would have been one hundred?"

"I don't know, an escaped convict dressed as Big Bird?"

"Right." Lincoln stuffed his hands in his pockets and looked around the place. "Big changes."

"Oh yeah, man. I redid the entire kitchen. New cupboards, counters, floors." He stepped past Lincoln and waved a hand in front of the fridge, gesturing the other at the oven. "Top of the line stainless steel." He opened the fridge and pulled out two Keith's IPAs. "New paint job in the living room, furniture *not* off of Kijiji. Catalogue, baby." He uncapped the beers and handed one to Lincoln. "I'm living large."

"Seems it." Lincoln took a sip of the beer, half looking at Andrew, half surveying the work on the cupboards, while Andrew kept his gaze one hundred percent on Lincoln.

"So?"

"So." Lincoln brought his gaze to Andrew.

"This, what, just a casual social call?"

"Can't a guy visit his cousin?"

"A guy, yes. You, hermit extraordinaire? Not without some questioning."

Lincoln gestured to the living room. "Should we sit?"

Andrew spread his arm wide. "Lead the way."

Lincoln settled on the couch. Andrew sank into the armchair across from him, his ankle resting on his opposite knee, a grin still planted on his face. "I can't wait for this."

Lincoln let out a puff of air. "It's not a big deal, man."

"All right. You want to chat first? How's the tree house?"

Now Lincoln was the one to grin. "Good. Really good. The base structure is done. I used a double wall design. Two-by-fours for the inner then local limbs and young trunks hewn for the outer."

Andrew laughed. "Rustic."

They spent the next ten to fifteen minutes talking about the design—Lincoln's attempts and small successes with solar power and storage, plumbing, heat.

Andrew shook his head. "It sounds awesome."

"It was supposed to be just for me, to get away, you know?"

"Oh, I know." Andrew took the final swig of his drink then motioned to the kitchen. Lincoln shook his head.

"Kali thinks I should turn it into a business. Either building them for others—not as a home necessarily, like I wanted mine to be. But for retreats. Either a weekend getaway or even in people's backyards. A man cave. A kid's tree house that's actually functional. She said there's this whole community of people interested in tree houses. It's kind of a niche interest right now, and some would even want them to live in. The tiny house people. Or I could just provide the blueprints, make it so people don't have to go through all the testing and research I've been—"

Andrew raised a hand. "Two things. Kali, that woman who was crashing with you? She's not gone yet? And like you

83

wanted it to be. You don't plan to live there anymore?"

Lincoln grabbed a coaster from the table beside him and tossed it between his hands. "She moved out. Around a month ago now."

"Okay."

"And I don't know. It may not be entirely practical to live out there. Full time at least."

Andrew laughed. "Oh, I know that. I just didn't think you did."

"With winter coming ... if I needed to get to town fast it'd be pretty difficult. I could leave my truck at the road but then it'd be at least a ten-minute hike just to get to it, providing the snow didn't slow me down. The reception is spotty too."

Andrew leaned forward. "And why would you need to get to town fast?" He leaned back again. "You're not looking quite so much like you woke up under an overpass. You seeing this woman?"

"No." Lincoln remembered the feeling of her arms around him, her head against his chest, how solid and soft she felt all at once.

"Look at that smile." Andrew laughed. "If you're not, you want to be."

"It's not like that."

"She's gorgeous, like she's some statue come to life."

Lincoln leaned in. "I know, exactly. She doesn't seem real sometimes."

"But she is real. And she has a kid. And you're a mess." Andrew set his beer on the table and stood. "No offence, but ... are you ready for all that?"

Lincoln looked away.

"Sure you don't want another?"

"Nah, man." Lincoln waited for Andrew to return and sit. "She has a brain tumour, too."

"Oh, wow." Andrew set his elbows on his knees. "That's heavy. She ..."

"It's not likely to kill her. But she's losing her vision. She's lost a lot of it already. And she lost her job ... well, unpaid leave until things are figured out."

"And you're trying to be a hero?"

"No."

"Then what is this all about?"

Lincoln stood and turned to look at a large painting on the wall behind the couch. "That grandpa's old place?"

"Had it done from an old photograph."

"We had some good times there."

"We did." Andrew crossed the room to stand beside Lincoln. "What are you doing?"

Was it so bizarre? Wanting to help someone? Changing your life to help someone? It's not as if he had much of a life to change anyway. Lincoln turned to Andrew. "You still have a job available?"

"For you? Always. Weren't you just talking about this whole tree house business, though? You don't have the funds to start that up?"

"I don't have the time. And I'm not touching money from the shares. We talked about that."

Andrew stepped back. "We did. What about savings. Weren't you making major dough in Montreal?"

"I went almost a full year not working, if you recall."

"Oh, I recall."

"I bought land. Some of the parts for the tree house weren't cheap." Lincoln inhaled. "And before that Lucy and I were spending major dough. Not as much savings as you'd think."

"And now this new woman and her son need a sugar daddy, so you're giving up your dream of a tree house, of starting your own business, to go back to the company that kicked you to the curb?"

"Andrew."

Andrew slapped Lincoln's back and crossed the room, one hand planted against the wall. "You've been going through a rough time. I don't want to see you taken advantage of. See this woman just use you and—"

"Kali. Her name's Kali."

"Okay, Kali—"

"And she's not trying to take advantage of anything. She's not going to want this. She hates accepting help. But she's going to need help. And if I can help her ... Besides, the part of the company you run and the part Joseph runs, they're worlds apart. I'm asking you for a job, not him."

Andrew shook his head. "You want a job, you got a job." He returned to his seat. "But you'll have to show up. Do the work, just like anyone else."

"Of course." Lincoln stayed standing. "It might be short term. I think for now something in construction or the warehouse."

"Not ready to be seen?"

"I'd rather ... well ..." Lincoln could see it, Joseph finding out. Walking in. Standing in front of Lincoln when he couldn't move, couldn't leave, was obligated not to. He could have worked anywhere, applied anywhere. But not in this field—construction. Not even in administration or management. Not in this city. This province, even.

Any competitor would be wary of letting a Fraser through their doors. He could go try a whole new field, but construction, building ... it was what he knew, from the bottom to the top. "I just don't see the need to make it public knowledge"

"What about family knowledge? That'll happen soon enough." Andrew shook his head. "Buddy, sit."

Lincoln eased back onto the couch.

"You're one of the two founder's sons. The current head-honcho's younger brother. As far as anyone knows you worked yourself up to a position of being second to running the empire then disappeared off the face of the earth after almost tanking a multi-million dollar deal. I can keep my mouth shut, but word will spread."

Of course it would. Lincoln stared at the shag rug under the coffee table. He could get a job somewhere else. A grocery checkout boy maybe. Would they hire someone with a Master's in Business Administration? With the top management experience he had? He could lie. But they'd still want past jobs, past references, and how would he hide almost a year of sitting around? The truth would come out.

Lincoln hadn't thought this through. The ball in his gut, which had taken some time off of late, seemed to grow in size and weight. Of course, people would know, wonder, talk. Most of them knew Lucy had been his, and that she was now Joseph's. They'd question. They'd wonder. They'd look at him like he was the pathetic loser he ... but he wasn't. Or he didn't have to be.

He'd had a breakdown, yes. He'd run away from life. But he had a reason to step back into it now.

Again he felt Kali's head on his chest, felt Theo nuzzling

up to him—and those reasons were more important than gossip. More important than the fear that gripped him. Kali might not want his help, but she'd need it—now more than ever.

If he could help, he would. Jumping in front of that car, a decision made so fast he'd had no time to think about it, meant more than just saving Theo's life. It'd saved his. Helped him believe again that people weren't worthless. That he could be happy.

Lincoln raised his gaze to Andrew. "You giving me the job or what?"

Andrew shrugged his shoulders, let out a laugh, and shook his head. "Yeah, man. Of course. I'll have to figure out where you best fit. But you've got the job."

CHAPTER THIRTEEN

A toddler on one hip, Mrs. Martin waved at Kali. She pulled Theo to her side and ruffled a hand on his head. "So nice to have this one back under my roof."

Kali smiled wide—both for Mrs. Martin and for Theo. It hurt, trying to keep a smile on. It had for days. But she did. Just like she kept striving to be the mother Theo deserved. Any tears she'd let fall were long after he'd gone to sleep. She pushed her anger and fear down deep, refusing to let it bubble to the surface. And they'd had good days. Sandcastles at the beach, hours at the park, racing cars and drawing pictures. Precious days. That's what she needed to focus on. The time she had, the sight she had, the moments she had. But how long would they last—with fading vision and a depleted bank account? A familiar pressure began to build against her chest.

Not now. She couldn't give in. Not now.

The bus had gotten them to Mrs. Martin's early enough that Kali decided to walk to the hospital. Lincoln probably would have driven her, but she hadn't called. While she could still do things on her own, she would. If this treatment was as bad as her supervisor said it could be, she'd need his help soon enough.

IN FRONT OF THE HOSPITAL, Kali paused and let the breath stream out of her. It made no sense to be nervous. This appointment, this treatment, might not make things better, but there was such a slim chance it'd make things worse. She should be excited, hopeful, or at least optimistic.

Kali didn't need to follow the green dotted line to Oncology, but she did anyway, fearful in her stressed state she'd take a wrong turn or end up leaving altogether. An orderly wheeled a patient past Kali, his head bandaged, his eyes glassy. Kali swallowed and looked away.

In just a few minutes that would be her. She was supposed to be the person giving care, not the one receiving it. She'd already stopped being a nurse; after this appointment, she'd officially be a patient.

Kali had given into research last night. Not a lot, but enough. Enough to jog her mind of the things she'd studied in nursing school. Enough to know the doctor would have a few options, none of which Kali was particularly excited about. Stereotactic radiosurgery seemed the most common treatment for tumours on the optic nerve or chiasm. A frame was bolted to a patients' skull then secured onto the treatment table.

Bolted.

Kali shook her head and kept walking. Bile rose in her throat. How many times had she told patients receiving similarly disturbing treatments that it was fine, that they'd be fine, that they were in good hands?

Kali checked in at reception and took a seat in the waiting room. A deep voice jolted her from her thoughts.

Jones. Eddie Jones. Now Dr. Eddie Jones.

Kali had seen him around the old neighbourhood growing up but only knew him by name. He was big then, and bigger now, at least six foot three with large shoulders and arms that made him look more suited for a football field than a lab coat. Though that wasn't fair. That was the kind of thinking that kept too many boys from North Preston away from trying.

Dr. Jones' smile warmed when Kali stood, but there was no recognition in his eyes. Why would there be? She was at least six years his junior. Notice didn't go both ways with that kind of age difference.

Kali sat across from him in his office, answered a few perfunctory questions, then half-listened as he went over the results from her visual field and acuity tests, her CT scan, her MRI results. He brought up the words she'd been dreading. Stereotactic radiosurgery.

"For your condition, I think that's too dangerous."

Kali zoned in her attention. "What?"

"The precision we'd need." He glanced again at his notes. "We're battling with the progression of your disease, which is swift, but we also don't want to risk further long-term damage by treating it too intensely. With radiosurgery, there's a strong chance of damaging the sensitive tissue surrounding your tumour. The chiasm and optic nerve can only tolerate so much. No, conventionally fractionated radiation would be much safer. Less risk of endangering the vision you have left. And really, just as effective."

Kali folded her hands. She'd heard of that treatment, vaguely, maybe a paragraph in a textbook years ago, but she couldn't remember much about it.

"Following standard doses of radiation," continued Dr. Jones, "healthy cells repair themselves more quickly and completely than tumour cells. As the radiation treatments continue, an increasing number of tumour cells die."

"I know all that."

"Yes." Dr. Jones smiled. "You would, wouldn't you? One of my colleagues mentioned you used to work here."

"Not in this department."

"But you're a nurse?"

Was she? She still had her nursing license. She just wasn't allowed to work. "Yes."

He made a sound deep in his throat. "Odd being on the other side, isn't it?"

A well of emotion shot through Kali. She nodded.

"With conventionally fractionated radiation the dose is relatively low. But we treat more often. Once a day, five days a week, for about six weeks."

Kali's pulse quickened. Every day for six weeks? An image of herself, metal frame affixed to her head, walking around like the female version of Frankenstein's monster, made her stomach lurch. "So, I mean ..." Kali raised a hand to her forehead, not sure how to get the words out.

Dr. Jones smiled. "You know about the bolts with radiosurgery."

Kali nodded.

"No bolts. Nothing that intrusive. We'll fit you with an aquaplast mask."

Kali made a noise of understanding. Six weeks.

Metal frame or not, six weeks of treatment, five days a week.

"You'll come in three days from now for your simulation."

Six weeks, at least, of unpaid leave. She'd had her work assessment the day before. They couldn't conclusively say her vision would prevent her from doing her job, but they also couldn't conclusively say it wouldn't create problems. The decision, of course, was in favour of the patients' safety, of avoiding an error that could jeopardize the organization and Westwood's good name.

"We'll do a CT scan and make the mask. It takes about a half hour."

The decision was to reassess after Kali's treatment, after they could see whether she'd regain any of her vision.

"Kali?"

Then, if her condition seemed stable, they'd look into assisted technology. They'd readdress the situation. Had Alison realized how long the process would take? How long Kali would be on unpaid leave? And how would it affect her probationary period? At the end of three months, would it be easier to simply let her go?

"Kali?"

Kali snapped her attention back to Dr. Jones. "Will it work? Will it heal me?"

Dr. Jones folded his hands on the desk in front of him. He couldn't answer that. Of course he couldn't. Eddie. Eddie Jones, who she'd watched play basketball while sitting on the sidelines with girls she'd never really felt were her friends as they laughed and cheered beside her. Who, she seemed to remember, had been a hero—saving a kid from falling through the ice at a skating pond one winter.

His brow furrowed. "Kali, I'm sure you know—"

"But stats, do you have—?"

"There's a good chance it will help. A high chance it'll stop the growth and it's possible it'll reverse some of the damage. Though things could get worse before they get better

... or seem to."

Kali kept her gaze focused on him.

"The tumour, the tissue surrounding it, can swell as a reaction to the radiation. Your symptoms can worsen too. Nausea, fatigue, dizziness."

The list went on, the words blurring in Kali's mind.

"In the future, you could have pituitary gland problems, which could affect fertility."

Fertility? Kali nodded slightly, processing the doctor's words. Did she want another child? She hadn't imagined herself having even one before Derek. Since, she'd resigned herself to a single life, a life focused on Theo. But things could change. She could change. She was so young.

"The best thing you can do is try to live your life as normally as possible. You'll be tired, but do what you can. Eat healthily. Sleep well. Stay active, but not too active."

"But when will I know?"

"Six weeks after treatment completes you'll have another MRI. You could have improvement at that time. But it's not likely."

Six weeks after treatment. Twelve weeks in total. Twelve weeks, but still not likely even then.

Dr. Jones smiled. "We need to take these things one day at a time. That's the best advice I can give you."

One day at a time. Kali fought to keep her breathing even. "Thank you." One gruelling, uncertain day at a time. "Of course." One day at a time, with no savings. With rent coming soon and only one more pay cheque left. Just one day at a time.

LINCOLN ARRIVED AT THE construction site twenty minutes early. As the rest of the crew trickled in, the workers glanced at him with surprise, suspicion, derision. Others shook his hand and clapped a hand on his back, welcoming him. These were the men he'd worked with as a teenager, older than him, the ones who were kind even then, knowing he'd one day be their boss. But he wasn't.

The work felt good. Natural. His months working on the tree house had prepared him for hard labour and he kept up with the best of them, surpassing many. At the end of the day his muscles were crying for relief, but he went home to the Gottingen Street apartment and worked them further. He wasn't sure how much time he had left before it'd be too late, so he was determined to make the best of it.

CHAPTER FOURTEEN

Cancer Centre. An apt title, but just walking through the doors ...

Kali thought of the invader inside her as a tumour, as meningioma. But cancer? Cancer spread. Cancer took over its host's life. Her tumour wouldn't. Not in the typical way. Still. It was cancer.

Pale green walls surrounded her. Large daisies, the green of their leaves almost matching the paint on the walls, hung as a massive print behind the receptionist's smiling face.

Kali handed over her health card and answered the woman's questions. She expected a wait but was greeted almost immediately.

"I'm Marissa." The woman looked sweet. Kind. "I'll be one of your radiation therapists."

"Kali."

"Yes." Marissa's large brown, almost black eyes smiled, and shiny black hair fell straight to her shoulders. She seemed ageless. Twenty-five? Forty-two? Either seemed a valid guess.

She looked around Kali to the waiting room. "Anyone with you today? They could go wait in the Sunshine Room, it's much more comfortable."

"No, no one."

"All right, then." Marissa kept her voice bright.

She led Kali down a hallway.

"The Sunshine Room is open to you too. We offer many great treatments: reiki, massage therapy, reflexology, healing and therapeutic touch. All free."

Kali rubbed her arms.

"Many people find it very helpful."

"Okay."

Marissa gently grazed Kali's shoulder as she directed her down a new hall. "Have you ever had an aquaplast cast made before?"

Kali shook her head.

"Well, we'll get you into a gown, fit the mask, then head over for a CT scan. Sound good?"

Kali pushed out a smile.

In the radiation room, Marissa directed Kali to the table then appeared with what looked like a flat pool net.

"Are you ready?"

Kali nodded and tilted her head to see Marissa better.

"We're going to need you to keep perfectly still."

Jonas, a second therapist, adjusted Kali's head. The mesh landed on Kali's face, warm and wet, and Kali fought the urge to raise her hands to peel it off of her. She flinched as Marissa and Jonas clipped the base of the mask to the table.

They weren't bolts. This was so much better than bolts. Kali breathed gently, willing the minutes to pass quickly as the mask dried.

"You'll feel some pressure." Jonas' voice was deep, matching his body—square and boxy. Unlike Marissa, Kali guessed Jonas to be in his mid-forties.

Green light shone on Kali's face.

"We're making marks on the mask. That's the pressure you feel."

Kali kept her eyes closed and concentrated on taking shallow breaths. She wanted nothing to mess this up.

Less than half an hour later Kali was in another room, on another table. The table was cold, as they usually were. Kali kept quiet as Marissa and Jonas directed her movements. She inhaled sharply as the now-hardened mask lowered onto her face and was clamped onto the table.

"Does it hurt anywhere? Feel pressure points?"

Kali started to shake her head then stopped. "No."

Marissa smiled, careful to keep her face above Kali's, where Kali could actually see her. Kali smiled back, thankful.

Red beams of light shone down on Kali when the therapists left the room. She closed her eyes, waiting for the clicking and whirring to stop, the table to still. "Stabilization," she whispered to herself, "cessation of growth."

KALI SAT IN A CHAIR ACROSS from Marissa, who explained the course of action. Dr. Jones and his team would need about a week to come up with a treatment plan. They'd merge the CT scan with her MRI from a few weeks ago. There'd been growth. Six more millimetres in three weeks. No wonder Kali's licence was gone. No wonder.

Kali nodded. She smiled. She knew how hard this may be for Marissa, what it took out of you to smile and be bright while sitting across from someone who was going through one of the hardest challenges of her life. A patient who was angry, accusatory, sobbing, only made it that much harder.

Would Kali lose her hair? Would her face swell to the point of being unrecognizable? Would she get insomnia, anxiety, increased appetite, decreased appetite, headaches more intense than she already had? All symptoms she knew were possible, but not predictable. She wouldn't ask.

LESS THAN AN HOUR later, Kali pumped her legs gently, watching the world shift as she rose and fell. It was weird being at the park without Theo. The last time she had been here without him was in her early months of pregnancy, Derek in the swing beside her. They'd talked about the life they'd have. He wanted a girl, her a boy, but they agreed they'd be happy with either. Besides, he'd insisted, they'd have a whole handful of kids, with that many, they were sure to get both.

Three, she stated. No more. Hopefully, no less. And in saying it a sense of wonder spread over her, how another person could change her so much. She'd always thought she wanted none ... and then she met Derek.

Kali closed her eyes, remembering what it'd felt like, that love. She'd gone on what could be called dates through high school—skating with a group of friends, someone to take photos with for a dance, but never more than once or twice with any guy, intentionally. She didn't want to get attached.

She had plans. Big plans. She wanted to dance. Not just salsa. Not just rec-centre ballroom or hip-hop or jazz. But really learn. Learn it all. She wanted to go to Broadway, even Off-Broadway would be fine. Heck, she didn't even need to dance on Broadway, she could just see the shows, dance in some community theatre. But she wanted to be there, among it all. For a time at least. She wanted to live a life bigger than anyone she knew could even imagine. She wanted to nurse too, of course. But after. Later. Once she'd lived.

A traditional life hadn't been her plan. Derek changed all that.

All these years later and she could still remember the feeling of his hand. They'd swung, hands clasped. Not practical, but as he looked at her that day, as he rubbed her thumb with his, she'd understood how women did crazy, thoughtless things for the man they loved. She understood the mystery of how, instantly, someone could go from being a stranger to seeming like your whole world. She'd understood how easy it was to put your dreams aside and make new ones for the one you loved.

She never thought she'd want to be wrapped up in another man's arms.

Lincoln's arms had felt safe. But they were risky, too. Anyone's were, obviously. Derek had seemed like the most solid man she'd ever met. Seemed.

Kali pumped her legs harder then dry heaved, nausea hitting her like a punch to the gut. She slowed the swing. She'd take Lincoln's help, but not rely on it. She needed to make her own plans. Be responsible for her own life. And being responsible meant facing reality. She couldn't afford her apartment. She'd contact ... whatever agency covered disability claims. She'd contact employment insurance to figure out what her sickness benefits would be. She'd apply for assisted living housing, something she probably should have done in the past, and pray it had no rats.

She'd do everything she could do. She wouldn't give up. And maybe, just maybe, God or the Universe would reward her. Her vision would return, her job would return. Life would be okay.

She couldn't think about herself, what she wanted. How much doing those things, relying on others, the government, admitting she couldn't take care of herself, felt impossible ... because relying on them, right now, was necessary. It was the best thing she could do for Theo. Her happiness, her pride, meant nothing. To even think about what she wanted was indulgent.

Kali kicked the dirt with her toe. She was stupid to think getting the job at Westwood meant her life would change, that for once, at last, she could be happy. Happy was for other people; her mother had said that more than once growing up. You had to make life work. That was the focus. Kali could hear her mother saying the words even now. She'd said them every time one of her boyfriends left them with even less money. Said them when Kali realized she was going to be a single mother too. Make life work. You just do whatever you have to do to make life work.

Making life work meant making sure Theo was safe. Cared for. Making sure no one took him from her. The thought took Kali's breath away. Was it possible?

It could be, if she didn't do what she needed to do, if she let herself sink into a place of despair so deep she couldn't get out of it, if she let her pride prevent her from getting the help she needed. But she wouldn't. And God or the Universe ... her sight would return or return enough. If it didn't, she'd find another job or use whatever assisted technology was available to make her old job work. That was it. She'd do that, and the world would answer. Life would answer. For once, would reward her. It had to.

Kali stood and adjusted her satchel. She took long strides

across the lawn on her way to Mrs. Martin's. That's all there was to it. Things would be okay. She'd make life work.

CHAPTER FIFTEEN

Walking up to Mrs. Martin's door felt like walking into a life Kali had taken for granted. She couldn't see the rose bushes she knew were to the right as she walked up the porch. The tree on the other side was barely a blur. And when Theo smiled up at her as the door opened, Kali felt deep loss for how much this tumour had already stolen from him ... a day care he loved, a social environment he was thriving in, and now his meetings with the psychologist. Today would be the last. If she cancelled now she'd have to pay anyway, so they'd go. And after Kali had her few minutes with Dr. Richards, she'd head to the receptionist and cancel all further visits.

Kali took Theo's hand, thanked Mrs. Martin, and turned back down the steps. She turned her head toward the tree— the brilliance of the orange leaves—she couldn't let the tumour steal it.

"SO, YOU'VE STILL NEVER heard Theo speak."

Kali raised her chin to Dr. Richards. "And neither have you, right?"

Dr. Richards folded her hands. "I'm not accusing you, Kali."

"I'm not saying you are." Kali looked at the paintings on the wall. Unlike the calm scenes in the waiting room, the images in Dr. Richards' office were bright and vibrant. "Theo had a huge disappointment after Lincoln's game. I had had an incredibly bad day. He wanted to tell me but I was trying to talk to Lincoln. I thought Theo just wanted to play, and I snapped at him."

"We all have bad days."

Kali kept her gaze on the array of colours. "We do. And then I had to tell him he wouldn't be going back to day care, which he loved. He hasn't talked since, but we also haven't seen Lincoln since."

"I'd encourage their games again."

"Of course you would."

"Kali, are you all right? You seem distracted."

Kali finally looked at the woman. She couldn't quite explain the reason just being in the psychologist's presence made her on edge ... or she could, but wasn't sure she liked what it said about her. "I'm fine, Dr. Richards."

"Theo's birthday is coming up soon, isn't it?"

"Mmhmm."

"Are you planning to throw him a party?"

"We'll do something."

"What about a big party, with all of his favourite friends from day care? The teacher too, if you have that type of relationship. It would be a great motivation for him."

And expensive. Kali rubbed her hands. A party, even if she made the decorations and food herself, would be expensive.

"Emphasizing that whispering is okay, you can tell him he can invite whoever he wants, their parents too—"

Parents? At the old day cares, Kali always felt intimidated by parents on the best of days. Most were older than her, more established. It'd be different this time, though. They'd be her colleagues. Fellow nurses. They may know her situation ... or simply suspect she'd been let go ... would they know it was a medical leave? Would they spend the time at the party looking at her, trying to figure it out? She'd only met a few in the short time she'd been at Westwood.

"—but as you don't know the names, he'll have to tell you." Dr. Richards continued. "Then, not only does he get a party, he gets one with the friends he misses. And when they come, when he realizes his words had the power to bring something so good and—"

"I get it."

Dr. Richards snapped her mouth closed.

Kali pursed her lips, regretting her words instantly. This woman wasn't her enemy. Uppity, maybe, but even if she hadn't helped much, she'd done no harm, and Kali was paying for her advice. "It's a good idea," Kali spoke softly. "And you think I should do it, not Lincoln?"

Dr. Richards sat quietly for a moment. "Yes. You could, perhaps, have Lincoln there with you. Or if it's not successful the first time, try again. Maybe he could whisper to Lincoln in your presence. But try on your own first. Or, at least out loud to both of you. Read his temperament. Try a day when Theo's in a good mood. Happy. Relaxed." Another pause. The woman seemed to study her. "This is going to happen, Kali. With some clients I'm uncertain, but with Theo I feel sure it's only a matter of time." Another pause. "He's well adjusted. He's extremely bright. And he has a mother who's invested and trying. He'll talk. And one day this will all seem like a blip in your past."

Pressure exploded in Kali's chest, working its way up her throat and to the back of her eyes. Maybe that was the tension today, knowing this would be the last time she'd see the first professional who had never seen Theo's lack of speech as a mental deficiency, who had faith in him, even if she hadn't always seemed to have faith in or support of Kali's methods. Kali nodded.

"With some patients, I would have suggested medication by now, but Theo's young and, as I said, otherwise well-adjusted. Otherwise, happy. The anxiety ... it may take a while to overcome, but once he sees it's safe ..." She reached a hand out, leaning forward, but still not close enough to grasp Kali's. "He's going to be okay."

But was she?

She would be. She resolved it. And if her financial situation got better before Theo did, Kali would come back to this woman. "Thank you. I think so too."

"Just guide him. Gently. From a place of silence to a place of expression. He'll open up. I've never felt more certain."

"Good. Great." Kali smiled. For the first time in a long time, hope bubbled within her. This might work. The Lincoln idea had worked, and Kali wasn't sure she would have thought of a party or thought to ask the names rather than figuring them out herself. The cost was, well ... if it worked it'd be worth it. Her smile grew. "Sounds like a plan."

"Now, I'd love to see that boy."

THEO CLAPPED HIS HANDS and jumped into a stance as if he was getting ready to surf—arms out, knees bent, smile on. Kali laughed. "You've got it down."

He grinned.

"We should take the ferry more often, shouldn't we?"

A huge nod.

Kali leaned over the railing and stared at the gently rocking waves below. She liked the ferry. It took longer, yes, but on a day when time didn't matter ... why not? And how many people lived in a place where they could take a trip on the water for no more than bus fare?

Theo sidled over and leaned into Kali's hip as he watched the waves. She put a hand to his head and he wrapped an arm around her thigh. She chuckled, amazed at how such a simple action could, at least for a moment, erase all the horrible in her life.

When she suggested the ferry, Kali worried that her nausea would make it a bad idea, but even that had slipped away for now. She was tired, the stress of the simulation had taken a lot out of her. Having to tell Dr. Richards' receptionist to cancel all their future appointments had taken even more. But Theo was happy. He'd had a good time at Mrs. Martin's, at the psychologist's, and now too.

Kali breathed in the ocean air, relishing how much fresher the harbour seemed from her childhood when garbage floated by in copious amounts. She took Theo's hand and led him to the open-air seats in the middle of the deck.

"I have an idea."

He tilted his head.

"You know your birthday is coming up."

A huge nod and hand clap.

"And I thought we should have a party."

Grin.

"A big party. With some of your friends from day care."

No expression, and then an explosion. Bouncing in his seat. He mimed blowing out candles.

"Yes, absolutely. A cake too."

Hands clasped. Nod.

"There's just one problem though, our place might not be quite big enough for everyone and their parents too. So I was thinking maybe ten friends and any parents who want to come. Does that sound okay?"

Theo tilted his head side to side then gave a closed mouth smile.

"Good."

"You just tell me the names then, and I'll work on getting things organized." Theo's smile fell. "We can even make invitations. You colour, I write."

He stared at her.

"I'm sorry, sweetie, but I'm not sure how else I can know who to invite."

He shifted away from her; the familiar look of betrayal.

"I know it feels hard, but we can't have everyone. There are over thirty kids there. So I need to know which ones are your friends."

He looked back, lips scrunched and twisted to the side.

"Do you understand?"

A group of kids, siblings probably, ran by laughing. A woman trailed behind, yelling at them not to run. Theo looked to his lap then back at Kali. He nodded.

"You do understand?"

Another nod.

"So?" She pulled her phone out of her satchel and swiped the screen open. "You tell me, and I'll make a list." She leaned close. "Remember, you can whisper."

He shook his head.

"You're not going to tell me?"

Brow furrowed, he slowly shook his head again.

"How about you take a day or two to think about it? I want you to have a party. A super amazing party. But I can't do it without your help. Okay?"

Brow still furrowed, Theo nodded. Kali swallowed. It was something. A start. Next time she'd try with Lincoln in the room.

Kali took a breath. "Want to look over the edge again, or show me your surfing skills?"

CHAPTER SIXTEEN

For the fourth night in a row, Lincoln slept in the Gottingen Street apartment. He woke with a smile on his face and stretched his aching muscles. A full eight hours at the construction site then another four here. And sleep. Deep. Solid. Renewing sleep. He hadn't bothered to set his alarm, certain he'd wake in plenty of time for today's appointments. The two extra hours of sleep plus waking up when his body felt ready, rather than to voices on the radio, felt indulgent in just the right way. Almost as good as having a specific reason to get up every day.

And tonight was his night with Theo. It'd been almost a week since he'd seen them, so he'd suggested dinner at their house, with him as the cook. Kali had agreed quickly.

He'd have time to get groceries after his appointment—one he still hadn't decided whether or not he'd tell Kali about.

LINCOLN WALKED BY THE building multiple times, only noticing its newness in a neighbourhood where many of the storefronts had existed long before him. But, as in most of the North End, that was slowly changing. Still, it was only last week that he'd really looked for the first time, realized what the building was, then stepped inside.

It felt like betrayal, walking through those doors. Once, in passing, Kali had mentioned her doctor's recommendation to do the same, but she'd dismissed the idea. He'd wanted to tell her it sounded great, wanted to encourage her, but didn't want to see her anger turn on him. So he was going instead. He felt committed to this woman, blindly so, and that part had to change.

He pushed through the door.

"Hi, there. Lincoln, right?"

"Yes."

The woman's jet black curls stood out against her pale skin. She was young. Thin, almost too thin, and had one of the brightest smiles Lincoln had ever seen. "Alika."

"Yes, I remember." Lincoln took her hand.

"About half of today's crowd has arrived. Just head on down that hall."

Lincoln stepped into a room with a long table where five others sat. There was an older man, his belly pushing against the table, his beard almost touching the top of it, two teenagers, most likely siblings, with their gazes darting about the room, and a woman and man, mid-fifties, tight, worried expressions on their faces.

Lincoln took a seat beside the woman. She turned to him, a look of desperation on her face. "I'm Suzanne."

"Lincoln." He met her grasp, her palm cold and clammy against his skin. When she let go, he fought the urge to wipe her touch off on his pant leg.

"You never think it will happen, do you?"

"No." Lincoln swallowed and glanced around the room. "I

guess not."

"It's our daughter. She's thirty-two. She has twins. And she'll never ... she ..." The woman's voice caught. The faintest squeak leaked out.

The man put an arm on her shoulder and leaned in front of her to meet Lincoln's eye. "Sorry about my wife. It's still very fresh. Our daughter's condition is degenerative. She'll be completely blind in three years at the most."

"It's visually impaired," said the male teen in a voice of authority. "Or suffering vision loss."

"It doesn't matter." The girl replied, annoyance dripping from her voice. "It's all the same."

"Not to—"

"It's my wife." The bearded man's voice was deep and gruff. "Your mother? Or father?"

"Our mom," said the girl.

"It does matter," her brother hissed. His gaze shifted and Lincoln followed it to see Alika entering the room with four more people. "Just wait, she'll tell you."

The girl rolled her eyes. "It's called the Canadian National Institute for the *Blind*, isn't it? If it's such a bad word—"

"It *used* to be called that." Her brother hissed. "Now it's CNIB. And that's—"

"Welcome." Alika stood at the back of the room in front of a large screen and waited as the new participants settled in their seats. "There's water and snacks." She gestured to two piles lined up in the centre of the table. Feel free to take whatever you like." She waited as several people reached out for water, granola bars, apples, and bananas. "Some of you are here just to get a better understanding of what your loved one is going through, others hope to participate, volunteer, which is wonderful in itself but will also help you better learn to interact with and be a support for whoever in your life is going through this difficult time.

"You're probably having a difficult time yourself, and we'll talk more later about a support group you can join, or just pop in any time we're meeting." Alika paused to smile. "Why don't we start with some introductions and then get started?"

That had been the hardest part when Lincoln stepped into the CNIB last week and first met Alika. What was he supposed to say? He's here because of this woman who used to be his roommate for a few months but isn't anymore. He had no real connection to her before that and a tenuous one even now?

He said he was here for a friend, a close friend, who had no family to help her.

Alika had smiled at him. Smiled in a similar way the mom at the day care had. Smiled like he wasn't the lost, misguided man he'd felt himself to be for the last year ... the last five years, if he was honest with himself.

Lincoln used the same explanation now, to highly different responses. Some looked confused. Some annoyed. One or two gazed at him as if he were a saint.

"You mean you're not even related to this woman?" The teenage girl's stare seemed to bore into him. "And she has a brain tumour and is going through cancer treatment and has a kid?" She shook her head. "That stuff is shit. She's going to get so sick. Our dad had cancer. Sick and blind. Dude, just walk away."

"Dayle." Her brother snapped.

"Unless you're trying to get in her pants." The girl snickered. "If so, trust me, there's easier tail."

The boy punched his sister in the arm. She growled at him and rubbed the spot but kept her mouth shut.

Alika seemed hesitant, her gaze on the teens before putting her smile back on. "Next."

Lincoln held back a grin, pleased the kid's words hadn't made his gut twist, hammering down the reality of what he was signing up for. He was scared, sure. Scared shitless at times. But not enough to walk away.

THE DOOR OPENED TO two smiling faces, Theo's smile, of course, outshining Kali's by a mile. Theo held up his arm.

"Oh my goodness!" Lincoln widened his eyes and made his smile wide. He set down the bags and grasped Theo's arm. "It's free!"

Theo nodded. His grin wide.

"How does it feel? All better?"

Another nod. Theo stepped forward and wrapped his arms around Lincoln's side. Lincoln put a hand on the boy's back and felt his own chest expand. He picked up the bags and held one up in each hand. "Who's ready for tacos?"

Theo clapped his hands and gave a little jump.

"Want to help me make 'em?"

Theo nodded and waved Lincoln inside.

Kali pulled her flowing cardigan against her chest and stepped aside for Lincoln to enter. She put a hand to Theo's head. "Why don't you go wash up?"

Lincoln looked to Kali. "How's it going?"

"All right." Kali ushered Lincoln into the kitchen and stood close. She smelled like cinnamon. Cinnamon and coconuts. Her eyes were bright but nervous. "The psychologist suggested we throw Theo a party, but it will only work if we can get him to tell us who he wants to invite."

Lincoln shifted away from Kali and her intoxicating scent. He took the tacos, lettuce, and tomatoes out of one bag and set it on the table. "Sounds like a plan."

"I already tried. He was intrigued but not ready." She unpacked the rest of the groceries. "I thought later tonight we could try again. Maybe he whispers to you, you whisper to me, then I whisper back to him to confirm. Kind of a broken telephone thing. And I can mess it up sometimes to make it more fun."

"That could work." Lincoln opened the cupboard to search out a pan.

"You think?" Kali spun to lean against the counter, one hand resting on her chin, the other propping her arm up.

"Could be great."

The sound of Theo's feet raced up the hall. He practically leapt into the kitchen.

Lincoln laughed. "You ready?"

A huge nod.

"Hands all clean?"

Theo held his hands out for inspection and flipped them up and down.

"You've passed."

He grinned.

CHAPTER SEVENTEEN

After dinner, Kali proposed her plan. Theo scrunched his nose, looking from Kali to Lincoln.

"Sounds like a lot of fun to me." Lincoln leaned back in his chair. "Both the game and the party."

Theo crossed his arms and sank lower into his seat.

"And it seems like it's all on you, buddy. Could you imagine all the day care kids and their parents in this place?" Lincoln shook his head and squeezed his arms tight against him. "We'd be stuffed in so tight there'd hardly be room for oxygen." He scrunched up his face and Theo gave a silent laugh. "So what do you say?"

Theo tilted his head side to side, looked at Lincoln and Kali again, then gave the slightest of nods.

Kali's face filled with fear and hope. As Lincoln's gaze caught hers, she quickly changed it to a smile.

Lincoln stood and pushed back his chair. "Let's head to the living room. More comfy."

"All right." Kali grabbed a pen and a piece of paper. She looked to Theo. "So, have you thought about who you want to invite?"

A nod.

"And you remember all their names?"

Another nod. Theo looked to his hands then held them up, fingers spread wide.

"That's right." Kali's voice shook. "Ten friends. Two full hands." She took a breath. "Go tell Lincoln."

Theo stepped over to Lincoln. He looked to Kali and raised one finger.

"Yep. Just one to start."

He tapped that finger against his chin. Lincoln smiled at the boy, nervous excitement tingling through him. He'd heard Theo's voice before but Kali hadn't. He could only imagine what she'd be feeling. Almost two years since she'd heard her son's voice and now ... Lincoln nodded at Theo, his smile growing. "You can do it, bud."

Unlike the other day, Theo didn't just whisper, he leaned in and cupped his little hands around Lincoln's ear. Disappointment flooded him. But, of course, that was the game. Kali wouldn't hear her son's voice. Lincoln would. But she'd know he'd spoken, hear the proof in just a moment. Theo's voice was so faint Lincoln could barely make out the word.

"Was that—?"

"No." Kali swallowed. "Just tell me whatever you think you heard, Lincoln. Then I'll check with Theo."

Lincoln looked to Theo then back to Kali. He moved to the couch and sat beside her, cupping his hands around her ear. He kept his voice a whisper. "Kenny."

Kali nodded then slid to sit beside Theo. He shook his head, crossed his arms in front of him then ran to Lincoln. Those small hands clasped around Lincoln's ear again. His breath was warm and moist, the word louder this time.

Lincoln nodded and moved to sit beside Kali. "Benny."

Kali gave a slight nod and moved to Theo. He gave two thumbs up and grinned.

"All right." Kali's smile was tight but pleased. "Benny is on the list."

Theo clapped.

They repeated the process again, and again, and again. Once, Lincoln suspected Kali messed up the name even when she'd heard it right. Lincoln studied her. She was happy, sure. But there was tightness behind her smile.

"Time for the switch!"

Kali and Theo both shifted their gazes to Lincoln.

"The switch."

They continued to stare.

Lincoln raised his arms in mock surprise. "That's how you play broken telephone. You've always got to make a switch. Reverse directions."

Theo's brow twitched. He bit his lip then looked to Kali. She shrugged, uncertain.

"Trust me." Lincoln's heart pounded. This could ruin things. This could send Theo stomping to his room, his little heart sour with betrayal. "Now you tell your mom, your mom tells me, and I confirm with you."

"We don't have to switch," Kali spoke quickly, the slightest hint of desperation and anger in her voice. She looked to Lincoln, shook her head, then back to Theo. "But if you want ..."

Theo stood between them, his little chest rising and falling. He walked to Kali, took a deep breath, and cupped his hands over her ears. Kali sat, her gaze raised to the ceiling as she listened. Her lips gave the slightest tremble. She nodded, smiled at Theo, then slid over to Lincoln.

"YOU DON'T HAVE TO be here."

"I know."

Kali stared straight ahead. "I'm fine."

"I know."

"It's ridiculous. I mean, what, are you going to come every time? All thirty times?"

"This is the first time."

Kali turned her head so Lincoln came into view. He smiled, just slightly, and something in her stomach flipped. She turned her head back to face the wall, all trace of him disappearing from her vision. "It's going to be fine."

She expected a response, an affirmation. But only the clap of shoes against the hallway, the receptionist chatting with a patient, and distant whirs and buzzes sounded in the room.

Kali turned her gaze to Lincoln again. "There's this room. The Sunshine Room. It's supposed to be really nice. You can wait there, though this shouldn't take long."

"Maybe I will."

Again, Kali stared at the wall. Lincoln's hand slipped around hers. She almost pulled it away but caught herself and stayed still. She didn't look at him. She couldn't. But her shoulders relaxed, her breath came more naturally. He'd come, even though she told him not to, even though she'd refused his offer of a drive. When she stepped into reception, there he was, one foot crossed over his knee, elbow resting on the chair arm, flipping through a magazine. He'd smiled at her, saying nothing, then brought his gaze back to some article while she checked in. She'd sat beside him and he'd nodded, still saying nothing, as if it was planned, as if she'd asked and so expected him to be there.

She stared at their hands. It felt familiar, comfortable, seeing her grasp in his, and entirely unnerving. So unnerving, she forgot for the briefest moment why she was here, why his hand was grasping hers.

"Kali, we're ready for you."

Her head shot up. Lincoln squeezed her hand then released it as she stood. Her voice came out louder than she anticipated. "Let's get this thing started." She didn't know who she was talking to, Jonas or Lincoln. She glanced back at him, sitting there, smile on, and smiled too, glad he'd come. Glad to know he'd be there when she came out.

THE TREATMENT'S OFTEN *worse than the disease.* True words, but there was no point thinking them, holding onto them.

After changing, Kali eased herself onto the treatment table. Marissa and Jonas stood on either side of her, checking this, adjusting that, explaining as the mask lowered down, as they clipped it onto the table. Kali fought the urge to push back, break away, say she didn't want radiation streaming into her brain, that there had to be another way. But that was childish. This was routine. Totally routine. And she was fine.

"It feel okay?"

"Huh?"

Marissa's face moved into Kali's line of vision. "The mask.

Not squeezing or pinching anywhere?"

"It's fine."

"We're going to leave the room, take a couple of X-rays to confirm everything is positioned properly, then we'll begin. We'll be able to see you and hear you the whole time."

"Right." Kali couldn't nod. She closed her eyes, opened them, closed them again, winced at the sound of the heavy lead door closing.

"You doing all right?" The voice came from speakers somewhere near the ceiling.

Again, Kali wanted to nod, not trust her voice. "Yep." No squeak, thankfully. "Doing great."

"We're going to begin now."

After a few moments, the machine's loud whirring increased to a heavy buzz as the arm moved. A sharp whine set Kali's teeth on edge as the radiation streamed into her. Helping. Healing. By destroying.

Kali's chest shook. Breathe in, breathe out.

The arm moved again, a teeth grinding whine. And Kali breathed.

At last, the whine dimmed, the buzz faded to the original whir, and Jonas's voice came through the speakers.

"That's it."

Less than ten minutes, barely more than five. That was it?

The door opened and Marissa's face was above Kali's. "How are you feeling?"

Marissa unclipped the mask from the table and Kali exhaled. "Like I can breathe again."

"A lot of people find it hard to be pinned down like that. It'll get easier. Sit up slowly."

Kali eased herself up and maneuvered off of the table.

"Any wooziness? Feeling okay?"

Kali hesitated, unsure. Not woozy. But unsure. As if she'd slipped out of her own skin and into someone else's. As if she wasn't herself. She should have been on the other side of the door, the other side of all of this. She should be the one asking the questions. "Good. Fine."

Marissa stared at Kali a moment then smiled. "It'll probably be a few days until you have any side effects, if you do. Watch out for headaches, nausea, increased or decreased appetite. Basically, make note of anything abnormal so you can let us or Dr. Jones know about it."

"Yep. Okay." Kali rubbed her hand across her opposite arm.

"Try not to stress or worry. Some people hardly have any symptoms at all. And you're young, otherwise healthy. Those are good things."

"Of course." Kali stared at the door.

"It's weird, isn't it?"

Kali turned her gaze back to Marissa.

"Being on the other side of all of this. I had an accident a couple of years ago and ended up needing surgery. There were complications. I spent three weeks in the hospital. And it just felt wrong the whole time. Out of place."

"Yeah." Kali let out a short laugh. "It's weird."

KALI WAVED TO MARISSA and stepped into the reception area. There he was, elbows on his knees, back hunched, staring at the floor. He looked up and stood. Kali's arms tingled; her legs too. What was she supposed to say? What was he supposed to say?

"I have about an hour and a half before I have to be at the

site." He picked up their bags and crossed the room to her. "And it's just about that time; want to grab lunch and work on plans for this party?"

Kali exhaled. "That would be great, actually."

Lincoln put his arm around Kali's shoulder, gave her a quick squeeze, then let his grasp fall. Kali caught her breath, surprised at how much she wanted his arm to stay.

CHAPTER EIGHTEEN

Kali rested her hands against the counter and stared at the bowl in front of her. The contents blurred. Her stomach twisted. Noise surrounded her. Laughing. Talking. The clink of drinks. The patter of footsteps. Her arms shook. Her head throbbed. She clenched her teeth and took deep breaths in and out. She jumped.

"God." She turned toward the owner of the hand on her shoulder. "Don't sneak up on me."

Lincoln hesitated. "I didn't mean to."

Of course he didn't. He hadn't. "Just ... say something, okay, please, don't ... Never mind." Kali reached for the bowl but Lincoln took it from her.

"Okay. And I'll get this." He grabbed an opened nacho bag and poured the chips into the bowl. "You okay?"

"Thanks. I'm fine."

He lingered. "Kali, are you *okay?*"

Kali pushed herself straight. "Fine." She smiled. "Just a little woozy. A little nauseated."

Lincoln brought his hand back to her shoulder and rubbed it twice. "You're doing great. And he's so happy. Like this wind-up bundle of excitement and energy."

"I know." Kali nodded. "It's great. So great."

"Yeah." Lincoln stepped away. "Take a minute. I've got things."

Kali waved a hand then leaned back against the counter, surveying the activity in the living room, careful to keep a smile on her face.

She'd finished her first two weeks of treatment and the symptoms had been plaguing her for days. Nausea. Fatigue. Lack of desire to eat anything. Spinning rooms. And though she couldn't be one hundred percent sure, increasing loss of vision.

But her face hadn't swelled. When she looked in the mirror, the same face she'd always seen, though wan and tired, looked back at her. It was vain, she knew, but that had been the symptom she feared the most—to see her body swell, her eyes bulge in their sockets. She already felt like an entirely different person, she wasn't sure she could handle looking like one too.

But the symptoms she did receive? They weren't fun. And this noise, this constant movement, constant need to smile and chat and act like her life was fine, like it wasn't unravelling ... she didn't know how much more of it she could handle.

Kali's chest was still tight from the shock of Lincoln's touch. She hadn't realized how much she'd been relying on her hearing these past weeks to alert her to movement in the peripherals she could no longer see. Today, with sounds and movement everywhere, half of the people who approached her seemed to appear out of thin air.

But the day was for Theo. And Theo was loving it. Kali grabbed a fresh tray of cut veggies from the fridge and stepped into the living room.

"We miss you at work."

Kali kept her jump within and turned to the voice. She barely recognized the woman but smiled with recognition anyway.

"When will you be back?"

"Oh," Kali kept her smile on and exhaled, "not quite sure, unfortunately."

"You seem to be doing okay?"

Kali shrugged. "Surviving."

The woman nodded, clearly wanting Kali to say more. Clearly curious as to how or why someone on medical leave could throw a party like this but couldn't work. But maybe she wasn't wondering. Maybe she was just concerned. Maybe the fear was nothing but Kali's insecurities. This woman was a nurse. She knew disease couldn't always be seen. Knew the ravages it could cause within a person who looked fine on the outside.

The woman's expression softened. "It's nice you have today."

"It is."

"And nice you have him." The woman—Cynthia, Cynthia with the most rambunctious kid in the day care—gestured to Lincoln, who kneeled on the floor with a group of kids surrounding him. He seemed to be arranging some sort of dinky car race.

Kali nodded. She smiled at the way he grinned, the way Theo leaned on Lincoln's shoulder with such familiarity. Aware of Cynthia's gaze, Kali turned back to the woman.

"He's your ..." Cynthia hesitated. "I don't see a ring. So, your   boyfriend?"

A streak of protectiveness shot through Kali. He wasn't. Of course he wasn't. But she wasn't about to give Cynthia the answer she hoped for. Instead, she shrugged and gave a smile she hoped was mysterious.

Cynthia's brow furrowed. She glanced to Lincoln then back at Kali. "So, he's your ... I don't want to encroach on—"

"We're close." Kali kept her smile on, surprised she didn't just speak the words Cynthia was pushing for. *We're friends. Go ahead.*

"You're ..."

"We're seeing where things go." Except they weren't. She wasn't. Or hadn't been. Laughter reverberated through the room as a child jumped, arms raised in victory.

"All right, then." Cynthia shook her head and laughed. "I get the message."

Kali bit her lip and stared at Lincoln. She'd been noticing him more, the way his muscles contracted under his shirt, how kind his eyes were, the expression they held when he looked at Theo, the expression when they looked at her. When he touched her shoulder or their fingers grazed as he passed her something, she no longer tensed. More often than not, she tingled.

But he was still a stranger, essentially. A stranger who could walk away at any moment. A stranger she was thankful for but couldn't rely on. Couldn't care for.

Cynthia's laugh tinkled through the room and Kali searched her out, relief washing through her when she saw the laugh came from chatting with another mother. Would Lincoln find someone like her appealing? Cynthia was clearly a single mom too, but one who smiled easily, who had a job, her sight, a little girl who didn't have weekly psychologist's appointments.

Lincoln stepped into view, a slow grin lighting his features. "Approach from the front, right?"

"Yeah." Something within Kali's chest fluttered. She moistened her lips.

Lincoln gestured toward Theo. "I can't get over how happy the kid is. He's just glowing."

"He is." Kali touched a hand to her throat.

Lincoln stepped closer, his gaze intent on hers. "How are you feeling now? Any better?"

She stepped away. "Yeah. A bit."

"It's a lot. But you're doing great."

"Mmhmm." Kali swallowed, aware of how close he was, how his body angled towards hers.

Lincoln looked back to the kids. "I was thinking it's probably a good time for cake. Then presents."

"Sure. Good."

"You want me to—?"

"I'm a little shaky. Yeah."

Kali turned to watch Lincoln walk away. He seemed so confident lately. So sure. Not of her, perhaps, but of life. He wasn't the man she'd met just months ago. He hardly talked about the lot anymore. She actually wasn't sure how he spent his days. He was elusive the few times she'd asked. Not that she'd pushed. Most of their talk centred around her and her treatment or Theo.

Large arms wrapped around Kali, shocking her once more. "Mrs. Martin. Hi."

"Sorry we're late, sweetie, but looks like we're just in time for the main event."

Kali turned as Lincoln entered, the lit cake in his arms. A

chorus of voices rose around her and Kali, turning her gaze to Theo, joined in. A father lifted Theo onto the ottoman and he stood, eyes shining, hands clasped, expectant. Lincoln waved to Kali and she rushed over. She smiled at her son. "You ready to make a wish?"

Theo nodded. He squeezed his eyes shut, his whole face scrunching, then opened them.

"You got it?"

Another nod.

"Then blow."

It took three powerful bursts of air before clapping and cheers spread throughout the room. Theo bounced as Mrs. Martin whisked the cake out of Lincoln's arms. "You three enjoy the fun." She tutted. "I'll take care of this."

Kali put out a hand. "You don't have—"

"Enjoy." Mrs. Martin turned.

"All right." Kali swooped Theo off of the table. "Ready for some presents?"

Theo nodded. Had he talked? To anyone? Several times she'd seen him, head bent low with Cynthia's girl and another child or two. If he hadn't, he would, eventually. And he'd spoken to her. Five names. Whispered. But they'd been words.

In the time between then and the party, he'd chosen his chocolate cake, mimed the baseball bat he wanted and some new cars. But there'd been words here and there, when something was particularly hard to mime or when Lincoln or she had made games out of it. Always in a whisper, but words.

Theo shredded the wrapping on his first present amid a chorus of children's laughter. He was an appreciative recipient. Bouncing, smiling, racing to give hugs. So different

129

than Kali had been, not that she'd ever received many gifts. Or had parties. But she'd always been hesitant, uncertain of the best way to show her thanks. Even with Derek, who'd been a good and exuberant gift giver, Kali had been quiet in her thanks.

As she passed Theo another gift and accepted a piece of cake from Mrs. Martin, Kali noticed Shelley in the corner, snapping pictures. She'd hardly spoken to her since leaving the ER and only invited her because one of her kids was close to Theo's age. But she was glad she'd come.

When the last present had been opened and Theo and the kids were busy playing again, Kali made her way to the other side of the room.

Shelley's smile was hesitant. "He's doing so well."

"He is."

"Like he's blossomed. And so comfortable with all of the kids."

"Yeah."

"Looks just like his father."

Kali shook her head. "Shell—"

"Just saying he looks like him. That's all."

Kali bit her lip and crossed her arms. "He does. Just as handsome."

Shelley elbowed her. "He looks like you too. He's got your nose. Your cheekbones."

Kali swallowed, her gaze on Theo. "You think so?"

"Oh, definitely." Shelley's voice lowered. "How are you?"

Kali glanced at her, then back at the kids. "Good. Great."

"I know."

Kali watched the children.

"Not the specifics. But I know you've been having

radiation therapy. People talk."

Of course they talked. Which is why Kali had started to dial and hung up four times before finally emailing Shelley an invite.

"I'd be pissed that I didn't find out from you, but I know you've always been private. And I don't want to make you dredge it all up ... here ... today. But I wish you'd let me be there for you. I wish you'd let me help."

"I'm fine." Kali glanced over again, pushing down the vulnerability that radiated through her. Shelley was her oldest friend, and although they'd never quite been 'besties'—Kali didn't really have besties—she was the closest thing Kali had ever had to a best friend.

"There's no way you're fine. You're dealing, perhaps. You're making it work, like you always do. But you're not fine."

Kali inhaled sharply.

"Promise me we can meet for coffee or tea next week." Shelley turned to Kali face on. "If you can't find someone to watch Theo I'll bring my devils and we can go to that play café that opened up."

"I'm—"

"Maybe I miss you. Maybe I want to talk. Bitch about my lazy husband and terror children."

Kali cracked a smile. "Right."

"Jake is getting lazy." She leaned in closer. "He's getting a gut. It jiggles all over the place when we're ... you know." She rolled her eyes. "I married washboard abs. And now this." She put a hand on her hip and winked. "Of course, I'm still the perfect hourglass that walked down the aisle."

"You were six months pregnant when you walked down

131

the aisle."

"Eh." Shelley laughed. "But I still had my waist. Anyway, after two kids I don't have too much to complain about. But that's the thing. I had the kids. I have an excuse. Him? Just plain lazy."

"You adore him. You don't need to bitch."

She sighed. "You're right. But I may want to. And I want to hear how you are without a dozen screaming children running around. Even if you truly are fine, I want to hear it. Promise and I'll shut up about this and let you join the party."

Kali nodded. "Promise."

"Next week."

Kali gave another nod.

Shelley leaned in closer. "Are you having fun?"

Kali looked at Shelley, realizing for the first time that she missed her, had been missing her for weeks, their comfortable banter on the floor or in the staff room, the knowledge that, if she wanted, she could tell someone her problems. Not that she often did, but she could. And despite the nausea, the discomfort, the fear, she was having fun. Theo was having fun, and the tumour hadn't stolen that. She could see his smiling face, his bright eyes. "Yeah." Theo ran in a circle around the coffee table, his new cape flaring out behind him. "I'm having a lot of fun."

CHAPTER NINETEEN

"A dozen kids." Andrew squatted on a box in the centre of the room and wiped a hand across his brow. "And you were orchestrating the thing?"

"Helping." Lincoln continued to roll paint on the freshly spackled and sanded wall.

"But you said she's pretty sick now?"

Lincoln turned. "Some days she seems good. Others ..." he turned back to the wall. "I think it's the treatment more than the tumour."

"It's wearing on you, isn't it?"

Lincoln stared at the wall. "It could make her better, or stop her from getting worse."

Andrew grabbed his brush and continued cutting in along the baseboards. "Why can you do all this for *her*, watch *her*, yet you haven't—"

"Don't."

"Buddy."

"Not now." Lincoln swallowed back a familiar tightness. Andrew couldn't understand, no matter how much he said he got it.

Silence passed between them.

"So, the landlord is cool with all this?"

Lincoln pushed the roller up the wall. "Didn't ask. I'm not on the lease. But they're all major improvements at no cost to him. So I can't see it being a problem."

"And you think she'll come?"

"If she doesn't, at least I'll have kept myself busy."

"Mmhmm." Andrew continued his cutting in.

"What?"

"Nothing, man. Nothing at all."

Lincoln turned to him.

"What?"

"You're working full time, which should keep you busy enough. But if it didn't, that tree house isn't done, is it?"

"I'm not giving up on it." Lincoln turned back to the wall. "It's just too far in case—"

"In case the woman you're not dating needs you."

Lincoln stared at the wall, then smoothed his roller over the spot that still held the faint stain of pizza sauce. "You've never heard of a friendship?"

"Not criticizing. Just trying to get you to admit it."

"Admit what? That I care about her? That I want to be with her? I'm not hiding—"

"No." The grin Lincoln hated as a kid, the I've-got-something-on-you-grin spread across Andrew's face. "That you're a romantic again."

Lincoln shook his head and laughed. "What?"

"A romantic. You lost it with Lucy. All business. And after her, you swore off not just love, but people. But when we were kids you had your dreaming, your high ideas, your intense desire to impress and woo whatever girl was 'the one.'

You were a romantic, and you are again."

Lincoln laughed. "If you say so."

"I do." Andrew, still in a crouch, looked at Lincoln. "And I'm glad. I've missed you, cuz." He looked back to the wall. "And I couldn't stand that corporate you. The suits. The slick hair. No time for real fun, for hard work and kicking back after."

Lincoln's arm paused mid-roll. "I hated it too."

"You love her?"

Lincoln continued rolling. "I love her kid. I'd rather be near her than ... just about anywhere."

"But you've never ..." He paused. "Not even a kiss, or—"

Lincoln set the roller down. "You getting hungry? I could do a run to Kut Korners—bring back some slices or calzones."

"Calzones." Andrew set down his brush. "Let's both go. You take a break, I take a break."

LIGHT STREAMED THROUGH the window. The wind blew her curtain out, then let it fall back again, the room dimming with the motion. Kali groaned. Her head ached. Another day. Another day of having to make it, to get out of bed, make breakfast, walk, move, smile.

She should be thankful. She should be ecstatic. Shouldn't she? She was alive. She could still see enough to get around without too much trouble. She had her boy. She had time to spend with her boy, and yet the past few days each moment of that time felt more like a burden than a joy.

She wanted to stay in bed. To not have to smile, move, walk. She rolled over and winced. Walking, especially, was a hazard. She tripped. She bumped into things. Her legs seemed not her own. She'd miss steps, bang into table edges or door frames. So much visual information she didn't realize she'd relied on, now missing. And her body was painted with the result. Never in her life had she been so bruised.

Kali counted to seven then made herself sit up. She counted again, then stood. One more count to make it to the dresser and put on her clothes. Another to cross the room and push open the door. It was ridiculous, but a way to rev herself up for each new action. A way to rest in between. In the bathroom, she stared at her reflection. Besides the tiredness that was a constant companion and made its presence known on her face, she still looked fine. No swelling. All her symptoms were internal, which is why that couple at the grocery store yesterday had looked at her with disapproving faces. Why the man had mumbled something about being a drunk when she'd bashed into their cart and then fell against the shelves, sending a pile of cans—chickpeas, Romano, and kidney beans—toppling down.

Her appearance, seemingly fine, was also why Theo looked so hurt and confused when she said she couldn't play in the park with him but would sit and watch. She cheered him on, but even that took up precious energy. Two to three hours a day, that's what she had to get things done, and then she was maxed out. Yesterday's energy had been spent at the Department of Community Services, checking on her application for income assistance. She'd already looked into disability, which would take approximately four months to come her way—if she was lucky. She'd also applied for low-income housing. She was on a wait-list, though she refused to move to the North End of Dartmouth, where drugs were more common than flowers. She hoped for the North End of Halifax. There were shady parts there too, but she knew the area, the community, and the community knew her.

She could just ask Lincoln. Should ask Lincoln. Lincoln who, actually, was taking someone else's spot in low-income housing. The spot of someone like her, who actually needed it. Not that it was his fault, really. It was the system's, for not keeping track, for letting thing's slide.

She'd only ask if she had to. She paid the last month's rent when she got her current apartment, so she still had two weeks left. Two weeks. Two weeks to make it work. Two weeks to tell Theo his life was about to change again.

CHAPTER TWENTY

"Why is this so important to you?" Kali turned her head to glance at Lincoln as he led her to the CNIB entrance. "You're the one who insists I'm not blind yet."

"You don't have to be fully blind to come here. Trust me, they do good work."

"How do you know?"

"I checked."

As they pushed through the door, a woman stepped away from the reception and smiled broadly. "You must be Kali. Lincoln's told us about you. I'm Alika."

Kali extended her hand and glanced to Lincoln. He'd told them about her? He knew this woman?

"Normally we'd give you a walk-through on your first visit, tell you about the services we offer, but there happens to be an Independent Living Skills meeting starting in a few minutes. You could join if you like. Meet some of the other clients."

"Oh, I don't—" Kali wrapped a hand around her middle as a man entered the building with a white cane. He didn't seem to use it the way she'd seen in the movies, tapping it in front of him side to side. It was just kind of there. He waved to Alika then flipped the cane up. It folded into foot long pieces; he deftly secured the parts and slipped it in his bag.

"There are a few types of white canes," said Alika, following Kali's gaze. "Three actually. Support, identification, and long, sometimes referred to as probing canes. Charles there has an identification cane. He has a fair amount of vision still, but using the cane lets people know he's visually impaired. It also helps with depth perception. Stairs and curbs, that type of thing."

Kali could almost feel Lincoln's urge to elbow her or say something. But they'd argued about this already, her unwillingness to take help, and the type of help she may need. Her being here was the result of an argument, one he'd only won by using the mom card. She couldn't deny her recent frustrations were being taken out on Theo more than she'd like, and if coming here could give her some coping mechanisms, make the day to day challenge of existing more doable, of course she'd be a happier, more relaxed mom for her son.

Kali insisted it was the treatment symptoms, not her vision, that caused most of the problems. But she'd resolved to make it work, and if this could help that ...

Kali watched the man walk down the hall without the cane. "So people use them even though they can see?"

"The canes are about independence, not dependence, though that's how many of our clients see them at first." Alika smiled warmly. "That using a cane is a sign they're disabled. But they're wrong. These canes are about the ability to navigate the world safely, without the constant need to rely

139

on someone else or the inconvenience of people not recognizing they may need a little space. A little patience."

"I see." Kali rubbed her arm. "And the other canes?"

"Both are very much what they sound like. Support canes are often used by the elderly or someone who needs an extra degree of stability, and long canes are what most people think of when they think of the white cane. The user holds them out in front to probe the area before them, make sure nothing's in their path." Alika's smile was brilliant. "We offer training on all three."

Kali nodded. Several more people pushed through the doors, chatting and laughing. One waved to Alika; the others didn't look over.

"So, what do you think? Want to jump into a meeting?"

She didn't. At all. But it might be the lesser of two evils. At least at a meeting, Kali could hide in the crowd. If she stuck with Alika, she'd be the one getting probed. Kali nodded.

"Great. It'll be about an hour."

Lincoln put a hand to Kali's shoulder. "I'll see you then."

Kali's natural inclination was to say no, that he didn't need to come back. But it'd been three days since she'd seen him and the moment she'd opened the door to him that morning a sense of relief floated over her. She offered a smile. "Sounds good."

Kali followed Alika down the hall to a bright room with six people seated in a big circle. A fancy speakerphone was set up in the middle of the circle.

Alika introduced Kali to the people in the room and the people joining through phone, then closed the door. Not everyone was blind, clearly. Some looked right at her, smiling their introductions. Others, still smiling, only looked in her general direction. One man, like Kali, seemed like he'd rather not be there.

The meeting was clearly more a discussion group than anything else. They talked about new devices they'd tried or wanted to. One woman shared a recent breakthrough with braille, marvelling at how good it felt to finally read for herself again rather than always being read to. She mocked a computer sounding voice and several chuckles rose in the room.

It all seemed a lie, like false independence. False acceptance of the shitty hand they'd been dealt. Tension rose within Kali. This wasn't her, wasn't for her. Sure, she'd been bumping into things daily, her hips and legs ached from the bruises, but she could see. She didn't need a device to magnify her can labels or a scanner to read them out. She didn't need raised stickers on her stove to know how far to turn the knob. She'd let tea and milk and juice overflow on the counter or missed the edge of the container while pouring more than once, but it just took focus, concentration; putting some beeping reader over the edge of the cup would be overkill.

Kali kept her gaze down as the people talked on about independence. None of them had independence. They couldn't sit in the driver's seat—not of their cars, not of their life. And not driving meant they weren't in charge. How many of them here, sitting here smiling like they were so lucky to be living in the age of technology, had jobs?

How many of them had to sit, after five years of university, after slogging their way through to dream jobs, in the community services office, just hoping for a handout?

Tricks of the trade, they called these life hacks. Tricks that took discipline. That took organization. That relied on systems. Systems, Kali could get. As a nurse, she relied on systems. But that was to keep patients alive, not to make sure she was wearing the same coloured socks.

"A place for everything and everything in its place," laughed one woman through the phone's speaker system. "It's the mantra in our home. My kids must hear it in their dreams I've said it so many times. But they're getting it. It's been weeks since I tripped over a dinky truck."

Kali rubbed her knee. One of Theo's cars had done that yesterday, sent her sprawling to the floor. She hadn't yelled, but she'd been sharp. Sharper than usual. Sharp enough to make Theo slink away before coming back to kiss her knee and offer a frightened smile.

"Your family needs to know the mantra. If you're alone, this will be easier, but other things will be harder. Your mind is going to improve. Your memory. Milk has its place. Sugar. Apples. Spoons and forks. Cell phone chargers. Everything. Let your family know the issues, the frustration it causes if they don't remember this, but let them know with love. They're adjusting too. They're scared too."

Kali hadn't told Theo yet, not about any of it—not the reason he only spent an hour at Mrs. Martin's most days. Not why she jumped when he walked up to her from the side, why she was so tired, so quick to anger. As a result, his fear didn't have a focus.

"It's normal to feel frustration, fear, overwhelm," said a burly man in overalls. "My whole life I was the one people came to for help, not the one who needed it. That was hard for me."

"I get that." A woman in a floral sweater and navy pants chuckled. "You may not know it to look at me, but I was feisty. In charge. The one who knew how to handle things. Who people came to." She smiled, gently, a laugh still behind it. "I've always been independent. I never married. Married to my Lord, perhaps you could say. I spent most of my years as a missionary in Haiti—all on my own, at a time when women didn't often do that, leave their homes, their families, go to a far away country.

"I spent forty years between here and there. One morning I woke up before my next planned trip to realize I couldn't see it was morning, and everything changed. Just like that, the independence I'd always known was stolen away, my ability to help, to make a difference in the world, gone."

The woman held her arms out, hands clenched. "But I wanted to hold onto what I still had. I grasped it with both fists, never realizing that when you hold something that hard, it's likely to leak out through your fingers." Her smile was radiant. "There's only so much we can control. When you start to lose your sight, your life becomes overrun with appointments. This doctor here and that one there. Appointments you didn't book, that you probably don't want to attend. But you have to. That time is no longer your own. And if your sight is far gone, if your license is taken or you live in a place without buses, as I did back then, you have to rely on people all the time."

Murmurs sounded throughout the room. "And you probably fight that. I did." Another laugh. "One day I was at an appointment. On my own. Got there all by myself, walking the streets with nothing but my memory and determination to rely on. And when I went to leave I felt someone hovering behind me. A man's voice. 'Lady, can I help you?' I jumped, then stiffened. Frustrated, angry that he was trying to take the independence I was gripping." She held out her clenched hands again. "'I'm just fine.' I said, all pert and proper. 'You are not,' the man laughed and my anger swelled. I ignored him, huffing my annoyance."

The woman paused, shook her head. "The man laughed again. 'As hard as you try, you will never turn that wall into a door,' then took my hand and led me to the door, a good four feet away from where I was groping." Another pause. A smile. "That day I said to myself, 'Madeleine, you need to come back to reality.'"

Madeleine sighed and let her arms fall to the side. "Sometimes we have to let go and be willing to accept what people are offering us. I spent my whole life giving, expecting people to accept it, and most of them did. Sometimes I wonder if this blindness came to me so I could learn what it's like, how much harder it is to receive than to give. At least for those fiercely independent types." She shrugged. "It was hard, and it didn't happen overnight. I had many similar trying-to-make-a-wall-into-a-door moments. But it's a good lesson. Letting go." She smiles. "Not give our power up, that's what this place is about, but accepting the reality of our situation. Accepting the help that will make life simpler."

The room stayed quiet.

Madeleine let out a huff of air, her voice shaky. "Letting go of the anger, too. The anger of not being able to do it all myself, of *needing* that help. For a while, it felt like that's all I had left. Anger. But we control that. We're in charge. I can get up in the morning and have a day that's restful, peaceful, full of thanks and joy for what I still have, or I can have a day that's restless, agitated, bitter. I'm the only one that can determine that. In the ways it matters, I'm still in charge. One hundred percent."

Kali glanced around the room at the nods, the contemplative faces. Kali did the math. Assuming this woman took her first mission trip when she was twenty, which was probably an early guess, she hadn't started to lose her vision until she was sixty. A full life. Time to experience, to live. And she'd had maybe up to twenty years since then to accept her fate.

What right did she have to preach to the people in this room? To Kali, to the girl across from her who looked hardly old enough to be out of high school, to the man who'd learned his wife was pregnant with twins the same day he'd learned he had a degenerative disease that would leave him blind within the next three years, five if he was lucky?

The woman had no right at all.

WHEN THE MEETING adjourned Kali left the room before anyone could say a word to her. These weren't her people. This wasn't the answer. Her answer was the treatment. Relying on it. Trusting that the lessening vision she'd been experiencing was nothing more than swelling, than her body fighting back. Trusting that her body would win, and for whatever vision the tumour wouldn't give back, she'd learn to make-do. She was fine. She'd adjust to the depth perception issues. Once the fatigue and nausea and lack of balance from the radiation faded, she'd be fine. She'd use whatever assisted technology was required to get her job back, but outside of that ... outside of that ...

Kali pushed through the doors, spotted Lincoln's truck, and hopped in the cab without looking at him. This place was not for her.

CHAPTER TWENTY-ONE

"What if it doesn't work?" Kali's head throbbed. She lifted her gaze to Lincoln.

"It will."

"But what—?"

Lincoln laid a hand on Kali's knee. She stared at it. If he hadn't arrived just minutes after, if he hadn't gone to Theo, comforted him when Kali was incapable ...? She closed her eyes, reliving the past hour. She'd come home from treatment in a fog. It was unpredictable, this fatigue. One moment she'd feel fine, almost normal, and then it could hit like a tsunami, drowning her and tearing away all the good parts—patience, understanding, kindness.

On the bus ride back to the apartment she'd wanted nothing more than to close her eyes, but Theo kept tugging on her, kept wanting to tell his day's stories through mime. She'd faked patience, saying Mommy needed to close her eyes, but her ears were still open.

He'd sulked.

And then they'd walked in the door. She'd turned to the kitchen to get her painkillers, stepped in, slid, and landed against the counter, head and shoulder banging with such force she'd had the wind knocked out of her. When she regained her breath she'd screamed. Screamed at Theo for leaving his truck on the floor, screamed and screamed as his little body shook, then fled.

"It'll be okay. He'll be okay." Lincoln rubbed her arm. "And you'll be okay."

A sob tore through Kali. She'd never felt so alone. Lincoln was here, right beside her. And she had the doctors and technicians and Mrs. Martin. She had Shelley, asking Kali to get in touch. But it didn't matter.

She was alone. Alone in a world that was slowly closing in on her. None of them, for all their wanting to help, could change that fact. Each day, with each treatment, her vision seemed to lessen. Dr. Jones had put her on steroids at her last appointment, which should help with all of it—the vision, the nausea, the fatigue—but it hadn't helped yet.

She knew her symptoms didn't mean the tumour was winning, that they could simply be a reaction to the radiation, but this shrinking world, it tore hope away. It made everything seem dark.

She hardly slept anymore. At night she lay in bed going over all the images she never wanted to lose: Her mother's smile. Theo in his crib. His first laugh, first step. Derek, when they were good. When the look in his eyes made her feel loved and precious and whole. When they had a future.

And then she'd think of all the things she'd miss if her sight kept failing, if her world went dark: walking along a new street, Sunday drives, seeing her first Broadway musical, Theo's growth through the years, freedom. Freedom to make her life something she could be proud of, something that was all her own creation.

"It's not working." Kali squeaked the words.

"You don't know that."

Of course she didn't know, but she felt it. She felt the tumour fighting back, growing, taking over her sight and eventually her life. She curled into the couch. "I'm such a bad mom."

"Most parents yell. All, at some points. It's amazing that you don't usually. He's just not used to it."

"I don't yell because he's amazing. He doesn't need—"

"And that's all on you."

She shook her head, feeling pathetic. Knowing she needed to stop this wallowing. Sit up and—

"You have to trust."

"Trust?" She laughed. Trust. Hope. It's all anyone offered. All they *could* offer, but it didn't mean anything. For the past week, she'd gotten dressed, gotten out of bed, gone to her appointments, most of the time feeling barely alive. Feeling, if it weren't for Theo, she'd just give up.

Kali raised her gaze to Lincoln's once more. "Those words are for children. Lies we're told. Trust. Hope. Dream. But there's no point. Good happens or it doesn't."

Kali stared ahead, her gaze focused on nothing. She felt trapped. No matter how much she wanted to escape the enemy growing inside her, she couldn't. Escape was impossible. The tumour would grow or it wouldn't. Would blind her or not. It was out of her control.

She turned back to Lincoln. "I can hope, I can try, but it all gets dashed. All falls apart. Every time something good happens, something worse follows. It's been like that my whole life.

"Hope, dream, plan, try ... it only works for the chosen few. Some get the stars. The rest of us get piles of shit."

"Kali, that's ridicu—"

Theo popped his head up from behind the side of the couch. His eyes moist, his expression fearful. Kali gasped. "I thought you were in your room."

The boy looked from Kali to Lincoln.

Lincoln said nothing. He shook his head and laid it against the couch, eyes closed.

Kali traced back her words. What had Theo heard? What would he understand? She motioned to him, urging her son toward her, anxious to hug away his fears. He stared at her, unmoving.

She looked again at Lincoln, whose eyes were open now, his gaze on Theo. He gestured and Theo cuddled into him, the motion slicing through Kali like a knife to the heart.

She didn't deserve them. Either of them. And maybe now Lincoln would realize that. Maybe he'd finally decide enough was enough.

Lincoln turned to her. "Why don't you go for a walk?"

"What?" Kali looked at the two as Theo's head pushed into Lincoln's side, his gaze away from Kali.

"Just go outside. Be alone. Walk. I'll stay with Theo, put him to bed."

Kali kept her voice low and even. "You're kicking me out of my own—"

"Kali, just—" His voice was sharp, frustrated. "Don't you think you could use some time alone? Some time to cool off?"

Kali's mouth hung slightly open. She stared.

"Walk it off."

She stood, wanting to fight back, wanting to defend

herself. But defend what, her assertion that life was shit? Her misery? She grabbed her satchel and headphones. Theo had heard it all. Heard her give up hope. Heard her say her life was miserable. *Please don't let him understand. Don't let him remember.*

Kali stepped toward the door. "I won't be long."

"Take as long as you like. As long as you need."

His tone was soft now. Tired, but soft. Not accusatory.

Kali backed to the hall slowly. She turned and left the apartment, careful to close the door as gently as she could. In the elevator she wrapped her hands around her middle, staring at the doors, not wanting them to open. She didn't know where to go, or what this exile was supposed to do.

At last the elevator doors opened and she stepped out. A walk around the park, maybe two. Some minutes on a bench. It wouldn't fix anything, but maybe it would calm her, remind her that whether she felt like it or not, she had to act. Had to pretend she was okay.

She slipped on her headphones and flipped through to a track she'd been listening to a lot lately. *Les Misérables*, again, Éponine's song this time: on her own, the way Kali felt. It was maudlin, she knew, indulging in this misery, but comforting as well.

Kali exited the building and turned down the drive. She stopped. Less than forty feet away from her on the small triangle of grass separating the drive from the sidewalk stood a figure in the shadows. No, paced in the shadows, hands slightly up, mouth moving. Marvin.

Kali slipped the headphones down to her neck and approached slowly.

Marvin's head rose. He darted toward her then stopped

midway, a glance back to his cart. He backed up as she approached, glancing behind at the cart every few steps.

Kali shivered as a breeze swirled around her. "What are you—?"

"You haven't been by. And I didn't know. I didn't—" He shook his head.

Kali looked from Marvin to the cart. "How did you—?"

"The bridge." He nodded. "I took the bridge."

Kali looked toward the harbour. "That's over five kilometres. And going through the toll, and those hills."

"You okay, Sweetness?" Marvin stepped closer. "With your ..." He raised a hand to the side of his head.

Kali shifted. "I'm doing treatment."

"It helping?"

She opened her mouth, closed it. He looked so weak. Frail. Concerned. "I'm not sure."

"You're going to beat this." He stood taller, the way she imagined he used to stand years ago. "Don't give up. You're obstinate, determined. From the first time I saw you, I thought, now that's a powerful woman."

Kali's stomach clenched. She couldn't deal with this right now, with him. "Marvin, are you okay? Do you need anything, or—" She raised a hand and let it fall.

"I came to see you. To see if you're okay."

Kali sighed. "I'm fine."

"You're not."

"I am. Just came out for some fresh air."

"Where's the boy?"

"Upstairs."

Marvin raised a brow.

"With Lincoln. He's fine. We're both fine."

He stepped closer. "You're strong, Kali. Doesn't matter if you lose your sight, your hearing, your limbs. You'll get through it."

Kali took a deep breath. Her chest shook. Anger flared. *Hold back. Keep it in.* "No."

"What?"

"No. You don't get to say that. 'I'm strong.' What do you know about strength? Who are you to say someone else is strong? To expect that?" Her voice rose. "You gave up on life. You're homeless. Not because you have to be, but because you're too scared to spend the night in a home. Like you think, what, just your presence is going to kill the people who share your roof?"

"Well, I—"

"Well, what, Marvin? You know," Kali leaned back, "I just realized it's basically the same thing as Theo. He's afraid to talk because he thinks it will hurt someone. You're afraid to live."

"No, no. That's not—"

"He's three, Marvin. Or four, whatever. Three when he finally had the courage to talk. How old are you? How—"

"I know." Marvin's head started that quick shake. Kali hated it. Hated the way it signified something wasn't right, that *he* needed protection, help, understanding. That she had no right to be standing here yelling at him. "He's strong. Like you. He'll figure it out and—"

"Bullshit." Kali stepped forward. "You talk about how wonderful Beatrice was. How perfect. Well, would some perfect woman fall in love with a loser? And what about the fact that you kept it together long enough to raise your boys? To provide for them. That takes strength. And yet now what are you? A scared pile of shit?" Kali flung her hand in the air, her body trembling. *Stop,* something inside her screamed. *This isn't you. Stop.*

"You tell me not to give up. Not to let myself fall apart. You say I'm strong. Well, if that's true it's only because I've forced myself to be. So why don't you do the same? What you've just been telling me, why don't you tell it to yourself? Say it in a mirror. Force yourself to be strong. Get your life together. Then come back to me. Then tell me it's going to be fine."

Marvin stared at Kali. He nodded slightly, then backed up to the curb and sat.

"What are you doing?"

"Thinking."

Kali stood, uncertain whether to stay standing, sit beside him, or walk away. "About what?"

"What you said."

Kali stayed staring. "Okay."

"You go on your walk, Sweetness. And I'll get out of your way."

"That's not—" Kali shook her head. Her shoulders fell. "What are you going to do tonight? You can't walk back across that bridge now."

He shrugged.

Kali let a long sigh escape. "Will you come up?"

He shook his head.

"At least come and get something to eat if you won't stay."

"I'm fine, Sweetness. I'm full. Promise. Just need a little sit. You walk now. Go."

Kali hesitated then waved a hand as she strode down the drive. She stopped. She should go back, force him to come inside. But he didn't want that. She couldn't force him.

She walked on. Marvin was not her problem. Marvin had figured out his sleeping situation for years. At the street she looked both ways, looked again, and crossed.

CHAPTER TWENTY-TWO

Almost an hour had passed by the time Kali pushed open the door of her apartment. She set down her satchel and leaned against the wall. The air had been good, the movement, the music, but still her whole body felt on edge. As she walked, dark shadows had stretched between the lampposts in the park. The cars nearby made it hard to hear approaching steps, and more than one quiet jogger or fast walker had overtaken her, shocking her with their sudden presence.

This was her life now. Never knowing who or what was on either side of her without having to turn her body, seeing so much less of the world than she should be; one day, maybe not seeing it at all.

Kali made her way to the living room. Her throat caught. It was empty. She resisted the urge to call out. Lincoln could be in the bathroom, or with Theo, helping him get back to—

"I'm here."

She turned to the kitchen. "Oh." Kali let out a nervous laugh. "Good." A mug and crumb dusted plate sat at the spot opposite Lincoln. "Theo wanted another snack?"

"Nope." Lincoln gestured for her to sit. "Marvin came for a visit."

Kali inhaled then let the breath out as she sat. "Really?"

"Says you're not doing too well. Not that I needed anyone to tell me that."

Kali stared at the table. She wiped some crumbs into her palm and dropped them on the plate.

"He came here. On his own. With no prompting?"

Lincoln nodded. "How was your walk?"

"Good. Thanks." She rolled her shoulders and sat, her gaze on Lincoln.

"Yelling at Theo, then heading out and yelling at Marvin."

"I—"

"No." Lincoln put up a hand. "I get it. I do. You have a lot weighing on you. You always have." He shrugged. "And I'm no one to talk. I don't know what it's like, having people rely on you." He paused. "I'm guessing it's hard."

Kali stared at him. He was right. He definitely wasn't one to talk. When his world crumbled he'd run from it. She opened her mouth to speak then closed it, waiting instead for Lincoln to finish.

"When I was going through my ..." he hesitated, "dark days I just turned off, pulled away. Became a hermit, as I believe you called it." Another pause. "It's not fair."

Kali eyed him. "What's not fair?"

"That you can't. That you've got to be stronger, do better."

She bit her lip.

"You've seen it all, right? Death, suffering, horrible pain?"

Kali gave a slight nod. What was he getting at?

"You've probably seen people give up."

She sat silent.

"But you can't. You don't have that luxury. And I know you might lose your sight, and that's terrifying—needing to relearn how you'll live if you do, and all you'll miss ... and for all you know, you'll have to deal with that all on your own."

Kali stiffened. Lincoln smiled. "I'm not planning to go anywhere, but you don't know that. And honestly, I don't either." He leaned forward. "I'll admit, there are times I wonder if you'd be better off without me. It's frustrating, all of this."

What exactly? Her? The tumour?

"We both know you're terrified and you're angry, and that makes sense, but you don't have the luxury I had. You don't get to fall apart. You have a son, and that son needs looking after."

Kali pushed her palms into the table. A vein in her forehead twitched. "You think I don't know that?"

"Of course you do. Marvin, though, you don't have to look after him. He's not your responsibility. So acknowledge that, but don't take it out on him."

Kali shifted in her seat. He'd known Marvin, for what, a few weeks. She'd been dealing with him for years.

"And like I said, I'm no one to talk, trust me. But someone has got to talk. Because you're doing what everyone wants to do, what I did. You're being indulgent with your misery."

Kali's chest tightened.

"And again, let me stress this, you have a right to be, at times, but you can't live like that. Not long term. Not when you're all Theo has."

She swallowed. Rage and guilt swirling within her.

"So let me in more for those times when you need to check out, to get away. I'll help out as much as I can." He paused again, and Kali felt her anger waver. "It's a slippery slope you're heading down. So think of this as a nudge back up. You have a son, an amazing son who I know you love like mad, so you can't let the misery pull you down. You slide down too far and it'll be near impossible to pull yourself back up again.

"Trust me, I know." He gave the slightest smile. "Theo doesn't need you to be perfect, but he needs more than you've been giving. He needs you to be honest. He has no idea what's going on. He just knows that something's not right with you, and he's scared, and he thinks it's his fault."

Kali fought tears as anger bubbled up again, her voice barely audible. "You don't know. You don't know what it's like. Not just the fear, the frustration. But the pain. The nausea. The mind-numbing fatigue. You have no idea. And my life," she shook her hand then pressed it into the table again. "I never planned to be a single mom. I never planned to be a mom, not until there was no turning back. I wanted to travel. See the world. Explore. Dance! Instead, I'm stuck. I've always been stuck. And now more than ever." She breathed heavily, her shoulders shaking. "You have no idea about my life, what any of this is like. So don't pretend we're the same. And don't tell me what my kid needs!"

Lincoln leaned back. She could see the tension in him, the way he fought letting his exasperation pour out on her. "You're right. I don't know what it's like. But I know all this worry, this fear and clinging to it, is making things worse. It's not going to bring back your sight. It's not going to determine whether the treatment works or whether it doesn't. It's just going to make you even more miserable than you already are."

Kali pushed back from the table. He expected her to let go, be fine, be happy? Her lips pressed tight. She wanted to yell, scream, let out the anger and frustration she'd let out twice already today. But what if she did and he walked away? She needed him. Theo needed him. She shook.

She paced. She whipped around as Lincoln stood.

"I'm leaving now. But I'll be back tomorrow around five-thirty."

Kali's brow furrowed.

"Okay?"

She crossed her arms. "Why?"

"I'm going to take you two somewhere. Don't worry about dinner, but be ready."

The stubbornness in Kali shot up. He wasn't asking. He was telling.

Lincoln smiled, his hair falling across his forehead and almost over his eye. "That all right?"

Kali's shoulders relaxed. Tension eased out of her like air from an old balloon. She nodded.

LINCOLN WALKED THE halls of his apartment, checking and double checking that everything was in place—all the paint brushes, tools, and tarps put away.

The place looked sparse, barren, even more so than the first time Kali had entered it. He'd disassembled and moved his work table to a large shed he'd built on the ground just adjacent to the tree house. It made more sense being there anyway.

But the place looked so empty. He'd tossed his couch,

which he imagined Kali must have hated, how could anyone not? He debated getting a new one, but that didn't seem the right choice either. If he wanted the place to feel like hers, she should be the one to decide on a new couch, or if hers alone was enough. So all that remained in the living room were a side table he'd refurbished, a bookshelf, and one lamp. The bedrooms weren't much better. He'd moved his bed, dresser and shelves into the spare room and his, now, was empty.

Fresh, bright paint covered the walls: no more peeling. The floors shone after he'd spent two days refinishing them, and new, real wood kitchen cabinet doors and counters replaced the old ratty ones. The place looked good. And with the help of equipment borrowed and old supplies scrounged from the company warehouse, he'd done it on only a few hundred dollars and a few weeks of hard work.

After one more quick glance, Lincoln stepped out into the stairwell and locked the door.

FORTY MINUTES LATER, Lincoln was putting his key back in the lock, Kali and Theo standing behind him.

Kali put a hand to her forehead and yawned. Her face looked drawn, like she hadn't slept at all, as she shifted the Chinese food bag in her arm. "What are we doing here?"

"Well, we'll eat."

"But we could have—"

"Just a second." Lincoln pushed open the door and stepped aside.

Kali stepped past him into the open space of the living room. Theo ran in, turning and jumping. He disappeared into the kitchen and then his footsteps sounded down the hall. Kali turned. "Wow. You've been busy."

"I have."

Lincoln shut the door behind him and took the bag of food from her. He walked into the kitchen.

"This is amazing." Her voice echoed in the expansive space. It seems so much bigger and brighter. Did you redo the floors?"

"Refinished."

She appeared before him, her mouth open. "Wow." She stepped forward, running her hand along the counter. "This is ... it's a whole new place."

He gestured to the lime green oven and fridge. "They don't quite fit anymore. They're probably older than the both of us."

Kali turned her body one way and then the other to glance at them. She shrugged. "Retro."

Lincoln laughed. "That's one way of looking at it."

"And clearly you did." She turned again, and he tried not to frown at the motion, the fact that where another person would only have to shift her head, Kali's whole body now moved to take in the space. "You've picked cabinets and a cupboard that make it work."

He smiled at her, the interest on her face, how impressed she seemed.

"But I don't get it. Aren't you moving into the tree house?" She met his gaze.

Lincoln's pulse quickened. "Follow me." He led her down the hall to his old room and pushed open the door. She stepped in, her mouth falling open again and her brow raised in question. Theo popped his head out from behind the room's divider, a grin on his face. Kali turned to Lincoln.

"What—?"

"Your place is too expensive. And it's far from your treatments."

"My treatments are half done." Her voice was wary.

"There'll be more. Follow-ups. And it's close to the CNIB."

Kali shook her head. "I don't plan to—"

"You need a new place. You said—"

"I know." Her voice shook. Theo tugged on her arm. She smiled at him, "Why don't you go explore the rest of the apartment, sweetie?" then turned back to Lincoln, her words tight. "But this is your place."

"Yeah." Lincoln rubbed a hand along his neck, then dropped it and waved a hand out. "But it can be our place. Not just mine."

She turned again, her gaze on the divider. "What's—"

"For you and Theo. So you have your separate space. I know it means neither area is big this way, but if it's really too small he can take the spare and I'll—"

"You?" She whipped back. "Aren't you planning to live in the tree house, isn't—"

"I have a job in town now, so—"

She turned both ways, as if looking for a place to sit. Finding none, she looked back at Lincoln. "A job?"

"Working for my cousin. Construction. I thought—"

"Construction? But that's not. I mean—" She rubbed both hands along the back of her neck. "Isn't... weren't you some big corporate hot shot? What are you doing in construction?"

"You don't know when you're going back to work and you need ... well, maybe not need, but it would be helpful to have someone close until you get bet—"

"I may never get better."

Lincoln furrowed his brow. "The effects of the radiation will get better. And until then, if you have a bad day or—" Lincoln took a deep breath. Had he misjudged how far they'd come? "If you want I'll live in the tree house. That was my original plan anyway. You and Theo could each have your own room. This place could be yours."

Kali's eyes widened.

"But it's not practical out there, to get to work, to get into town if there's an emergency. Especially when the snow comes. It may be impassable when the snow comes."

Kali bit her lip and nodded. "You got a job for ... I mean ..."

"I got a job for me. It feels good working again. But yeah, I imagine times are tight for you and I figured if we shared this place the rent's practically nothing."

She stared at him, her head tilted.

"And it didn't work so badly before. This would be even better. Our place. Not mine. Ours, and—"

Kali flung her arms around him, making Lincoln stumble back with the shock. He cradled his arms around her.

"Thank you." Her words were barely a whisper. She held tighter as Lincoln regained his footing.

"I know it's pretty barren, but once we move your stuff over."

She nodded against his chest then stepped away, looking embarrassed but resolved. "I've applied for sickness benefits, E.I. It should start soon, and disability too, though that will take longer."

Lincoln nodded, his arms crossed just below the spot her head rested a moment ago. "Okay."

"So once it does, I'll put in my fair share. For food and rent and ..." she hesitated. "Everything."

"Great."

They stared at each other. "Theo will be excited." Kali's voice was high, uneven.

"Definitely."

She shifted foot to foot. "Maybe a little confused. All these changes. But excited."

"And it's close to Mrs. Martin. To Cherie. He'll like that."

"Definitely." Kali looked away, then back at Lincoln. "Well, that food's probably getting cold."

"It would be, yeah." Lincoln gestured toward the door, indicating Kali go first. She wrapped her arms around him again. "Thank you. I don't even ... with all I ... and after last night." She let out a breath and pulled away, her smile tight. She walked past him, her step lighter than he'd seen it in weeks.

Lincoln lingered a moment.

Kali and Theo were moving in. She'd be closer to treatment, closer to affordable childcare—Mrs. Martin and him—and so much of the worry and fear he'd seen building in her these past weeks, it seemed to slide off of her the moment she pulled out of his embrace. This didn't solve the biggest problem, but a lot of the smaller ones.

Lincoln felt his own body relax as he watched her walk down the hallway to start unpacking the Chinese food. He'd be close by if she needed him. He wouldn't lie in bed at night wondering if she had a day she could hardly handle, if she needed help but was too proud to ask for it, if this time the unseen truck barrelling toward her hadn't missed.

CHAPTER TWENTY-THREE

A half hour after gorging on Chinese food, Lincoln sat on the floor, his back against the wall, one hand rubbing his stomach. "Do you think it's possible for a stomach to actually explode?"

Kali chuckled and Theo grinned. "Possible, perhaps," said Kali, "but highly unlikely."

Lincoln winked at Theo. "Well, that's good." He kept his gaze on the boy. "So you like the new look of the place?"

Theo put two thumbs up.

"And you're glad to be coming back?"

He made the thumbs dance, then put a finger to his chin. He mimed climbing what seemed like a ladder then stood, his arms out, fingers outstretched, slightly swaying.

"What about the tree house?"

He nodded.

"It's still there. I'll just be staying here most of the time."

Theo frowned.

"You don't want me here?"

He waved both hands in front of him, shaking his head, then made a walking motion, followed by the climbing.

Lincoln glanced to Kali, who was shaking her head out of Theo's view. Lincoln rubbed his chin. "I'm sorry. I'm just not following you, buddy. Why don't you come on over, tell me what you're trying to say."

Theo stomped one foot on the ground then wavered. He walked over to Lincoln and cupped a hand around his ear.

"Oh!" Lincoln feigned realization. "You want to see the tree house?"

Theo nodded.

Lincoln gestured to Kali. "Ask your mom."

He turned to Kali, arms out to the side, head tilted.

"Good things come to those who speak." Lincoln gave Theo a little nudge toward Kali.

Kali wore a gentle smile as Theo's hands cupped around her ear. "Yes." She grinned. "We can go to the tree house." She listened. "Tomorrow? I don't know ..."

Lincoln grinned. "Tomorrow's fine with me."

Theo stepped back from Kali and pointed at Lincoln.

"Well," Kali looked between the two, "tomorrow it is."

Theo clapped.

Lincoln pulled his knees up and rested an arm on them, staring at Kali and her son. "You ever been to Musquodoboit?"

Kali shook her head then paused mid-shake. "Oh, the Train Museum. Yeah, when I was in school."

"Railway museum," said Lincoln. "That the only time?"

"I think so."

A shot of excitement tingled through Lincoln. This would be fun, would be exactly what Kali needed. "I have a buddy who has some boys about Theo's age. They don't live too far from the turn off to the tree house. It might be nice to drop

Theo off there and you and I have an excursion."

Theo's brow furrowed. He pointed to his chest.

"This excursion wouldn't be so fun for you," said Lincoln, "but visiting those boys, that would be a blast. They have a trampoline and a great big field to play catch and soccer and are always up to lots of great fun."

Kali looked uncertain. "I'm not dropping Theo off with strangers."

"Strangers to you. I've know them since I was Theo's age. The mom, she's just about the sweetest woman you've ever met. They're good people."

Kali looked to Theo, who was practically bouncing. "I don't know."

"The day care was full of strangers too."

"You want to go?" Kali asked Theo. "To meet these boys and use their trampoline?"

He nodded.

Kali turned to Lincoln. "And this excursion?"

The corners of Lincoln's lips twitched up. "It'd be a surprise. A good one, I'm sure."

Kali's brow rose. "You're not giving me any more than that?"

"It'd require good shoes."

Kali laughed. "The trampoline have a net?"

Lincoln nodded. "Their mother insisted."

THEO JUMPED UP AND down on the lawn outside the apartment, his face lit with excitement. The bouncy castle at city events was the closest he'd ever come to a trampoline. Kali looked up—blue skies and white fluffy clouds. A warm breeze. Surprisingly warm for early October.

Yesterday's forecast of light showers had apparently blown away. And she was glad, definitely, but when the alarm sounded at seven-thirty this morning, the earliest she'd set it in weeks, she'd hoped that maybe the rain would cancel their plans ... whatever those plans were. Lincoln had told her to wear sturdy shoes with ankle support and layers. The rest, he said, he would handle.

His truck pulled into the drive at eight-o-clock on the dot. He waved out the window then switched off the truck and hopped out of the cab. Kali's breath caught. His eyes seemed to gleam as the light caught them. She hadn't paid much attention before and perhaps couldn't have answered if asked the colour. Brown, deep blue, hazel? Today his eyes seemed green against the rich tone of his shirt. His face, free of another inch or two of beard, seemed more chiselled. She liked the scruff.

Not that the state of his facial hair should matter to her.

Lincoln swung Theo in the air to the sound of laughter: real, audible laughter, then set him down, his gaze on Kali. "Did you bring your pills? We'll be gone all day. I forgot to mention that."

Kali patted her satchel.

He looked at it, uncertainty on his face. "We'll leave that

in the truck or you can run it upstairs after taking out your wallet and pills. Anything else of value?"

"My phone."

He nodded. "That can go in your pocket or my pack."

Kali headed toward the passenger door.

"Why don't we do that now, to make sure we don't forget. Your pills, especially."

Kali shrugged and gestured to the back of the cab. Lincoln nodded and she pulled open the door as Lincoln helped Theo into the cab on the other side and oversaw the adjustment of his booster seat, a now permanent fixture in Lincoln's truck. It wasn't as if Kali needed it.

"We going camping?" asked Kali as she slipped her wallet and pills into Lincoln's pack.

"That would require a much bigger pack." Theo safely buckled, Lincoln slammed the door and met Kali in the front. "But it's got our lunch, first aid kit, water, binoculars."

"First aid kit?" Kali slid into her seat and fastened the belt. "Do I want to know?"

"You mean you haven't guessed?"

Kali shook her head.

"Well, then a little mystery may be part of the fun."

About forty-five minutes later the truck turned down a long and bumpy drive. Kali's nausea hadn't made a show today, the steroids were definitely helping in that department, but it threatened to arise as she bounced in the seat. She gripped the armrest and door. "This the road to your lot?"

Lincoln laughed. "The road to my lot makes this seem like smooth sailing, not that you could call the way in a road."

They continued along until the thick trees parted, revealing a bright clearing. The lawn was expansive, almost as big as a baseball field, with bright-leaved trees spread throughout. The house seemed proportionally as expansive. A white, wooden structure with a wrap-around porch, red roof and trim. Kali would have thought she'd travelled back in time if not for the trampoline she could spot behind the house, the satellite on the roof, and the shiny truck parked just in front of theirs.

Four boys seemed to tumble out of the house. A woman with curly red hair and a broad smile trailed after them, wiping her hands on an apron.

Kali glanced at Lincoln then gestured to Theo. "They know?"

"They know."

The boys clambered around the truck. Lincoln stepped out and they chatted at him, so fast and so hard Kali could hardly make out the words. One boy started climbing up Lincoln's side while two others pointed to the truck. Kali walked around to open the door for Theo, whose eyes were wide. "It's okay," she whispered. "They're nice. You're going to have tons of fun."

He peered over her shoulder then looked back at Kali, skeptical.

"I'm sure of it. So much fun. Did you see the trampoline when we were driving in?"

Theo nodded and crawled out. What looked like the oldest and the second youngest boy practically pounced on him, talking away but not asking questions. They led him toward the back of the house, Theo twisting to look back with a nervous smile. Kali smiled back, trying to mask her own nervousness.

The woman approached and wrapped her arms around

Lincoln then kissed him on the cheek. An obvious bump sat beneath her apron.

"I'm Jennifer," the woman smiled, turning to Kali with a hand out. "Like just about every fifth woman my age you'll meet."

Kali took the hand. "Kali."

"Ah," the woman winked, "your mother had a little creativity." Her laugh was light and fresh. "So he's taking you to the wilderness, is he?"

Kali looked to Lincoln.

"Oh, he hasn't told you?" Another laugh. "Well, just don't let him push you too hard. Back in the day, this one and Johnny used to leave me winded." She leaned in toward Kali. "I've learned though, if you just stop, they will too. You wouldn't know by the looks of 'em, but they're gentlemanly enough not to leave a lady by her lonesome in the woods."

Lincoln rubbed a hand through his hair. "You could handle yourself no problem."

"Of course I could." Jennifer shifted her gaze to Lincoln, a look of fond familiarity on her face that made Kali feel like an outsider. But that doesn't mean you two, or Andrew for that matter, would let me."

"Johnny around?" asked Lincoln.

"Nah, he got a call about an hour ago. His mother's facing some plumbing crisis. Hopefully, he'll be back to say hello when you pick up the boy." Jennifer looked to Kali again. "Theo, right?"

"Yeah," Kali nodded. "Are you sure you're all right watching him?"

"I'm sure." Jennifer's smile was warm. "Are you? You must be a little nervous, not knowing me or anything about me."

Kali pursed her lips.

Jennifer gestured her head towards the boys in the back. "I've got a lot of experience. And I'll keep an eye on him like a hawk."

"Thank you." Kali swallowed. "He's pretty easy but sensitive at times."

"A sensitive boy." Jennifer shook her head. "Wish I had myself one of those." She raised a hand to Kali's shoulder. "But they're kind. Don't worry about that. They'll treat your boy like a prince." She laid a hand on her belly. "I'm really hoping for a girl with this one. I'd love a boy, of course," she rolled her eyes, "but someone to put in dresses, to watch movies with that don't involve trucks and bombs and general destruction."

Kali smiled, not knowing what to say.

"So, we'll be three or four hours," said Lincoln. "Possibly five."

Five hours? Kali studied him. What excursion in the woods could possibly take five hours?

"I'll have him fed and most likely worn out." Jennifer laughed and wrapped her arms around Lincoln again, this time without a kiss. She rubbed her hand on Kali's shoulder. "You two have fun."

Back on the road, Kali turned to Lincoln. "You said you've known her long?"

"Jennifer?" He glanced over. "Oh yeah, since we were kids. Johnny, her husband, is my cousin's cousin and she lived next door to him growing up. We were always up to something."

"You seemed so natural with her."

"Natural?" Lincoln's brow rose.

"Comfortable. Easy. Open."

"Like I said, we've known each other since we were kids."

Kali stared out the window. "That's nice."

Lincoln chuckled. "Yeah. It is."

CHAPTER TWENTY-FOUR

Lincoln looked over at Kali. She sat with her arms wrapped tight around her middle, her lips slightly pursed. "You feeling okay?"

"Hmm?" She drew her gaze from the window. "Oh, yeah. I'm fine."

"Your head? Your stomach?"

She offered the slightest smile. "Pretty good today."

So rarely now did he see that strong, larger than life woman he'd first seen racing for the bus. She was still there, of course, but only in glimpses. He brought his attention back to the road. What would she think of today? He'd lain awake for several hours the night before, wondering if he was pushing too hard, if she wouldn't be interested in this hike even in the prime of health, but she had mentioned wanting to travel, to explore. This was a taste of it. Lincoln pulled the truck into the Trailway parking space.

Kali looked around. "We're going on the rail trail?"

"It'll get us to where we're going."

Kali eased out of the truck as Lincoln hopped out and grabbed his pack from the back. "Where we're—?"

Lincoln pointed to the woods, growing higher in the distance.

"I can barely get up the stairs to your apartment."

"The doctor said the more you do, as long as you don't push it too hard, the more energy you'll have."

"But—"

"You haven't been doing much lately." Lincoln swung the pack over his back. "No offence."

"I can hardly see. I trip over steps and curbs and toy trucks."

"So you'll have to pay more attention than usual. I know it'll be a bit hard. But it'll be worth it."

Kali took a step away from him. "Worth what?"

"The experience. The view." Lincoln leaned against the doors of the truck. "This is an incredible system of trails. And so many people who live so close never see it. I wanted you to see it."

"In case I never have another chance?"

Lincoln stared at her. She was standing taller now, ready to fight, to refuse. "Or to show you still can."

Her brow furrowed. "What do you mean 'system?'"

Lincoln gestured to the hills. "A series of trails and loops with access points to the Trailway. We'll just be doing one of the first ones today. Nothing too intense. Just under 9K."

"Nine kilometres?" Kali shook her head.

"It's not as far as you think. We'll take it slow." He reached back into the back of the cab and pulled out two hiking poles. "These will help."

Kali stared at the offering.

"They're not canes. They're just there for support. They ease the pressure on your joints and will help you if you stumble. When I do a full day hike on uneven terrain I sometimes use them myself."

Kali reached for the poles and looked to the trail.

"We'll start on the Trailway. A nice, easy stroll."

KALI LOOKED TO THE Trailway. Not another car was in the lot, but it was early and Lincoln seemed the type to know his way around the wilderness. He'd planned to live there after all. "There cell service, in case something happens?"

Lincoln grinned as he slammed his truck door closed. "In places. I have a radio in the pack, and Johnny knows the frequency I'll be on."

"He'll check it?"

"Not usually, but today, considering the circumstances." He shrugged.

Kali still wasn't sure. Not that that was her, not being sure. Or at least it hadn't been her. She was the woman who did things. Who made it work. And though she'd never spent much time in this type of terrain—not that she even really knew what the terrain would be—she'd enjoyed the times she spent in the woods as a child, running through the trees with the other children, making their own trails to the lake. That was mostly flat land, and the excursions had ended with the start of puberty. But she'd loved them. "Okay."

"What?"

"Okay." Kali stepped past Lincoln to the trail entrance. "Let's go."

They started along the Trailway. Birds chirped, the river bubbled, and Kali felt something inside her well up. She filled her lungs then released them again, surprised at the way her shoulders relaxed. The leaves were a blaze of orange, yellow, and every now and then a fiery red. They kept silent as they walked.

About forty-five minutes in, Lincoln stopped. Kali turned to him, a question in her eyes. He pulled a bottle from his pack and offered it to her.

"Thanks."

He gestured to a sign and what looked like a foot path leading into the woods.

Kali's gaze travelled up the ascent. "So this is where it begins."

"This is where it begins."

Kali fell into step behind Lincoln. The path was uneven and rocky in parts. Roots crept up unexpectedly, making her thankful for the poles to steady her. Once or twice she had to put the poles to the side to scramble over or around rocks, but Lincoln was always there, arms out to steady her or offer a hand up.

It wasn't the same peaceful experience the Trailway had been, where she could let her mind free. It took focus, concentration, which was a different type of freedom.

The air was cooler under the cover of the trees, but within minutes Kali shed her jacket and wiped a gleam of sweat from her brow.

"How much farther?" she asked with a laugh.

Lincoln laughed back, but the pace seemed to slow.

Kali had no idea how much time had passed when they stepped out into the sun. It took a moment for her eyes to adjust. She gasped. As far as she could see there was nothing but colour. Red, yellow, orange of the leaves, green of the pines, and blue of the lake and the sky. "It's ..." She struggled for the words.

"Worth it?"

Kali turned to Lincoln, her pulse racing. "Yeah." Her breath came out in a laugh. "It's worth it."

He gestured to a make-shift bench, and Kali eased herself onto it, setting the poles to the side. She took the water he offered.

"A snack?"

She turned to him. "What do you have?"

"Apples. Trail mix. Egg salad sandwiches, though I'm thinking we could save those for the next stop."

"An apple sounds great."

Kali bit into the crisp fruit and watched several crows soar in the distance. She leaned back and closed her eyes, revelling in the warmth of the sun on her face and arms. She let it soak in, wondering the last time she'd sat in the sun, allowing herself not to worry about anything or anyone. Before Theo for sure. Back when life seemed full of so many possibilities. When she believed she'd get far away from Nova Scotia, from Canada even. When she thought she'd travel, explore, live a life nothing like her mother's had been—stuck in the same town where she'd taken her first breath.

When she opened her eyes, Lincoln was staring at her. Kali shifted slightly then relaxed, smiling back at him.

"You like it so far?" he asked.

"It's rough." Kali directed her gaze back to the horizon. "But yeah, I like it."

Lincoln leaned back on his elbow, a satisfied smile on his

face.

"So, I take it you've done this whole trail before."

"The system of them, yeah. To do the entire network you either have to start super early and end late—only possible in summer—or overnight it. I did that once with Romper. Before that, though ... I don't know. Years. In undergrad, probably." He glanced at her. "I'm glad you like it. I was worried I'd drag you out here and ... I don't know. I wanted you to like it."

"It'd be hard not to."

"It's so close, these amazing sights. And the fact that you have to work for them, I don't know, it just makes them better. Yet so many people never see them. I rarely encounter anyone else on these trails. The trailway, yes, but ..."

Kali stared at his profile as he sat, knees up, arms resting on them, eyes toward the distance. "It is hard work."

He let out a little laugh. "I couldn't get Lucy out here if my life depended on it."

Kali propped herself up.

Lincoln shook his head. "Sorry, I—"

"It's okay."

"Don't know why I brought her up. I guess just ... the difference you know, of my life with her compared to my life without. Somehow I thought that was the life I wanted, she was the life I wanted. But this is the life I missed."

"Have you seen her again? Since your Mom's birthday party?"

"No." He rubbed a hand through his hair, the strong lines of his biceps in full display. Kali swallowed and shifted away from him. Lincoln glanced at her before looking back at the view. "But I will be. She's pregnant again and engaged to my brother."

"You seen him?"

"Nah." Lincoln shook his head. "Just my mom a couple of times. My younger sister has reached out. She wants to get together but ... I don't know."

"What about your dad?"

Lincoln glanced back at Kali. "No." He stood and offered his hand. "You ready to get going?"

Kali felt cut off, and not quite ready to end the moment, but she accepted his hand and let him pull her up.

By the time they returned to the truck almost three and a half hours had passed. Her muscles ached, but her mind felt alert and something else—her spirit?—invigorated.

"Another one tomorrow?" asked Lincoln as he held open the truck door.

"Definitely not." Kali groaned.

"But it was good?" Lincoln stood inches from her, the door open in his hand, as she buckled up.

"It was amazing." Each viewpoint had been just as incredible as the last, though in different ways, and after a few tutorials from Lincoln she'd become much more adept at using the poles to guide her past the rocks and rogue roots while simultaneously taking some of the pressure off of her joints. And most amazing of all, there'd been whole stretches of time where she'd forgotten her fading vision, her fear.

Lincoln closed the truck door and made his way around to the other side. "I promise the rest of the day will be more relaxed. You'll have to climb up the tree house, but after that, I'll wait on you hand and foot."

He reached to a cooler in the back and handed her a thermos before starting the ignition.

"I'm fine."

"Drink it." He reversed the truck and pulled out of the parking area. "Your muscles aren't used to this exertion, it'll help ease potential soreness."

She took a sip. "What's—"

"A protein shake."

She grinned, letting the smooth vanilla mix cross her lips. After taking a long drink, she swallowed. "Anything you didn't think of?"

He winked. "Well, I considered setting up a hot tub in the tree house for you to soak any sore muscles, but I didn't want to look like I was trying too hard."

Kali grinned, feeling a flutter in her stomach she hadn't felt in years. "Yeah, I suppose that would be a bit overkill."

CHAPTER TWENTY-FIVE

Lincoln eased the truck over the ruts, stumps, and old roots as cautiously as he could on the way to the tree house. He glanced at Kali, who seemed fine, but continued slowly. He didn't want a wave of nausea ruining the night. A look in the rearview mirror told him Theo was more than fine. A smile spread across his face, hands pressed up against the window. The boys had been good for him. It'd taken almost ten minutes to get him in the car after arriving at Johnny and Jennifer's. He was so full of descriptions he even let out a few unprompted words amongst his miming.

Only the promise of seeing the tree house had gotten Theo in the truck. Lincoln hoped it wouldn't disappoint. It was simple, not elaborate like some of the ones he'd looked up on Pinterest after Kali's suggestion, but it was beautiful. At least *he* thought it was beautiful.

At the site, Lincoln helped Theo out of the truck then turned to Kali. Her gaze was turned toward the tree house, an unreadable expression on her face. Theo jumped up and down and pointed to the ladder.

"Just a minute, buddy." Lincoln pulled his pack and the

cooler out of the back of the truck. He slung the pack over his shoulder and positioned the cooler on the pulley. Four heaves and it was level with the little wrap-around porch he'd built. He turned to Theo and noticed Kali quickly shifted her view, a hand to the side of her face.

"You go in front of me, and I'll stay close behind," said Lincoln.

Theo nodded and immediately started climbing.

"It's safe?" called Kali.

"It's perfectly safe."

At the top, Theo raced around the porch, his hand on the middle of the triple layered railing Lincoln had installed; he wanted no chance of Theo slipping through a too large gap. He looked to the ground. "Do you need help, or—"

"No." Kali stepped to the ladder and reached for the rung closest to her outstretched arm.

Once she reached the top, Lincoln latched the gate opening to the ladder. Another precaution added with Theo in mind, and Kali too, he supposed, once he'd learned her diagnosis. Kali walked around the porch then stopped at the view of the lake. "Not bad." She turned to Lincoln, one hand resting on the railing. "People would pay a lot for a view like this."

"The land was a steal." He stood inches from her, the smell that now seemed definitively Kali still lingering. It must be something she put in her hair. How else could it still be there after all those hours in the breeze and sun? She gestured toward the door.

"Inside. Yes. Of course."

The tree house was still one level, but Lincoln explained how and where there was space to expand. The inside was sparse. A love seat he'd gotten from a Kijiji ad. Two lawn chairs. A bookshelf. Small cupboards with a scant amount of dishes and cutlery. It looked threadbare. Cheap. Kali was silent as he talked, as he explained the heating system, the rudimentary plumbing. He should have waited until he'd had time to make the place more appealing, a place where she could see herself spending time.

"It's incredible."

He turned to her and swallowed.

"You did this all on your own?"

Lincoln caught Theo in his arms as he dashed across the room. "Yes. A labour of—"

"Love." Her smile grew gently. "It's really great. I was expecting ... I don't know. Less."

"It's going to be more," said Lincoln, his hands still on Theo's shoulders. "With the other levels. And I want to actually craft my own furniture, build shelving."

"Why are you giving this up?"

"What?"

"To be in town. To work in town." She hesitated. " Is it for us?"

"Oh, well," Lincoln stepped outside and grabbed the cooler, "it's for me too. As I said, it would be rough in winter. To get in and out. The walls could use another layer of caulking, too."

"You're going to finish it though, the way you wanted?"

"I plan to."

She turned again. "You really could make money off of this—the design, the plan, or building it for others. People would love it." She laughed and gestured to Theo. "It would fulfill their childhood dreams."

"Maybe one day."

Lincoln looked to the cooler. "It's a little early for dinner. Want to take a ..." he paused, his gaze locking with Kali's as he grinned, "a short, easy walk to see a bit of my land and then start a fire for roasted hot dogs?"

Theo clapped and nodded. Kali looked to the love seat. "Do you mind if I just rest here for a bit? I'll join you for the roasting, I promise."

Lincoln assessed Kali. Had he pushed her too hard? She looked tired but was smiling. "No problem." He led Theo out the door and down the ladder.

LINCOLN SET UP THE campfire by the water and several hours later the three of them were sitting around the firelight, stomachs filled, with Theo asleep on Kali's lap. She smoothed her hand over his brow. "I need to tell him soon." Kali kept her gaze on Theo but could feel Lincoln looking at her.

"Tell him?"

"About my sight ... the tumour."

"Oh." Lincoln shifted and Kali turned to him. "I figured you were waiting until you knew more, how permanent it would be."

Kali sighed. "Do you see how fully I have to turn just to see you? When I look forward I wouldn't even know you're there." She paused. "I get so mad all the time because he doesn't understand not to creep up on me, because he leaves his toys and I can't see them. But he doesn't understand why."

She stopped again. "Because I haven't told him."

"Well, then it sounds like a good idea."

"I don't want to scare him."

Lincoln was silent a moment. "You already have. Maybe this will be less scary, knowing what's happening."

Kali wanted to be angry, defensive, but she knew he was right. "I spend minutes sometimes, hours when I can't sleep, just staring at him, memorizing every ridge of him, in case ..."

"There's no reason to think you'll lose all your sight."

"I know." There wasn't, not really. Her fading sight these recent weeks meant nothing. But it was possible. Even if the treatment worked for now, in one year, two, ten, the tumour could continue its growth. "I want to be happier for him. Better for him."

"You're doing fine. You've had some rough patches, but who wouldn't?"

"I've changed. I'm not the same mother I was. I don't know if I ever can be again."

Lincoln took a deep breath and let it out slowly.

"I'm not a nurse anymore. I may never be again. I can't play with him at the park, not in the same way. I get so tired."

"The tiredness will fade after the effects of the treatment fade. And you'll find another job."

"And when he joins a soccer team or needs me to take him to a friend's house on the other side of town? I may never get my license back."

"Which is why there are buses." He elbowed her. "And me."

Kali's voice grew quiet. She knew she was being indulgent, as he'd accused her of days before. She knew her life wasn't over. "I feel like half a person. Like I'm no longer in control."

Again, Lincoln was quiet. Gaze on the water, he finally broke the stillness. "Some of those people at the CNIB, they're amazing. The things they do, the lives they live, and many, sight-wise, are far worse off than you."

"Don't."

"None of us are ever in control of our lives. Not really."

A flock of Canadian geese soared above then landed in the water with a near silent flourish. Kali wanted to be on the hike again, immersed in nature in a way that required her concentration, stole her thoughts. "I don't actually remember my father."

Lincoln turned to her.

"I remember remembering him perhaps, stories of him—all from my mother's perspective, which wasn't exactly flattering—so I have this image, but I don't actually remember him. I know he was a sucker, my mother's words. Always investing in things he knew nothing about, trying to catch a big break, taking money from my mother. Then he left, got himself a new woman, a new child. Apparently, he made it big after that. Some investment paid off." Kali pulled Theo closer. "My mom never saw any of that money. And whenever money was tight, as it often was, she'd go on and on about him, how he ruined us, how I should never get with a man like him. She did though. She had a string of boyfriends who didn't treat her right. They weren't abusive or anything. Just pathetic, lazy. They used her."

Kali watched as the birds took off again, amazed at their coordination, their community. "She said I needed a solid educated white man. Some man with his feet on the ground who'd take me out of this place. This neighbourhood." Kali glanced at Lincoln. "Someone like you ... or who you used to be. You're still educated, still white, though I don't know how solid you are." Her laugh cut off quickly. "It's weird, how my mom thought race had something to do with it. Racist against her own kind I guess. To an extent. She liked Derek. At first. She just didn't like that he convinced me to marry him so young. She thought I'd drop out of school and never have more. She wanted me to have more."

Kali's throat tightened. "After ... well ... when I was left pregnant and alone, her opinion certainly changed. She never said I told you so out loud. She was great, actually, took me back home, watched after Theo like he was her own child. But messages can be passed loud and clear without words."

Lincoln's voice was hesitant. "Surely she couldn't have blamed Derek for—"

Kali turned her head. "Are you afraid of the dark?"

"Uhh ..."

"I am. I always have been a bit. It's childish, I know. But there's just something." She hesitated. "Every night when I go to bed I don't know what it'll be like when I wake up. The fear is always there. And so sometimes when I wake up I keep my eyes closed—so scared of what I'll see when I open them. Will my vision be worse, better, gone completely? It could, you know. Despite the treatment. Maybe even because of the treatment. The swelling, or the tumour fighting back, the radiation not working; I could wake up tomorrow with nothing."

"That's not likely."

"No. It isn't." Theo sighed and shifted and Kali readjusted him, her hand smoothing across his brow once more. "Do you remember what it felt like though, to be afraid of the dark? To wonder what ghosts and goblins waited? But then you grow up, you know there's no ghosts or goblins, but there could be something worse. Far worse. A few years ago I cut through a trail to save some time on the walk home. And the darkness was so thick. So heavy. I heard things in that short stretch of wood. Rustlings. At any moment I knew a hand could reach out—" She rubbed her fingers along her neck, remembering the shiver that had passed through her. "That could be my whole life. Never knowing. Never being certain. Trapped in the dark."

"Maybe you'll get spidey senses, or some other kind of sense. Didn't you mention your hearing had already improved?"

Kali let out a small laugh, though she didn't find it funny. "Somewhat."

"And you're not in the dark. Isn't it more like you have blinders on?"

"Yeah." She smiled, her chest tightening. "For now." He didn't understand. He couldn't. She grunted as she stood with Theo in her arms. He was getting so big. "It's getting late. We should probably head back."

He nodded in the encroaching darkness then reached for Theo as she let the boy slip into his arms.

Kali smiled through tight lips, her heart pounding. He didn't get it. But he was here, holding her son as gently as if he were his own.

CHAPTER TWENTY-SIX

When Lincoln showed up at Kali's apartment two days later, an array of boxes, laundry bins, and large plastic bags lined the hall, each item pushed tight against the wall to leave a clear walking space.

"Kali?" He'd knocked three times then tried the doorknob. Music thumped from her closed bedroom door. "Kali?" He knocked. "Kal—" The door swung open. "Oh."

"Hi." She wore an old long-sleeved t-shirt, the sleeves pushed up to her elbows, her hair tied back in what looked to be a rag. Her eyes were bright and a gleam of sweat shone on her brow.

Lincoln stepped into the bare room. "You okay?"

Kali lifted her phone off the dresser. "You're early."

"Thought I'd see if you needed any help before the guys come to move the furniture."

"I'm good." She waved a hand to encompass the bed, dresser, and armchair. "All cleared and ready for transport."

"Okay." Lincoln stared at her. Yesterday when they'd packed up the living room and kitchen she'd been lethargic, moody, as if the entire process was an admission of defeat.

Today ...

"Was just starting some of the cleaning." She pointed to a rag and spray by the windowsill. "Won't be too intense considering we weren't here long."

"Everything else is packed? The bathroom? Theo's room?"

"Long done now."

Lincoln ran a hand across the scruff on his chin. "When did you get up?"

"Don't know if you could really say I got up."

"That's, uh ..." Lincoln looked around the room. "Where's Theo?"

"Theo. Oh!" Kali brought a hand to her mouth and raised her voice. "Shoot." She put her hands on her hips. "I must have packed him away."

Lincoln's brow furrowed.

"Darn it. Darn it." Kali paced the room, her voice still loud. "Now where would I have packed a little boy?"

"Ah ..." Lincoln joined in. "It would have to be a big box."

"Very big," said Kali, her tone serious and concerned. "Huge."

"Are you sure you didn't just sweep him under the bed?"

"No. Definitely not." A slight shuffling sounded from a box in the corner of the room. "He would have been too big for the bristles.

"Hmm ..." Kali checked a box near her feet. "Not that one. Gee, I hope it isn't one I taped already."

"You'd never find him if that's the case." Lincoln kept his gaze on Kali, surprised by her joviality. Unnerved by it. "You'd have to just ship him over to the apartment and unpack them one by one."

"Well, that could take hours. A day or more. What if he

wasted away?"

"We better look harder." Lincoln raised the lid of several boxes far too small for Theo to fit in then went to one of the two big enough—the one that hadn't shifted first. "Not here." He walked to the next box. "Maybe—" Theo popped out like a jack-in-the-box. Lincoln stepped back in false alarm, a hand to his chest, as Theo grinned.

"You found him!" Kali exclaimed. She rushed to Theo and wrapped her arms around him, attacking him with kisses. Theo giggled. Really giggled, sound and all.

Theo turned to Lincoln, his voice small but audible and pointed. "Got you."

Lincoln shook his head. "You sure did."

The boy grinned.

Kali lifted him out of the box.

Lincoln stared at them both. This was good. Of course it was good. It was what he'd been hoping for: Kali feeling better. Kali laughing again, playing again. But there was something different to this play—an edge to it almost. From Kali, not Theo. "Your head feeling better?"

She shrugged. "Not really. But it is what it is." She looked to Theo and winked. "Adventures have no time for headaches."

"Adventures?" asked Lincoln.

"Moving," she said as if it were self-evident. "A new adventure."

"Oh, yeah."

"We're going to start having more adventures. We decided." She looked to Theo, who gave a definitive nod. "Go give your room a double check. Okay, sweetheart?"

Theo gave another nod and zoomed from the room.

"Adventures, huh?" said Lincoln.

"Yeah." Kali picked up her cloth and went back to her cleaning. "How, I don't know—for the big adventures anyway. I've got no money, a kid I hardly feel I can care for on my own. Kind of makes me want to scream." She laughed. "Not Theo, but the situation. The absurdity of it, of years of slaving to give us a better life, of making it on my own." Her hand paused then continued scrubbing. "But little adventures we can do. Like going to the park, the museum, the discovery centre." She glanced at Lincoln. "On their free days."

She grabbed a broom and slipped into the closet. "I just need to decide to do it, you know, even if I feel tired. I'm tired no matter what, anyway. The world is out there and I have to get back to conquering it."

"That's, uh ... great."

"Of course it's great." She held her chin high then continued sweeping. "And if this tumour wins I know I'll have tried, that I didn't waste away my final days of sight sitting around feeling sorry for myself."

"You're not going to lose all your sight."

"Correction," she said without looking at him. "I'm probably not going to lose all my sight ... yet. If the treatment only calms the tumour for the time being, well," she raised an arm, "all bets are off, aren't they?"

Lincoln took a deep breath. This wasn't her. Wasn't the way she talked, even when she was her determined, brazen self. She didn't use clichés. She didn't have this edge. An edge, yes, but a defensive one. Not desperate.

THE FIRST MORNING IN Lincoln's apartment, Kali stood under the hot stream of the shower, letting the heat soothe her aching shoulders. Lincoln and his friends wouldn't let her lift a single box, but she'd insisted on doing the cleaning. Once everything was moved, Lincoln came back and helped her, but still it had been too much. Her body ached. Every inch of it.

Kali sighed and reached for the conditioner. She worked it through her hair, separating the knots as best she could. She shifted her neck side to side. Then, the biggest offenders untangled, pulled her hand away to reach for the comb. She froze. Long strands of hair hung off her fingers. She was used to seeing that in her comb, especially on a particularly battle filled tangle session, but in her hands? Never. She put her fingers back through her hair, feeling around the areas where the beams of radiation shone through and came back with another clump.

Her throat itched and clamped, her breath came in short gasps. Her hair. Her hair was part of her. Defined her. Those curls standing up on end was how people pointed her out from a distance, knew to call if they saw her walking up ahead. They were Theo's comfort as they lay on the couch together or sat in bed reading stories, his fingers twirling her curls again and again.

She put her hands against the wall to steady herself. She was losing her hair.

She pushed back, squeezed the excess conditioner from her locks, and rinsed it off of her shoulders and back. She was losing her hair.

So what? Who cares? It was just her. Or hair. It was just hair.

Kali switched off the water. Afro or not, her hair didn't define her. She defined her. She slicked the water off her arms, torsos, and legs—even that motion causing pain—and reached for a towel.

She'd fight back. In her own way. Prove to this disease that her life wasn't over. She may not have the money, it could be a challenge to find someone to watch Theo when she was gone, but she knew exactly what she'd do to prove she still had a life, to prove the tumour wouldn't win.

CHAPTER TWENTY-SEVEN

A long wooden spoon in his hand, Lincoln hovered over the stove, stirring the walnut pesto gently. The scent of garlic and fresh herbs wafted up around him. He smiled, imagining Theo's face when he saw the bright green pasta. Would his nose scrunch up? Would he think it was gross or interesting? No matter, at the first bite he'd be won over. Lincoln brought the spoon to his lips to have a little taste. The motion called to mind his mother, the way she'd test the sauce, taking the smallest of tastes, and then offer it to him as if uncertain of the flavour when she knew it'd be great. It always was. Homey. Traditional. Solid. Just like her.

This sauce was nothing like hers. And it was incredible. One of his best yet, but could use a dash more salt. Lincoln held the shaker over the pan, returned the spoon to the sauce, and stirred.

His mind travelled to his mother's kitchen once more. He had to answer the invite. His family knew he was here, knew, most likely, that he'd started working for Andrew. He hadn't been to a family dinner since moving back to Halifax, but this was more than a typical family dinner. He lifted the spoon to his lips again.

"I'm going to New York."

Lincoln held back a sputter, then turned. "What?"

Kali stood firm, legs wide. "New York. My whole life I've wanted to go. My whole life I've wanted to see a Broadway musical. Can you watch Theo?"

Lincoln stared at her. Her eyes were bright, that determined edge he'd seen yesterday back with a vengeance. "Well, I have—"

"Work. Right." She tossed her head and raised a hand up. "Well, maybe you can watch him in the evenings and I bet Mrs. Martin will take him during the day."

"New York." Lincoln set the spoon down. "That's, uh ... How are you going to—"

"Credit." Kali walked to the fridge and pulled out the orange juice. She squeezed by Lincoln and grabbed a glass from the cupboard. "Never not paid off my credit card in my life. But there's a first time for everything, right?"

"There is ..." Lincoln followed her with his gaze as she downed the juice then crossed to the sink. "But not everything needs a first time."

"I'll pay it off. I'll figure it out. My sickness benefits start soon, then disability in a few months. But hopefully before that I'll find a job. If it's not full time I think the disability will supplement it. Gotta look into that. Another thing to add to the list."

Kali perched on the kitchen table. "I'm thinking four days, five with travel. Take in a couple of shows. See the sights. Broadway." A soft smile covered her face. "I've always wanted to see a Broadway show."

"Yeah, you just said." Lincoln turned back to the stove to

stir the sauce. Broadway. New York. Why not? He turned back. "That's great, Kali. When do you think you'll go?"

"One more week of getting zapped, figure it'll be best in the in-between, before I know whether this monster inside me is hibernating, or ready to keep on the attack."

Lincoln winced. "I guess that makes sense."

"What are you making?" Kali rose from the table and leaned over his shoulder. "Smells great but looks ..." She raised an eyebrow.

"Looks aren't everything."

Kali stepped back, a tight smile on her face. "You are absolutely right. Looks aren't everything." Kali looked past Lincoln. Her jaw clenched and her chin rose ever so slightly. "I'm going to tell Theo. Tonight. If I have to tell him something worse later it will be better if it's not such a shock, don't you think?"

Lincoln's eyes narrowed. Would it be? "Sure. That makes sense."

Kali bit her lip. "I think so. It's best." She nodded. "Definitely." She hovered beside him. "How long till dinner?"

"Five minutes."

"Five minutes." Kali let a hand hover around her jaw then fall to her neck. "Maybe I'll tell him at dinner. Not really enough time before."

Lincoln turned. "I can just leave it to warm."

"No." Kali shook her head. "Maybe it will be good if you're there anyway. A buffer to confusion."

"A what?"

Kali let out a pinched laugh. "I don't know."

Theo stared at the green pasta then looked at Lincoln, his brow raised just the way his mother's so often did.

"It's good. I promise."

He pushed the plate away.

"You don't want to be that kind of person," said Kali, her voice soft. "Afraid to try new things just because they're different."

He crossed his arms.

"Remember the first time you went down a slide?"

He shook his head.

Kali smiled softly. "Well, I remember. You watched those other kids climbing up and soaring down and you wanted none of it. You looked at them like they were crazy and pulled me in the other direction. But I encouraged you to try it. Eventually you did, and what do you think of slides now?"

Theo's lips twisted.

"You love them."

He let his crossed arms rise then fall with a silent humph.

"You love them." Kali gave his shoulder a little push. "And don't deny it." She tickled his side. "You love them."

Theo struggled to hold back a grin, his eyes laughing.

"So maybe you'll like this too. You like some green things." Kali tapped a finger against her chin. "Kermit. Kermit's green."

"And Oscar the Grouch," said Lincoln.

"And Brobee," said Kali.

"Brobee?"

"Yo Gabba Gabba. A TV show." Kali turned from Lincoln back to Theo. "And Brobee has a hard time trying new things too, right? But when he does he always likes them." She poked his side again. "Doesn't he?"

Theo's brow furrowed once more.

"Make Brobee proud."

Theo let out a long breath then reached for his fork. He scrunched up his forehead then looked at Kali once more.

"You can do it," she urged, her smile gentle. Lincoln fought the urge to rest his hand upon hers. She'd jump if he did, not just because of the unexpected motion, but because she wouldn't see it coming. Just the way she couldn't see the way he was looking at her now, wanting to take this platonic arrangement further. Wanting to know that when she figured out this phase of her life, she'd want him to remain a part of it.

"Almost there."

Theo looked at her, a bit of pasta on his fork now. He was playing it up, Lincoln could tell, getting a kick out of this urging. He raised the fork half way to his mouth then stopped, waiting for more encouragement.

"Just a couple more—"

He popped the fork into his mouth. His brows raised and he chewed slowly.

"So?" asked Lincoln.

Theo scrunched up his nose and put out his hand, tilting it back and forth. So-so.

"I think it's delicious." Kali turned her head to Lincoln. "Restaurant delicious."

Theo took another hesitant bite.

"It's new to me too, you know. Never in my life have I had green pasta."

Theo tilted his head. He set his fork down and spoke softly. "Never?"

Kali grinned, her chest expanding. "Nope. Never. It's a first time for both of us."

Theo nodded and took another bite. Kali looked to Lincoln, her eyes asking a question he couldn't decipher. She turned back to Theo. "I've been experiencing something else new too."

Theo looked to her while taking another bite.

Kali set down her fork. "You know how I've been a little more ..." She looked to Lincoln, as if expecting him to hold the word she was looking for. "Angry. And clumsy. Bumping into everything. Tired. Bruises all over." She held out her forearm in display.

Theo nodded, hesitant. He looked from Lincoln to Kali. "Well, it's because I have a little problem inside my head." She stopped, searching again, this time looking to the wall. "It's like ... well, something started growing inside of me that's not meant to be there, like a seed."

Theo's eyes widened.

Kali continued, not looking at him. "And it's taking up too much room. Taking over the space that's meant to be for other things in my head. Invading."

Theo's eyes were wider now. The hand holding his fork sunk to the table.

"Like ... like ... an alien."

His mouth fell open and at last Kali looked to him.

"No, no. Not an alien. Not like ..."

"More like a sponge." Lincoln swallowed. "Like it's soaking up some of the things in your mommy's head that are meant to be responsible for other things."

"Exactly," said Kali, looking thankful. "Just like a little sponge. And what it's soaking up is my vision."

Theo's nose scrunched up again.

"My ability to see."

Theo glanced between them then made a wringing motion.

"No." Lincoln shook his head. "Maybe a sponge wasn't the best description. It can't be wrung out."

"Where I go every day though," said Kali, "That's to try to make the sponge smaller, stop it from taking up so much room." She hesitated. "You know when you get sick and I give you some medicine to help you get better?"

Theo nodded.

"Well, I've got sickness inside my head and I go every day to get medicine for it." She took a deep breath. "So that should help. But I didn't find out I was sick fast enough. So it already did some damage." Her voice lowered. "Kind of like how even though the doctor helped you when you fell and hurt your arm it was already broken, so you needed a cast to help you get better. But that medicine didn't make you better right away ..." Her voice faltered. "It was broken. And even though it's mostly better now, inside, it'll always show that it was broken ... so my eyes, my ..."

Kali took a deep, shaky breath, and again Lincoln fought the urge to take her hand in his. "That's why I didn't see the truck that day. Why I walked out and—" Lincoln grasped her hand. She looked at him and smiled but pulled away, bringing both hands up to the side of her face, using them as blinders. "When I see now, it's kind of like this. Unless I'm turned right to you I can't see you. And really," she put a hand over her left eye, "I can't see much out of this eye at all. So, I don't see when you leave things on the floor so well. And you know how I spill things all the time now. Cereal. Milk. Juice."

Theo nodded.

"It's affected my depth perception."

His forehead furrowed.

"My ability to know how far away something is, or how deep."

Lincoln put his hands to his face the same way Kali had. "Why don't you try it?"

Theo raised his hands slowly.

"Now pull them away, see how much more you can see?"

Theo did and nodded again; the little lines on his forehead seemed permanently etched. He repeated the motion several times, covering his left eye, while still holding up the right to the side of his face. He turned his head far to the left, far to the right, his bottom lip quivering. He slid off his chair and sidled beside Kali, his hand resting on her thigh. "Mommy okay?"

Kali blinked and gulped her breath.

Theo looked up at her. "It hurt bad?"

Kali scooped Theo onto her lap. "Sometimes it hurts. A lot. And it's a little scary. That's why I cry sometimes. Or I'm grumpy. Cause I'm in a lot of pain."

Theo snuggled into her.

Kali let out a shattered breath and closed her eyes as she hugged Theo against her. A tear escaped. She wiped it then pulled him away so she could look at him. "But the medicine's going to help. And I take other medicine too, and it helps."

"So you see good again?"

She pressed her lips tight then smiled. "Maybe. Or maybe I'll just have to learn to," she shook her head and kept the smile, "to get used to seeing differently than other people." She held his hands back to his face. "It's harder, but if you take some time and move your head the right way you can still see everything, right?"

Brow scrunched and lips tight, Theo moved his head back and forth and up and down. He dropped his hands and nodded.

"Yeah. So it's not so bad. Just different. Like it was different for you to have the cast. You had to be careful while washing your hands and taking a bath, but we made it work, didn't we?"

Theo nodded.

Kali looked to Lincoln, then back at Theo. "So we're going to make this work."

Theo looked solemn. He nodded. "I help."

"Oh, well ..."

He jumped from her lap and ran to the living room. They could see him collecting the toys he'd strewn across the cardboard track Lincoln had made him and toss them in the toy box. "Not now, sweetie," called Kali. "Finish your dinner."

Theo looked up. He started taking bigger armfuls of cars and dumping them in the box. Kali shook her head and smiled.

"That's great," called Lincoln. "But you don't want your green pasta getting cold. What would Brobee think?"

Kali let out a tired laugh. "I guess I should have waited till we were done eating."

"You did great," Lincoln whispered.

Kali picked up her fork. Lincoln watched Theo collect the last few cars then fold up the track. He re-entered the room with a grin on his face and sat down in front of his plate.

The two of them ate as Lincoln watched. Eventually, he picked up his own fork. The sauce was lukewarm now, but it didn't seem to matter.

CHAPTER TWENTY-EIGHT

After dinner, Lincoln and Kali stood shoulder to shoulder as he washed and she dried the dishes. Lincoln handed Kali the saucepan. "That went well."

"Really well." Kali let out a short laugh. "I feel silly." She swiped the dish towel over the pan several times. "I should have told him weeks ago."

As he absentmindedly scrubbed the blender, Lincoln looked at her, taking in the exquisite profile he'd stared at so many months ago while creeping her on Facebook. This had an aspect of creepiness to it too, watching her like this when she couldn't tell. He brought his gaze to the blender then, satisfied it was clean, passed it to her. "Maybe if you'd told him weeks ago, before the angry outbursts, before the tripping, it would have been harder for him to understand."

She shrugged. "No changing the past."

"No. There isn't." Lincoln passed her the cutting board. "I'm proud of you anyway."

"Proud of—"

"You were scared, but you did it. That takes guts."

Kali pushed up her sleeves and let out a slight smile. "Thanks, I guess."

Lincoln took a deep breath, his chest tightening. "I need to get some guts. Or have guts, or—" He stopped. "I was invited to my sister's birthday party."

"Oh?" Kali turned so she could look at him. "You going?"

"I should."

She took the grater from his hand. "Family."

"Yeah. Family." Lincoln looked to the sink. He couldn't see anything more in the soapy water so passed his hand through the liquid, searching.

Finding nothing, he looked back at Kali, his smile too quick. He opened his mouth, closed it, looked away. Stupid. This nervousness. With all he'd done for her; not that he'd done any of it to get favours in return... "Want to come?"

"What?" Kali dried her hands on the towel. "To your sister's birthday party?"

"Sure. Yeah. Won't be a ton of people. Mostly family. Maybe a few close family friends. It'll be fun."

"Fun?" She raised an eyebrow. "Your face isn't doing much to convince me."

He laughed then stepped around her to hang the towel on the oven door. "Fun for you. Maybe not so much for me."

"Your brother will be there and," she hesitated, "her."

"Probably. But my sister, Rachel, she's really nice. Linda is ... Linda, but her kids aren't too bad. And my mom, she's ... a good mom."

Kali leaned against the counter. "Have you seen them? Since her party?"

"My mom a couple of times. No one else."

Kali lowered her gaze. "I don't know. I'm never the best at

people meeting."

"You're a nurse."

"Was a nurse. And that's different, I'm not being social. I'm doing a job. And crowds ... people talking, walking by, popping out of nowhere...."

"I'll tell them—"

"I don't know if—"

"It'll make it easier if people are aware, if you don't have to worry about snubbing someone simply because you didn't see them or didn't realize they were talking to you."

Kali looked at him, a question in her eyes. "How did you know?" She shook her head. "Never mind. I just don't—"

"I need you."

"Linc—"

"As a buffer. Or support, or ... simply to let them know I'm not spending all my time hiding away by myself, licking my wounds."

Kali stared at him. His chest tightened with each moment that passed. He wanted to step into her head, know what was going on in there, know what questions or resistance or excuses she was thinking through. Her expression softened into an uncertain wariness. "Okay."

"Okay?"

"Yeah. Sure. When is it?"

"This Sunday."

She turned from him. "Just after my treatment is done. Perfect time to celebrate."

There was that edge again, the false joviality.

"I'll be your wingman, but don't tell anyone I'm your girlfriend."

ON THE MORNING OF THE party, Kali woke with nausea that sent her running to the bathroom. Dry, painful heaves wracked through her as her head throbbed. Hands shaking, she reached for her pills in the medicine cabinet, having to stand on her tiptoes to reach the top shelf—far out of Theo's reach even if he crawled on the counter, and almost out of hers. She let water flow into the sink, cupped her hands, and slurped the water to gulp down her pills—one for her stomach and two for her head.

She slumped onto the toilet seat cover, her head in her hands. The last few days of treatment her symptoms had seemed to get worse, not better. She'd minimized them while talking to the radiation therapists and later on to the oncologist, not wanting him to up her dose of steroids and their possible side effects. Already her appetite was strengthening, too much, and her ankles seemed swollen. She was almost through treatment, after all. But perhaps she'd been wrong to downplay the pain.

Kali took several deep breaths then raised her head. She had five hours to feel better. Five hours to put on a smile and be pleasant, to—as best she could—act as a buffer between the tension sure to pulsate between Lincoln and his family.

One hand grasping the towel rack, Kali rose to her feet and, hand pressing along the wall, made her way back to her room. She gasped as Lincoln stepped into her line of vision.

"Sorry. Sorry. Damn." He stepped back. "Are you okay?"

Kali pushed out a smile. She was making it work. That was her resolution. Stop feeling sorry for herself. Stop letting the misery of her circumstances make her so miserable. "A little queasy."

"Can I—?" His brow furrowed and that unfamiliar feeling that was cropping up more and more lately fluttered through Kali. "Maybe just keep an ear out for Theo. Grab him when he's up so I can sleep?"

"Absolutely."

Kali slipped past him, into her room, and under the covers. She set her alarm to 10:30, enough time to get up, shower, make it to the Fraser home and, hopefully, enough time for the pills to do their work.

WHEN KALI WOKE HOURS later, she lay in bed motionless, scared her first movement would bring the nausea back with a rush. She took several breaths then, ever so gently, rolled over. No nausea. She eased herself onto her forearms and took another breath. Not bad. She swung her feet to the edge of the bed and sat. Her stomach clenched. But not horribly. A monumental improvement from several hours earlier, the pain in her head was nothing but mild tension. Her shoulders relaxed and she stood.

She could have pulled out, of course, she still could. Lincoln would understand. But with all he'd done for her, she'd go to this party. She'd make sure she had her pills, not that she went anywhere without them anymore. And she'd smile and she'd make small talk, and she'd defend him if need be. Tell that cheating ex and wretched brother ... Kali's brow furrowed. She placed a hand on her chest, surprised at the swell of angry protectiveness that surged. She'd felt this way about Theo dozens of times—when the day cares wouldn't take him, when kids at the park gave him odd looks. She'd felt this way about Marvin, she couldn't even count the times. But Lincoln?

She shook her head and grabbed a towel before crossing to the bathroom. Now she felt that way about Lincoln.

The realization left Kali nervous. She'd been wary before … of meeting strangers, of the confusion and uncertainty she was sure to feel about who was talking to her, who was looking at her. But beyond that, it hadn't mattered what anyone at the party would think of her. She was going to support Lincoln, plain and simple. But this was his family. For better or worse, they would be in his life and their opinion of her—she closed her eyes and let the water stream down—it mattered.

CHAPTER TWENTY-NINE

In the car, crossing the harbour to Dartmouth, Kali quizzed herself. "So your mother is Marilyn. Your sisters are Linda and Rachel. Linda is older, but does she look it?"

Lincoln laughed. "Yes. Linda looks like a soccer mom. Rachel looks like ..." A smile spread across his face. "Rachel. Slightly bohemian, slightly corporate. A traveller. Though she hasn't really travelled yet. At least not as much as she wants."

"And she's turning thirty. And your brother," Kali glanced at Lincoln, "is Joseph. His fiancée is Lucy."

Lincoln's smile faded. "There won't be a test."

"I know." Kali looked away. "Will Andrew be there?"

"Most likely. I didn't get a guest list."

"And your dad?"

Lincoln's jaw twitched. "I don't know."

"When's the last time—?"

He shook his head.

Kali looked ahead then turned around to Theo. "You excited for cake?"

He gave a huge nod.

"And meeting some new kids?"

Theo's nod was less defined this time. He pushed his lips tight and gave an uncertain smile.

"They'll be nice, bud," said Lincoln. "Or I'll hold them upside down and spin them."

Theo giggled. A real giggle. Kali rested her head against the seat back. It didn't happen often, these unprompted noises from her son, but they were more and more frequent, and every time they made her heart clench with joy, pride, and relief.

Lincoln slowed the truck in front of a large house. No. Large didn't cover it. It was huge. But not grotesquely so, and not in comparison to the house beside it. It didn't look showy, with its welcoming large wrap-around porch. The house was painted a deep forest green with white trim, two large maple trees on the lawn, and a fire bush just to the left of the steps. "This is it?"

"This is it." Lincoln turned off the engine and stared at the building.

Kali waited a moment. "We going in?"

Lincoln nodded but didn't move.

"It wasn't so bad last time, right? I mean, you got through it."

"Last time I sat in the car for hours before going in. Last time ..." His voice trailed off.

"Well, I don't think hours will work today." Kali turned back to Theo. "We're hungry, aren't we?"

Theo nodded vigorously.

"And they're expecting us." Kali undid her seat belt. Lincoln's body seemed rigid. His jaw clenched. She put a hand on his arm. He flinched then turned to her. "You can do this." She hesitated, not knowing if the words would anger or calm him. "And all in all they did you a favour, right? Forced you out of a life that was making you miserable."

He looked at her, his eyes piercing in a way that scared her, then his expression softened. "Yeah. Absolutely." He unbuckled his seat belt and stepped out of the cab.

LINCOLN PUSHED OPEN THE door and stepped inside. Two boys who looked to be around eight or nine zoomed past them. Laughter, and voices talking over each other carried down the hall. Lincoln bi-passed a room to the right of the hall where Kali could see several people chatting and made a straight line for the kitchen.

It overflowed with people, the mass crowding onto the back porch. Despite the chill outside, the door was wide open, but with the crowded bodies, the air inside still felt toasty. Kali leaned into Lincoln. "I thought it was a family dinner."

He spoke through clenched teeth. "I guess an extended family dinner."

"Lincoln!" A woman with long wavy hair, eyes the same hue as Lincoln's, and an inviting smile pushed through the room. She wrapped her arms around Lincoln. Kali felt sure she'd seen that smile before, but couldn't place it.

"Hey, sis." Lincoln held her tight. "Happy Birthday."

"I wasn't sure you'd show." Her eyes glinted as she grinned at him then turned her gaze to Kali. "And you must be—"

Kali shot out her hand. "Kali. And you're Rachel. Happy Birthday."

Rachel laughed and Kali gave herself an inner kick for her eagerness. She wasn't used to it—this desire for approval. She didn't like it. "And," Rachel bent down to Theo's level. "Theo, is it?"

Theo nodded.

"Well, it's very nice to meet you."

Theo smiled then wrapped his arms around Kali's leg.

Rachel stood, her gaze back on Lincoln, who scanned the room. She put a hand on her brother's arm. "They're not here yet."

Lincoln looked back to her.

"Dad isn't either. We really hoped he'd get a pass but," her brows furrowed, "all the people at Mom's party, it upset him. I'll stop by later today. Maybe you could—"

Lincoln stepped away from the reach of her hand. "I should find Mom. Introduce her to Kali and Theo."

"Sure." Rachel nodded, pain obvious in her eyes. "I think she's in the dining room."

MARILYN WRAPPED HER arms around Kali, pulling her close as if they'd known each other for years. The motion shocked Kali, but she relaxed into the embrace, feeling something stir within her. This woman, too, looked familiar. She was darker than Lincoln, a shade between them, and Kali did a double take, realizing Lincoln was mixed-race. Marilyn's hair was in a tidy afro, several inches shorter than Kali's. She didn't look like a woman to be trifled with, but her eyes were kind and welcoming—reminding Kali of the way her own mother had softened in her final years.

"We're glad you could make it." Marilyn squeezed Kali again. "Lincoln's told me so much about you." She looked to Theo but held back a hug. "And you. I hear you've got quite the throwing arm."

Theo grinned, mimed his pitching stance, then let an imaginary ball fly.

"Wow!" Marilyn clapped her hands together and leaned back. "Have a favourite team?"

"More playing than watching at this point," said Lincoln.

Marilyn turned her gaze to Lincoln and offered a soft smile. "Just like my boys." She pulled him into a hug. "That's probably a better way to be."

Lincoln's words came out tight. "Joseph goes to games."

"For business," said Marilyn with a wave of her hand. "He couldn't care less otherwise. You know that."

Lincoln barely nodded, his jaw twitching again, and Kali wanted to step inside his mind, know what he was thinking and what she could do to help. She smiled at Marilyn. "Your home is beautiful."

"Lincoln's daddy built it." Marilyn barely looked at Lincoln before returning her gaze to Kali. "With some help, of course."

"Oh," Kali shifted her head to take a better look at the room, "so he's a carpenter, too? That must be where Lincoln gets it. Did you see the tree house he built?"

"Not yet." Marilyn glanced again to Lincoln, a surprised smile on her face. "Although I hope to soon. And yes, Lincoln gets his skills honestly. As a child, he and his daddy were always building things, and then he begged to join a work crew at the company before he was even old enough. When did your uncle first let you—?"

"Fifteen," said Lincoln, his brow still furrowed.

"The company?" asked Kali.

"Fraser Construction."

"Fraser—" Kali tried not to let the shock show on her face.

215

Fraser Construction, the most known locally owned construction company in all of Nova Scotia, maybe in all of the Maritimes. She'd seen an article in the paper a few months earlier about them, how they were giving companies like Home Depot and Kent a run for their money. How the son of one of the founders was working to expand the company through the rest of Canada. They already had major holdings in Montreal, Ottawa, and Ontario and were working their way West, as well as looking at partnerships with companies in the states. The son. Joseph. Joseph, who'd taken over the business due to his father's diagnosis with Alzheimer's. Kali looked to Lincoln, not believing she'd never pieced it together. But why would she? Why would she think the homeless looking man who'd lived in income-assisted housing was the son of a multi-millionaire, was one of the heirs to a massive corporation? Had, she now realized, worked for that corporation at the upper levels and, due to his grief, either lost or thrown it all away.

Lincoln looked at her, and she could almost see the tension building in him, the desire to know the questions running through her mind. Kali looked away. His father had Alzheimer's. That's why he wouldn't see him? That's what Lincoln meant when he'd said he'd disappeared?

Kali tried to replay the conversation as she said goodbye to Marilyn, who was pulled away to handle some problem in the kitchen. She'd seen the article because Dianne had shown it to her, bragging about how she was tending to a millionaire. Alexander Fraser. Kali had never tended to him herself, but she'd seen him in the common room, her heart clenching at how sad he looked. How alone and confused. And that's why Rachel looked familiar. And Marilyn. She must have seen them in the halls, or as she passed through the common room. She'd been wrong about the house, about it being big. Considering the family's wealth, it was modest.

Kali looked to Lincoln; she opened her mouth to speak, then shut it.

"That's my story." He put a hand on her shoulder and led her to the kitchen. "You two said you were hungry, right? I saw some appetizers."

CHAPTER THIRTY

"What about the time the four of them decided they'd build their own village in the woods?" An older woman, Lincoln's aunt, if Kali remembered correctly, raised her arm to start the story.

"Not that one again—" Rachel shook her head, a hand half covering her face.

"And it wasn't a village," said Andrew with a grin. "It was a commune."

"A commune, right." The woman, who she now guessed was Andrew's mother, gave a nod. "A commune in the woods behind your grandparents' property. With everything you could find stolen from the house."

Rachel shook her head again and sighed.

"Andrew and Lincoln built the structure while Rachel swiped the best china and the curtains your grandmother's grandmother had made."

"Was it really the best china?" asked Rachel. "Or merely the oldest? They're not necessarily one and the same."

"The best and the oldest," said Marilyn. "Most definitely."

"And if it wasn't for my little angel they all would have

been ruined."

"Instead of just half the set," laughed Marilyn.

"She wasn't an angel. She was a snitch," accused Andrew with a laugh.

"Still am." A woman Kali couldn't remember the name of gave a grin to match Andrew's. "I bet Mom would love to know about—"

Andrew wrapped a hand around her mouth. "Whatever *you* think Mom needs to know about, trust me, she doesn't."

"Oh ho, ho." The aunt waved a hand toward her daughter. "We'll slip away later and you can tell me all about it."

The sister winked as Andrew released her. The adults were all sitting in what seemed to be a drawing room—the larger living room on the other side of the house—while the kids sat at the table in the dining room, with a teenager overseeing the group.

Kali glanced at Lincoln, who sat a few places down from her. He was smiling but seemed distanced from the fun. Joseph sat across from him, looking less stiff and uncomfortable, though he never let his gaze fall on Lincoln. Or her. If someone in their vicinity was talking he'd skim past them, never making eye contact. Lucy, on the other hand, seemed to be darting her gaze every time Kali looked her way.

Slim and delicate with bright blue eyes and flowing blonde hair, if not for her lack of height, she could be a model. Even her little baby bump looked picture perfect. There was something in her eyes though, a strained desperation. Like she wanted the people there to like her, approve of her, and wasn't sure they would. Kali could relate to that, but there was something more—guilt? Shame? Everyone seemed pleasant enough, but they certainly didn't hold the easy camaraderie with Lucy as they did with each other.

Of course, both guilt and shame made sense. Kali guessed everyone in the room knew Lucy had gone from Lincoln to Joseph, breaking Lincoln's heart and creating a rift in the family in the process.

The couple had joined lunch late, so Kali hadn't had an introduction, she'd simply watched Joseph and Lucy sit down with their plates. It was hard to imagine Lincoln and this woman together. She was poised. Every hair in place—the dress, the heels, the diamond bracelet—Perfect. Joseph, in his made to seem casual dress shirt, slacks, and slicked back hair, seemed the better match for her.

Kali glanced at Lincoln. Had he looked that way once? She tried to picture him without the scruff and hair that fell almost to his shoulders, without his standard plaid shirt. Take those things away and the brotherly resemblance was striking.

Someone asked Joseph for an update on the business dealings out West and he went into a spiel—his shoulders held back, his chin high, clearly in his element. Kali turned to see Marilyn place a hand on Lincoln's thigh and squeeze. She didn't draw attention to the motion, didn't look at Lincoln—her gaze on Joseph. Lincoln's pasted on smile softened just slightly.

As people finished their first servings of food they rose to the kitchen for seconds or to get another drink. Kali stayed where she was, happy with her position where no one could sneak up on her and she didn't have to worry about accidentally bumping into anything or anyone. As the seats beside her opened up then vacated again, several people slid in beside her, asking friendly questions she wasn't sure how to answer. "How'd you two meet?" In the neighbourhood.

"What do you do?" A nurse, but she was on leave right now. Mostly, eyebrows raised or heads nodded, sensing her desire for them not to dig deeper. No one asked about her sight—either Lincoln had restricted that information to the immediate family or hinted it wasn't a topic she wanted to talk about. Maybe some didn't even know. "And are you two ...?" Friends, she said every time. Just friends.

A HUSH FELL OVER THE ROOM then erupted in a loud chorus of Happy Birthday. Linda entered with a massive candle-covered cake. Thirty flames at least. Rachel's face glowed and her eyes widened. "Seriously." She laughed as the song ended—including an extra verse by the nephews having something to do with a monkey that Kali probably hadn't heard since she was their age. "Are there any candles left in the province?"

"Oh, a few," said Linda with a laugh. Her husband sat in the corner, face concentrated on his phone. He'd been like that half the meal, but everyone else had their eyes on Rachel and the love felt palpable, as if you could reach out and touch it.

"Make it a good wish," called Joseph. "Nothing wishy-washy, no world peace or anything."

"Wish for a man!" called someone from across the room. "It's about time you got yourself a man."

"She'll get a man when she's good and ready," scoffed someone else. "She's living her life."

Rachel laughed off the comments and held a hand to her chin, presumably contemplating her wish.

"Hurry up!" Another voice called. "That cake looks heavy, your sister may collapse." Linda pretended to wobble.

"And the candles, they'll melt to stubs."

Kali's chest tightened, amazed at the easy jokes, the closeness. Her mother, an only child, both parents dead, had come from Ontario as a young girl, met Kali's father, and never gone back. She knew she had cousins out there somewhere—second cousins to Kali. But she'd never met them. Never met her father's family. It had only ever been her and her mom.

Derek, she'd thought, would give her family. There'd been one dinner—her Mom, Marvin, Derek, Jason, and Jason's girlfriend. It'd been nice, but nothing like this. Never had she been a part of something like this. At least twenty-five people were in the house. They all knew each other, loved each other, had a common history. Tensions existed, obviously—Lincoln and Joseph's the most palpable. But there were others, too: little side glances, rolled eyes here and there among the other guests, something was going on with Linda and her husband, but still they were all here, all connected.

Rachel blew out her candles in four gusts among a chorus of cheers and shouts about the number of babies that meant. No, said someone else, number of husbands. The number of cats, shouted a boy just between childhood and becoming a teenager. "It's cats. She's going to be the crazy cat lady."

Rachel grabbed him to her side and gave him a noogie. "Thirty hardly makes me a spinster and I've just got one cat, thank you very much." She released him and put a hand on his shoulder. "Besides, I want to make sure I find the right person—" she glanced to who Kali suspected was the boy's mother. "Make sure I don't create such an awkward looking kid like you."

"Aww," the boy groaned.

"Ha!" shouted the mother. "You're just jealous. You know you could never find a man good-looking enough to produce such a handsome specimen."

"You're right, you're right." Rachel put an exaggerated hand to her chest and cupped the boy's chin. "You're just about the most handsome fella I've ever seen."

He waved a hand and stepped away from her, his neck reddening.

"Where's the cake?" shouted a man with massive shoulders who looked like he'd spent his whole life working hard labour and had a cast up to his thigh. "I expect to be served."

"Aye, aye!" Rachel sent the man a loving wink and, arm pointed out, headed to the kitchen.

"No," the almost-teen's mom stopped her, "today you do no work."

"If you insist." Rachel scanned the room then crossed to the open seat beside Kali. She put a hand on her shoulder. "How are you handling the madness?"

Kali swallowed. "It's great. I've never seen anything like it."

"Not overwhelmed?"

Kali tilted her head back and forth. "Maybe a little. But it's good. It's nice."

"Don't come from a big family yourself?"

Kali gestured to Theo, who sat in the dining room, eyes wide at the large piece of chocolate cake placed in front of him. "Just the two of us."

Rachel nodded. "Keep hanging around Lincoln and you'll be one of the gang in no time." She leaned back and Kali shifted so she could see her better. "He's a good guy. Has been through a rough time, but I think he's going to be a better man because of it."

Kali glanced to Lincoln, who had a toddler on his lap and was wearing the first unrestricted smile she'd seen on him all day. "He is a good man. Kind. Generous. I'm not sure what would have happened if he hadn't stepped into our lives." When Rachel didn't respond, Kali turned to her.

Rachel's smile was soft. "How are you? Lincoln told me ... not details, but about your treatment. The vision issues."

"It's hard." Kali bit her lip. "Really hard. Your brother makes it a bit easier." She shook her head, uncomfortable with the mix of emotions swirling within her and not wanting them to pour out. "I'm just hoping for the best."

"That's all we can do, isn't it?" Rachel put her hand on Kali's shoulder again, so casually, as if they'd known each other for years. The almost-teen's mother stood before them, a piece of cake in each hand. "Now this," said Rachel, taking her piece, "is some of the best cake you'll ever eat. Aunt Gertie's specialty."

"I helped her this year," said the woman in front of them. "So if it's not the most amazing thing you've ever tasted, blame it on me."

Rachel grinned up at her and took a bite. Her eyes widened and her mouth formed a little 'o' after she swallowed. "It's divine." The woman gave a wink and turned back to the kitchen. Rachel patted Kali's knee. "I've got more rounds to make."

A moment later Lincoln filled the seat. "Having fun?"

"Yeah," Kali turned to him, "I am." She lowered her voice. "How about you?"

"It's nice," he said, "being around family again." He looked away. "Awkward too." He gestured toward Joseph and Lucy, who stood in the corner, Lucy smiling uncomfortably as some woman placed a hand on her stomach. "The elephant in the room."

"Has anyone—?"

"No one's said anything. I almost wish they would."

Kali took a bite of cake. It really was divine. The rich and creamy chocolate melted in her mouth.

Lincoln eyed her plate. "When you're done do you want to—" he looked to the hall. "I could use a little air. I'll give you a tour. Show you my old room."

"Sure." Kali finished quickly, then stood. "Theo?"

"He's well taken care of." Lincoln cupped a hand around her elbow and led her through the crowd.

CHAPTER THIRTY-ONE

I n the hall, Lincoln's shoulders seemed to relax. He released Kali's elbow and gestured to the stairs. Kali took the lead, stopping on the landing.

"Down this way." Lincoln passed Kali and pushed open the third door on the left. "The realm of Lincoln Fraser, circa 1987 to 2005."

Kali stepped in. The room was large with bunk beds against one wall, a writing desk, and posters: Nickelback, Cold Play, Green Day, and The Black Eyed Peas. Kali pointed to the last one.

"I had a variety of interests," he laughed. "I listened to a lot of folk music, some country. But those weren't as socially acceptable." He pointed to a CD tower. "You'll find the variety represented there."

"And bunk beds? You shared with Joseph?"

"Until I was nine. After that, he took a room in the basement. He was fifteen and I cramped his style. Kept the bunk beds though, they were good for sleepovers."

Kali turned slowly in the room, trying to imagine the Lincoln who'd lived here. Was he quiet? Did he plan to go into the family business? Could he ever have imagined he'd be shacked up with a woman going blind and her semi-mute son ... yet in separate rooms? "You talk to Joseph?"

Lincoln tapped his hand on the dresser. "I have not."

"Will you?"

"I won't seek him out. The desire to smash his face in hasn't been quite as strong this time. That's improvement."

"You get a twitch whenever he speaks." She put a hand to his jaw, barely touching it. "Right there."

He stepped away and sat on the bottom bunk.

"You two were close once?"

"Off and on. Close as young kids. Not so much when he reached teenage years or after he moved out. I thought we were close again when I graduated university and went to work with him." Lincoln paused. "I was all about making him proud. Being worthy." Lincoln shook his head slowly, a look of mild disgust covering his face. "And all the time he was sleeping with my girlfriend."

Kali sat beside him. "So, you're a millionaire?"

Lincoln let out a little laugh. "Not me. The business is rich. A multi-million dollar corporation now."

"But you—"

"I have savings from work, though I didn't save as much as I should have. Now they're running thin. Back then, I didn't think I had to. I had earnings from the shares to back me up if I ever needed it."

"And now?"

"They're there. But I don't touch them. It's his money."

"His? Joseph's? But your dad started—"

"It's Joseph's company now. Joseph who handled the expansion. In the past thirteen years he's transformed the company from two local stores and a modest construction company into an empire."

Kali spoke her words carefully. "And your Dad. His disappearance. It was Alzheimer's?"

Lincoln looked at her then turned his gaze. "Early-onset."

"I read an article a month or so ago. One of my co-workers tends to him. I never thought ... there are lots of Frasers."

Lincoln's jaw clenched again.

"When did—?"

"I was eleven when it started. He was so young." Lincoln paused. "My dad was the strongest man you'd ever meet. Smart. Funny. Solid, you know?" Lincoln rubbed a hand across his thigh. "He started forgetting little things: Rachel's recitals. Picking me up from soccer practice. Work meetings." Lincoln's brow furrowed. "We thought he was overworked. We teased him about it. Then one day he couldn't find his way home. I was in the car with him and he just kept driving around town but didn't say why. Eventually I asked, and he looked at me like he didn't know me. Just for a second. He tried to turn it into a game. Said I should direct us home. But he didn't sound funny. He sounded scared."

Lincoln took a shaky breath and wiped the back of his hand below his eyes. "He didn't want to go the doctor, was angry when I told Mom what happened. It went so fast after that. Less than a year later it was a good day if he remembered who we were. He remembered his brothers and sister and mom, though he'd look at them funny, like they were playing a trick on him. But he didn't remember me. I was the first one he forgot."

Lincoln hunched over, his shoulders shaking, his breath coming in short gasps. "I tried to help out. He needed a lot of help with simple things. Buttoning his pants, preparing toast. He'd yell at me for no reason, like my existence made him mad. Nothing I did was right." His head shook. "It was just ... with the girls ... I don't know. Maybe because they were girls it was easier for him to accept their help.

"I adored him. He was my dad. Power Rangers had nothing on him" Lincoln let out a rough laugh. "He was my hero. And then he wasn't."

A puff of air streamed out of Lincoln's cheeks. "I don't know how they do it. Linda and Rachel. Joseph. They were older, maybe that made it easier to understand. And Dad didn't take it out on them the way he took it out on me. Joseph wasn't even around in the beginning. He was off at school in Montreal. But still, how they visit, how they can see him like that? He's just this shell."

"He's your dad."

"No." Lincoln's mouth hung open, his eyes closed. "He's not. He's the ghost of my dad. He can't even walk. He can hardly talk." Lincoln raised his head and stared at the wall in front of him. "Maybe he can't talk anymore."

"When's the last time you saw him?"

Lincoln looked to her and released a shaky sigh. "Over a decade ago. I was seventeen, had just graduated high school, and went over in my cap and gown, diploma in hand. Hoping it'd be a good day—not that he really had those by then. But sometimes he was placid, you know? Like he wouldn't know it was me but he'd be friendly. I could be some nice boy coming to visit.

"It wasn't a good day. He swore and shouted garbled words, but I could get the gist. He tried to throw his clock radio at me, but it fumbled to the floor. He told me never to come back. So I listened."

"Lincoln."

"Don't." He stood and crossed to the window. After a moment he waved her over. Kali rose slowly and stood beside him. "It's a nice backyard, isn't it?"

"Beautiful." Like the front yard, it was immaculately landscaped. Trees and bushes and several plots with bright fall flowers.

"We spent so much time out there. Playing catch, soccer, building snowmen." Lincoln pointed to a large patch of lawn to the left. "That's where the rink would go." He folded his arms. "No room for a tree house though. I always wanted to build my own tree house. That was a hard talk—dad sitting me down to tell me we didn't have the right kind of trees. After he was sick I tried once to change his mind. His knowledge of carpentry was still intact so he shut that down."

Kali touched a hand to his back.

"It's genetic."

Kali nodded. "Did you—?"

"No. Joseph did. And Linda. Joseph's safe. Linda's not. But she used preimplantation genetic testing or something like that when she got pregnant. So the boys are safe. It's part of why she started so young, so she'd have as much time with them as possible.

"Rachel and I—" Lincoln shook his head and stepped from the window. "We didn't test. It'd be worse to know." He paused. "But now you do, so—"

Kali stepped back, her mouth open at the implication.

"We should get back to the party. Don't want to be rude."

"Linc—"

"Come on." He crossed the room and entered the hall.

Kali followed behind, thinking she should say something, anything, but the words wouldn't come.

CHAPTER THIRTY-TWO

"Lincoln. There you are."

Lincoln's arms tensed. Kali glanced from him to Joseph. Joseph's smile was slightly tight, but beyond that, he seemed perfectly at ease.

Joseph pointed toward the drawing room. "People were asking about you. Thought you'd dashed." Silence. "They're about to open the presents." More silence. Joseph turned to Kali. "Well, you must be—"

"Kali." Kali kept her hands crossed over her middle. "Kali Johnson."

Joseph nodded, his smile engaging. "Yes, I've heard about you. You and your boy." His smile grew. "Saw him around, too. He's a cutie."

Lucy walked into the hall and stepped beside Joseph. Her gaze darted between Kali and Lincoln. At last she took a deep breath, her focus on Kali. "HELLO!" Her voice resounded over the din from the other rooms. "YOU MUST BE KALI. IT'S SO NICE TO MEET YOU."

Lincoln spoke softly. "She's not deaf."

"What? Oh." Lucy's cheeks coloured. "No, I know. I—"

She turned to Joseph. "Was I talking loudly?"

Joseph nodded and put a hand to her waist. "Just a bit."

"Sorry." Lucy turned back to Kali. "I'm a little nervous."

"Oh?" Kali raised her eyebrow, her pulse quickening. "Why's that?"

Lucy glanced between the men and put a hand to her throat. She laughed. "Just, uh," her gaze was on Lincoln, "meeting new people. I always get a little nervous around new people."

Lincoln let out a rough gust of air, half laugh, half scoff. Lucy kept her gaze on Lincoln. "How are you doing?"

"Great."

She nodded and bit her lip. Kali stared at the two, wondering how long Lincoln could keep it together. Wondering how he and this woman had once fit. What he had seen in her. She was beautiful, that was for sure, but again, Kali couldn't help but think she seemed more suited to someone like Joseph. Of course, she reminded herself, Lincoln had once been like Joseph. Joseph, who had replaced the role of Lincoln's father and then ...

Kali put a hand to Lincoln's arm, wanting to get away from this moment, and started past the couple. "You said they wanted to open presents?"

"Yes." Joseph followed behind them.

Rachel sat in a chair toward the centre of the room, expressing excited thanks over a book. Several eyes turned toward their way as the four of them walked into the room, expressions of surprise or confusion covering the faces. Most, however, kept their attention on Rachel. Kali whispered she was going to find Theo as Lincoln nodded and took an empty seat.

In the kitchen Kali leaned against the wall, her heart still pounding. She wanted to go back in time. What had she even said in that room as Lincoln's shoulders shook? As he expressed the grief and anger he'd been holding for years? She couldn't remember but was sure it hadn't been good enough. Should she have wrapped her arms around him? Should she—

A body crashed into her from the side. Kali yelped then looked down to see a smiling Theo staring up at her, arms wrapped around her legs. She laughed. "You having fun?"

He nodded.

"Make any friends?"

Another nod.

"Where were you?"

He pointed to a door with stairs leading down. "The basement? What were you doing there?"

Theo put a hand to his chin, thinking for a moment. Then he held out his hands close together, thumbs on top and tilted them back and forth, his whole body joining in the motion.

"Video games."

He gave one big nod.

"Very cool."

He grabbed Kali's hand and led her downstairs. Several boys and one girl sat on bean cushions, a fierce competition clearly going on between them. A Nintendo 64 racetrack flashed on the screen of the large projection TV on the far wall. Theo pulled Kali down to a bean bag and cuddled into her.

ABOUT TWENTY MINUTES later Marilyn called down the stairs and two of the children rose from their seats with groans. Marilyn's expression turned to surprise as her gaze fell on Kali. "That's where you got off to."

Kali eased Theo off of her and stood. "I hope it's not—"

"The Fraser/Simmonds brood can get a little overwhelming at times." Marilyn led Kali away from the kids to the back of the room where a pool and ping-pong table were set up. "Big families are like that."

"It's nice."

Marilyn laughed. "At times." She gave her head a little shake. "Anyway, it's lovely to have you here. For us, and for Lincoln." She paused. "He's told you? About his brother?"

"Most of it."

Marilyn nodded. "We're glad he came. It's a hard situation without easy answers. They're both my children. And my soon to be grandchild."

Kali pursed her lips.

"You don't approve."

"No, I ..." Kali looked at the floor, searching for the words. She turned to Theo. "I don't know if anything he ever did could make me turn from him."

"Just so." Marilyn put a hand on Kali's arm, very similarly to the way Rachel had. "I wanted to say thank you. For being there for Lincoln."

"It was the other way around," said Kali. "Lincoln was there for me."

Marilyn raised her other hand. "You brought him back to life. Back to us. You and that boy."

"It was nothing I did." Kali looked past Marilyn. "If anything I pushed him away. I was rude and ungrateful and ... suspicious."

Marilyn laughed. "Maybe that's what he needed.

Someone who'd make him work to be in their life. Who was worth working for." Marilyn glanced to Theo. "He's a sweet boy. You raised him all on your own?"

"My mom was there for the first two years."

Marilyn looked back to Kali. "Then she passed?"

Kali nodded.

"Well, you've done good. Must have been hard."

Kali took a quick breath. "I made it work."

Marilyn laughed. "That's what we do, isn't it?"

"Well, you and ... four kids."

"I had Alex through the roughest years ... or at least the busiest ones." Marilyn let out a soft sigh. "Those teen years, they're a challenge. But I had Alex. And my family. A lot of friends. A whole community."

The corners of Marilyn's eyes crinkled. Kali felt certain she had more to say. Kali could guess it, too—the assumption that Kali didn't have a community. If she had, she wouldn't have moved into some strange man's apartment just to keep off the street.

"Teen years, huh?" Kali kept her tone light. "Have to admit, I'm a little scared of those."

"He'll be fighting off the ladies." Marilyn put an arm around Kali's shoulder. Kali surprised herself by not flinching. The touch felt natural. Warm. Marilyn smiled at her. "Want to head back up? The crowd will have thinned out a bit by now."

Kali walked alongside Marilyn, stopping to ask Theo, who now had the remote in his hand and was being directed by a very patient boy, if he wanted to go upstairs. His head gave a vehement shake.

At the top of the stairs, Kali's stomach roiled. Not now.

She took several deep breaths as her head spun. Where had she put the pills? "Bathroom," she gasped. Marilyn pointed and Kali ran. She heaved into the toilet just as she realized she hadn't stopped to close the door, which meant anyone in the kitchen could hear her, maybe even see her. Before she could even groan in embarrassment she heaved again. The click of the door sounded behind her and a hand fell on her shoulder.

Kali wiped her mouth and turned. Lincoln was smiling. His hand rubbed her back in circles. She heaved again then reached for some tissue, wiped her mouth, and flushed the toilet.

"Anything left in there?"

Kali shook her head. "Not that that necessarily means I'm done."

"Well, let's hope so, 'cause I gotta say, I'm feeling pretty useless."

Kali raised an eyebrow.

"I should be holding your hair back," he gestured to her afro, "but it just stands up on its own. Nothing for me to do."

Kali laughed. She put a hand on the spot that was thinning. "Pretty soon there may be nothing to hold back anyway."

"It's coming out?" He shifted closer to her without looking at the spot she'd touched.

"Has been for a few days now."

"I didn't notice."

"It's thick. At least I have that."

Lincoln leaned against the tiled wall beside her. "Can I get you anything? Water? Your pills?"

Kali reached for his hand and laid her head against the wall. "Just sit here a moment."

Lincoln squeezed her hand, saying nothing.

"Will they think I'm pregnant?"

Lincoln shook his head. "It's mostly close family now. My mom and sisters know; they'll gently turn people from that assumption."

Kali closed her eyes and took several long breaths. "Why does your mom still live here? Couldn't she have a mansion?"

"A mansion?" Lincoln laughed. "Not her style. Joseph offered to buy her a new place once, not that she couldn't have done it herself, but this is the house we grew up in. The house my father built. The first house he built under his own company. Mom doesn't want to leave it. Anyway, it's plenty big for just her, except on days like this."

Kali nodded, realizing it was the first time he'd mentioned his father without tension and hedging. A shiver went through her and she breathed slowly, warding off another wave of nausea. "How was it, seeing Joseph and Lucy?"

Lincoln exhaled. "It's going to be a long time before it's easy. If it ever is."

"I get that." Kali sat silently, uncertain if she should say the words that were pulsing through her. At last she spoke. "Come to New York with me?"

"What?"

She sensed Lincoln shifting and opened her eyes to turn to him. "Would you? I know you'd have to take time off of work—"

"What about Theo? Didn't you want me watching him?"

"I did." Kali bit her lip. She'd thought about taking Theo with her before, briefly. But when she was planning the trip on her own it wouldn't have been possible. Theo with her in a new city when she'd have enough trouble taking care of herself ... Now that Lincoln was coming, should Theo too?

No. She needed this. For herself. Not to be a mom, but to be her, travelling, experiencing something new. Guilt crept up, but she pushed it down. She needed this one thing for herself.

"Maybe Mrs. Martin would finally accept him not sleeping in his own bed, or Sheila, if it were just for a few days, or ..." Kali tilted her head, remembering Marilyn's warm smile, the nurturing touch of her hand. "Do you think your Mom would watch him?"

Lincoln smiled. "I think she'd jump at the chance."

Kali bit her lip. Was it crazy? Leaving her boy with a stranger? She looked at Lincoln. A stranger who had raised this caring, sensitive man. Who had a loving family surrounding her. But still ...

"Maybe Mrs. Martin during the day, as planned, and then your Mom in the evenings, so it's not too overwhelming for Theo, being with someone new."

"That could work." Lincoln looked away then back at her. "You're sure, though? I thought this was supposed to be some independent exploration, some—"

"I want you there."

Lincoln gave her hand another squeeze. "Then I'll be there."

Kali nodded and released his hand, exhaustion washing over her. "How about that water? And maybe then we head home?"

Lincoln jumped up and offered her his hands. Kali took them, and an entirely different type of shiver ran through her.

CHAPTER THIRTY-THREE

As Kali sat in his office, Dr. Jones talked about monitoring, not just in the near future, but for years to come. Tests for pituitary gland function, luteinizing hormone, FSH, estrogen, prolactin, cortisol ... all in addition to the testing of her sight, of the tumour's growth or decline.

"But nothing today?" asked Kali.

Dr. Jones leaned back, his broad shoulders spanning the width of his chair. "Six weeks and we'll do a scan. That should give enough time for the swelling from the treatment to start going down."

"And if it hasn't?"

"Then we give it another four to six weeks. Every body is different. If it has gone down, we'll see you again in eight to twelve weeks. Then three to six months. After two years, every six months until you're five years past. If everything is stable after that, once a year."

"For the rest of my life?"

Dr. Jones nodded. "It's not likely you'll ever have an MRI that looks normal. You'll always have something there. And that something needs to be monitored closely. Residual meningioma, dead meningioma, scar tissue—they all look a bit similar. So we need to ensure, in case what remains is residual, that it doesn't come back."

Because it could come back. It could always come back. Kali knew this, had known this from the start. But somehow ... "And if it's not stable? If this treatment doesn't help or a year from now it starts growing?"

Dr. Jones leaned in. "Then we'll have a new discussion. Treatments are improving, changing all the time. On the West Coast, they're using a form of laser therapy that's had some fabulous results."

"But if it does come back, if the residual tissue reactivates and treatment doesn't work, radiation or laser, I could lose all of my vision?"

"You could."

Kali's brow furrowed. Again, nothing new.

"How is your nausea doing? And the fatigue?"

Kali shrugged. "Both are problems. But I'm pushing through."

"There's no need to be a hero. The medication's there for reason."

"I take it," said Kali.

Dr. Jones looked at her like he doubted her words. "It'll be about twelve weeks before the fatigue really disappears. It may feel like you're climbing out of a rut for a few months, each day a little better than the last." He counted off his recommendations on his fingers. "Eat nutritious food, get enough sleep, take rests when you need to. All of that will help."

He paused and wrote something on a pad of paper. "Time

to reduce the steroids. It'll take a few more weeks until you're done with them entirely." He passed Kali the paper and explained the weaning protocol directions.

"And my vision, when should I be able to tell if it's improved?" Kali looked away, noting the way the doctor vanished from her vision. "It's gotten worse since treatment started. I'm sure of that."

"Maybe eight weeks after treatment. Maybe. It could be longer." Dr. Jones paused. "I have to remind you, there may be no improvement."

Kali's gut tightened. She knew that. Of course she knew it. As long as it didn't get worse. "I'm planning to travel. Next week. New York."

"Oh really?" Dr. Jones' hesitancy was clear. "You sure you up for it?"

"The tickets are booked."

He reached for his prescription pad. "I'm glad you told me. I want you to buy a pair of compression stockings." He scribbled something on the pad. "Here are a few places nearby you can find them. It's not a long flight, but try to get up and walk the aisles every twenty minutes or so and stay hydrated."

Kali raised an eyebrow.

"You're going to be at high risk of deep vein thrombosis."

A blood clot in her leg. Of course. Kali couldn't believe she hadn't even thought of that possibility.

"And take it easy. Have fun. But not too much."

Kali let out a nervous laugh. "I've never been. And if the tumour comes back."

Dr. Jones held her gaze. "I get it, Kali. Minus the flight, I think it's good. These next few weeks are often the hardest for people. The uncertainty. The lack of routine after so many weeks of coming in, doing something about your condition." He paused. "Having something to focus on, showing yourself you can still make new memories, good memories, that this doesn't have to define your life; it's a good plan."

Kali shifted in her seat, his words echoing too strongly her own hopes and fears.

"Have fun. And if you have any drastic changes, call my office."

Drastic changes. Like what? Kali didn't ask. She pushed her chair back and stuck out her hand. She took a deep breath, pushing back her fear and holding onto the belief that things weren't so bad. That no matter what happened, she was going to be okay. "I'll tell you all about it at my next appointment."

KALI SLIPPED INTO 16A and reached for her seat belt. She fiddled with the latch until she heard a click then turned to Lincoln, hoping he hadn't seen. He had and was smiling.

Kali smiled back, fighting to keep her grin steady. "I feel like a grandmother."

Lincoln raised an eyebrow.

"The compression stockings." Kali pointed to her legs. "They don't feel quite as weird as I thought they would. It's just the idea."

"Hmmm."

"You know tonight will be the first night I've spent apart from Theo. The first night in over four years. More if you count when he was inside me." She was rambling. She knew that. And she wasn't a rambler. "It'll be fine though. I'm sure. It'll probably be worse for me than for him." Kali lifted in her seat to see around the plane. It was big. Really big ... not that she had much to compare it to. Bigger than a bus. And it was packed.

Kali rubbed her hands on the armrest. "He'll be fine. He's sleeping in his own bed almost all the time now." She tapped her feet. "When we first moved into the new ... well, now the old apartment, he was so excited about his new room. But he climbed in with me almost every night for the first two weeks. Now it's maybe, I don't know, once every two weeks."

Lincoln nodded. He looked so relaxed, so at ease. But why wouldn't he? He'd flown dozens of times. He didn't have to worry about a blood clot or a son who was about to be a country away. Kali opened her mouth then closed it again. She glanced at Lincoln, reached for her water bottle, and took a long swallow. She stared ahead. A TV screen was built into the seat in front of her. Not that it surprised her. She knew that was likely. She'd seen movies where people watched a film during their flight. What she wasn't sure of was the credit card reader to the side of it. Would she have to pay?

She looked to Lincoln. "You going to watch something?"

"Maybe later."

Kali nodded.

"Most of it doesn't cost anything. There'll be a variety that's free."

"Oh, yeah." Kali let out a little laugh. "I figured that."

She swallowed then closed her eyes and took a long but gentle breath. There was nothing to be afraid of. Hundreds of thousands of people travelled every day. She was doing everything she should be doing to prevent any clot issues, and she was going to New York City—the place she'd dreamed of since she was a child. She was going to see *Les Misérables* and *The Light Princess* on Broadway. She'd see Times Square.

The Empire State Building. The Statue of Liberty. Madame Tussauds. Central Park. And other things, too. Places Lincoln said were off the beaten track but that she'd love. Culture. Food. Obscurities.

A voice sounded and Kali strained to see the flight attendant's safety presentation. She followed along with the pamphlet in her seat back, noticing as far as she could see, she was the only one.

Shortly after, the plane started moving. The wheels left the ground and Kali's stomach flipped. She put her hands against the wall and gazed through the window as the earth stretched farther and farther away. She turned to Lincoln. "Nova Scotia's practically all trees."

Lincoln laughed. "Practically."

Kali leaned back in her chair as they cut through the clouds. The earth disappeared, right along with her fear. This trip was going to be good. Wonderful. And she was going to be fine.

CHAPTER THIRTY-FOUR

fter clearing customs, Kali stood close to Lincoln as swarms of people rushed past. Nausea swam over her—not from the treatment, but from the sheer mass of bodies surrounding them. People seemed to appear out of nowhere. She turned her head back and forth quickly as Lincoln guided them onward. One hand clutched her bag, she hoped the other wasn't cutting off the circulation in Lincoln's arm. A man cut her off without even a glance or apology and Kali nearly tripped trying not to hit him.

"So," she looked to Lincoln, trying to exude calm as her heart raced. "I guess we should find a taxi?"

"Nah." Lincoln, again, looked perfectly at ease. "We'll take the train."

"Oh." Kali nodded as he walked on, her chest tightening.

She'd been on busy buses, standing room only, and the train was no different. But when they made it to the street the crowd made the airport seem spacious. Kali kept her hand clenched on Lincoln's arm. She was a fool, thinking she could have done this by herself. Maybe the old her, the woman who was brave and fearless, the woman who strode through life, knowing she'd make it through, would have been fine. But that woman could see clearly. She didn't stumble and fall and bump into things or people multiple times a day. Curbs didn't terrify her. Gaps in the sidewalk weren't a cause for concern.

Kali wanted to stop, to pull herself out of the crowd, squeeze up against the side of some building, and sob. But if she even slowed, the crowd would trample over her. She stumbled and clutched Lincoln's arm harder. His hand wrapped around her middle, holding her firm. She looked up with thanks but felt weak. They turned the corner and the crowd thinned.

Lincoln pulled her to the side.

Kali looked around, her chin held high and not trembling. At least she hoped it wasn't trembling. "Is this ... are we close to the hotel?"

"A little ways yet." Lincoln's brow furrowed. "Are you okay?"

"The trip? Tripping, I mean. Oh, yeah. Fine. You think I'd be used to it by now."

Lincoln stared at her. "Kali, are you okay?"

She breathed out a smile. "I'm fine. I'm great. Just," she paused, "it's a little overwhelming."

Lincoln nodded and looked away. "We arrived at a busy time."

"So, it's not always this crowded?"

"No," he smiled, "it pretty much is. It's the city that never sleeps. But it depends where you are, what time. One street can be breathing room only then turn a corner," he held out an arm, gesturing to the almost empty street, "and you get this. A quiet little oasis."

Kali's breath came easier. "This isn't a shortcut to get to

where we're going by any chance?"

"It is not." Lincoln offered his arm again. "However, just another minute or two and we'll be on Jane Street. It should be pretty tame."

They stepped back onto 8th Avenue and into a crowd no bigger than Spring Garden Road on a weekday. "Ah, see," said Lincoln. "It comes in waves."

Kali nodded and fell into step beside Lincoln. They turned again.

Jane Street felt like the New York she'd imagined and longed for—from movies and TV shows of adventurous and quirky young people, full of struggle but striving nonetheless. Tall leafy trees grew out of little fenced in plots in the sidewalk. Flat faced brick buildings, some six stories high with metal fire escapes, wrought iron railings, and no space between them, went on as far as Kali could see.

Her tension eased as excitement flared. Lincoln looked over at her. "You like it?"

She nodded.

"Wait till you see the hotel. It was a good pick."

"You've stayed there before, right?"

"Once."

He wasn't wrong. The building was even more impressive than on the website. Set on a corner, red brick from another era made it seem like she was stepping back in time. The Jane wasn't the cheapest of the hotels she'd looked at but she liked the fact that it was different. Built for sailors, the rooms were designed after ship cabins. Small, but it wasn't as if they planned to spend much time there anyway. And it was in the West Village, a place Lincoln said was perfect for not getting pulled into too many tourist traps.

Though she wouldn't admit it, Kali liked the idea of staying in a place with a 'Grand Ballroom' and a past—from sailors to Titanic survivors, to drug addicts. She'd researched the hotel and nowhere else looked appealing after. One step inside the lobby and Kali knew she wouldn't be disappointed. The wood panelled walls were dark and rich, chandeliers made to look like candles lit the space, and green tiles coated several of the walls half way up. "Let's look around," she whispered as she stepped away from Lincoln.

He followed behind. "We could look around after we put away our luggage."

Kali grinned. "I want to see it now. At least some of it." The ballroom was more than she could have imagined. Victorian? Not that she knew these things, but she was sure that was what the article had said. A Victorian base, perhaps, with pieces from various eras thrown in. Either way, it was massive. More wood panelling, thick red curtains, low retro looking couches, cushioned bar stools, long armless chairs she could only think to call chaises, bigger, grander chandeliers than in the entry, and a disco ball. Kali drank it in.

Lincoln put a hand on her shoulder. "We'll see it all. I promise. But let's check in. I need to use the washroom and don't feel like lugging my baggage into a stall."

Kali nodded and followed him back to the lobby. A frustrated looking couple was just stepping away from the desk as Lincoln and Kali approached. Kali let Lincoln take the lead, her gaze on the couple. She couldn't hear them, but an argument was definitely brewing. The woman did not look pleased.

Just as the receptionist was about to hand Lincoln their keys, Kali's attention shifted. "No." She held her hand up to the receptionist. "We're supposed to have two standards."

The receptionist looked at the desk. "I have two Captain's Cabins. The booking was changed."

Lincoln turned to Kali.

"I upgraded."

"You—?"

Lincoln put a hand on her shoulder and turned her from the receptionist.

Kali shook her head. "The Captain's are more than twice as much. Each."

"The Standards don't have bathrooms."

"I know, but—"

"And if you're trying to get there in the night, strangers popping out at you, or if you have more nausea?"

"I haven't been bad this week."

"Captain's are better. They have ensuites. And our rooms are beside each other so—"

"No." Kali stopped him. "It's too expensive."

"I'll pay—"

"Lincoln."

"I'll pay the difference, okay?"

Kali shook her head.

"For me, then. Not you. If you're in a standard I won't sleep. I'll be listening to every footstep down the hall wondering if it's you, if you're okay."

Kali glanced at the receptionist then leaned in. "I don't like this."

"The other rooms are probably booked by now anyway."

Kali pursed her lips then turned to the receptionist. "How big are the beds?"

The receptionist answered immediately. "Two queens

were requested, but as I just mentioned to Mr. Fraser we were all booked so I upgraded one room to the King."

"We'll take the King."

Lincoln and the receptionist stared at her.

"Just the King."

Lincoln cupped her elbow and drew her close. "Are you sure?"

"A King is plenty big for both of us. It solves the bathroom problem. It's fine."

"But—"

"With our one-day cancellation policy, you'll still have to pay for both rooms the first night."

"We'll take it!" The woman from the arguing couple stepped forward, determination on her face.

"Well ..." the receptionist faltered.

"What's the problem?" The woman turned to Kali. "My oh-so-romantic husband thought bunk-beds would be fun. For our five year anniversary. Bunk beds and public bathrooms." She rolled her eyes. "I don't think so."

The receptionist leaned forward. "There'd still be the problem of the cancellation fee for your room."

The woman leaned on the desk, her red lips turned into a smile. "These people were staying for four nights, you said?"

The receptionist nodded.

"Well, we were staying three. But we'll extend it."

"Honey."

The woman raised a hand, silencing her husband. "We'll bump our other reservations back a day." She looked to Kali. "We're here for a week and a half. Three nights in three boroughs. But we'll make it four nights here." She turned her gaze back to the receptionist. "So we'll be paying a higher fare, more than double, and for an extra day. Surely that should warrant waiving the cancellation fee."

The receptionist hesitated.

"You two go on." The woman waved to Kali and Lincoln. "I'll take care of this."

Lincoln shrugged and looked to the receptionist. "The King key?" He accepted the key and flipped it in his hand with a grin. "Problem solved." He extended his grin to the woman and her husband, who looked chastised. "If we see you in the bar in the next few days, there'll be a round on us."

The woman nodded and returned to the receptionist.

KALI STEPPED INTO THEIR room. She'd been expecting a cabin style room, 7x7. Instead, the room boasted a massive bed, large bureau, table and chairs, patterned wallpaper, and full-length mirrors. White and black tiles and a claw footed tub made the bathroom seem like something out of Alice in Wonderland. She crossed the room to the two patio doors. "Lincoln, come!" She stepped outside. "Our own terrace with a view of the river." Wrought iron chairs, red cushions. Another table.

A smile crept onto Lincoln's face. "Better than a glorified closet?"

"Oh yeah." Kali stepped back inside and sunk into an antique looking chair by the bed.

Lincoln shrugged off his backpack and sat across from her. "What do you want to do first?"

Kali tilted her head. "Call Theo." She quickly continued. "Just a check in. Then maybe explore the neighbourhood."

"Sounds like a plan."

Kali took one more look around the room before searching

for her phone. She was in New York. She was out of the country. She was about to have the time of her life.

CHAPTER THIRTY-FIVE

Kali stood in front of the mirror carefully applying mascara. Earlier, she'd popped into a pharmacy near their hotel to pick up the makeup. She couldn't remember the last time she'd done this. A year? Two? Clearly, before her vision had started to go. If she'd done it more often she may have caught the vision loss sooner, the tumour sooner.

It was near impossible. Applying the mascara to her 'bad' eye wasn't so bad. But when she went to whisk the wand over her 'good' eye, her reflection all but disappeared. It became an awkward game of swiping her wand, opening the eye to check, then swiping again. She'd bought eyeliner too, but felt certain it would only result in her looking like a clown.

The lipstick went on easily enough, as did the matte powder. She styled her hair to minimize the thinning section—not that she really thought anyone but her would notice.

Still.

Kali slipped into her dress. She debated heels. She'd brought them, after all. But considering the last two days of exploration, the tripping, the bumping into things and people or having them bump into her... even with Lincoln's arm to hold onto, heels wouldn't be worth the risk.

Kali relived those hours as she smoothed lotion over her skin. The past two days hadn't been all awkward mishaps. The Staten Island ferry—a better way to see the sights than paying for a tour, Lincoln insisted. The museums. Central Park with a crowd and bustle that made her feel alive rather than terrified.

And now tonight, dinner and *Les Misérables*. Dancing—if she felt up to it. Her energy was waning, but excitement carried her through. That and a few mandatory naps.

Kali paused, remembering the odd sensation of Lincoln sleeping beside her. The bed was massive and almost two people could have fit in the space between them, but still he was there—close enough to touch.

Four years.

Four years since she'd shared a bed with anyone but Theo. Four years since she'd felt the touch of a man. That first night Kali had lain, her back turned away for what felt like hours, unable to sleep, wondering if he was thinking the same thoughts she was, if a part of him wanted to roll over and pull her close.

The thought made her shiver, awakening parts of herself she thought had died. She'd shifted in a way she hoped imitated sleep and inched closer to him. He hadn't moved, but his breathing halted before returning to normal. At last she'd fallen asleep.

Waking held its own type of intimacy. When she opened her eyes and rolled over he'd been sitting on the chair by the terrace, a book in his hand and a coffee beside him. He'd looked over, their gazes meeting, and smiled.

She'd seen him in the morning dozens of times—book and coffee in hand, hair mussed from sleep. But never as she lay in a bed beside him.

In that moment, something shifted in Kali ... a shift she realized had been coming on for weeks and was amplified by the way he kept his arm out for her these past couple of days— without making her feel like an invalid. Rather, she felt cherished.

"Morning," he had said, his voice still gravelly from sleep.

Kali had almost shivered with the casual intimacy of it.

And now she was preparing for an experience she'd secretly dreamt of for years, thinking it would probably never come—at least not until Theo was old enough to take care of himself. A Broadway show. And yet her excitement paled compared to her nervousness about what was outside that bathroom door.

Lincoln in a dress shirt and slacks, waiting for her. Not even his mother or sister's birthday had gotten him out of the plaid. The sight of him, looking like that, had made her pulse quicken. She wanted the sight of her to cause the same reaction.

Kali stared at her reflection. On the surface, she didn't look so different from the woman who was out salsa dancing the night she'd first met Derek. Inside, she was almost unrecognizable.

She remembered preparing for that night too. A night of dance. Meeting a man was the last thing on her mind. Inspiring lust... not even a thought. But tonight...

Kali shook her head and turned from the mirror. Tonight was about the show. About a nice, fancy dinner rather than the cafes , bakeries, and street vendors they'd been visiting to conserve cash and, if she was up to it, they'd dance.

Lincoln's arm around her waist, his hand in hers, then maybe after that...

It could just be tonight. Just this trip. They could go back to life as normal afterwards. Roommates, both too broken for a relationship to work, to be healthy. They'd have to go back to normal.

But tonight they could pretend, just like this whole trip was pretend. Not reality, but a chance to live as if she was a different woman, with a different life. A woman whose husband hadn't jumped into an ocean, abandoning her and his child. Who didn't have a ticking time-bomb in her brain. Who hadn't struggled to finally make a good life for herself, only to have it stripped away. Who wasn't forced to rely on charity. Lincoln's charity.

She could erase it all. Just for tonight. And if the evening led to more, to Lincoln's hands trailing over her neck, her arms, her thighs...

If, when they sat across from each other at dinner, she let her eyes show what she wanted, it wouldn't be a promise. It would just be a woman, out with a man, seeing where the night took them. There were reasons not to, of course, multiple reasons. But they didn't matter. Not really. Not for one night.

Kali gave one last glance into the mirror. For the first time in years, she wasn't a mom or a nurse or a patient ... she was a woman. She took a deep breath and opened the door.

THE DOOR OPENED AND Lincoln turned from his perch on the bed. He set down his book and rose. Kali stood, her hand resting on her stomach, as if uncertain. Lincoln stepped forward, speechless. A red dress hugged every part of her— not tightly—but perfectly. Snug enough to hint at the shape beneath without giving all the mystery away. Her afro was pinned to the side with a matching red flower clip. Her lips were rosier than he'd ever seen them.

"Wow."

She put a hand on her shoulder somewhat self-consciously.

He looked to her feet and grinned. "Finally ditching the combat boots?"

She looked down and turned one black ballet-slippered foot. "For tonight. I mean, Broadway."

Lincoln let out a soft laugh. "Broadway will approve."

She nodded and swallowed, that perfect throat convulsing. "Are you ready?"

Another nod.

"Excited?"

"Yes."

Lincoln stepped to the room door and held it open. Kali looked just as incredible from behind. He glanced away, but in the elevator he looked at her again. When the doors opened, she exited without looking at him. It wasn't until they reached the stairs leaving the building that he finally let himself put a hand to her waist—steadying her. She smiled thanks, her gaze lingering longer than usual, and his stomach clenched.

Their conversation flowed easily at dinner. Normally. Except something wasn't normal. Those lingering glances. The long, slow smiles. Something had shifted. If it wasn't Kali, if it were any other woman sitting across from him, Lincoln would be sure she wanted more. But it was Kali. They'd been growing closer, sure. But that only indicated increased trust, comfort with his friendship and his help. She could feel that way with a brother. Tonight though... he didn't think she'd look at a brother like that.

CHAPTER THIRTY-SIX

At *Les Misérables*, Kali sat entranced, her hand casually on the armrest between them. Lincoln rested his hand beside it, expecting hers to draw away. It remained. He glanced at her, her gaze still ahead. Energy pulsed between them. Could she feel it?

They'd held hands before. In fear. In sadness. But this ...

Lincoln shook his head. He was acting like a fourteen-year-old. Thinking like one. He eased his fingers over and looped his hand around hers. Her gaze remained forward, but she let her hand settle in his. One breath, two, three, she looked over and smiled.

Lincoln swallowed and returned his gaze to the stage. That smile. No, it wasn't one you'd give a brother. His heart raced. All these months. And now...

Was his palm sweating? He stilled his thoughts to focus on the sensation. No. It was fine. He was fine. He looked at her again. Kali. Kali, who'd brought him back from the depths. No. He smiled to himself. She hadn't done that. He had pulled and struggled to lift himself out of the mire. Her existence had just given him the extra boost of motivation he needed, had reminded him it was okay to care.

As the musical ended Kali leapt to her feet and clapped furiously. Her eyes shone. He could almost feel the tingles of happiness emanating from her, and then she looked at him. Their gaze, again, locked longer than necessary. She leaned into him, her torso pressed so close he could feel the heat of her; her lips brushed his ear. "Thank you."

"Thank—?" Lincoln pulled back and shook his head in question.

She drew her mouth to his ear again. "For this, for being here. For everything."

Her hand lingered on his shoulder, her face remained inches from his, and Lincoln leaned in. The kiss was soft at first, questioning, and then she responded. Hands at the side of his face, she pulled him closer. Deeper, but gently. He wrapped his arms around her back, pressing her into him. Her mouth opened first. Her tongue searched his, delicately, cautiously, causing him to tremble. As he met her search, the months of passion he'd tampered down erupted within him. One hand travelled to the small of her back and held her tighter. The other caressed the skin of her bare arm.

A third hand tapped firmly on Lincoln's back. He ignored it; nothing existed but Kali.

The hand thumped this time. "Buddy, you mind? We're trying to get out."

Lincoln forced himself to release Kali and stepped out of the man's way. Kali reached for her purse and clutched it to her as they walked down their row. The kiss probably hadn't lasted seven seconds but Lincoln's whole body felt on fire. He looked to Kali and she grinned at him—nervous, embarrassed, electrified?

At the end of the aisle, they mixed with the throng of people entering the lobby and exiting the theatre. A woman bumped into Lincoln and dropped her bag, the contents of her purse scattering out on the ground in front of her. He crouched beside the woman and helped her gather her items amid the rushing feet.

When he stood, Kali was gone. Lincoln nodded to the woman's gushing thanks and scanned the crowd. Faces rushed by, blurring. He pushed through the throng, hoping she'd remember the way they came, his eyes constantly scanning. Halfway down the block, as the crowd thinned out, Lincoln still couldn't spot her. He jogged back to the Imperial Theatre and pulled open the lobby door.

Plenty of people milled in the space, but no Kali. He went to the desk and asked if anyone had seen a woman looking lost, or like she was searching for someone. He described her. They shook their heads.

Lincoln stepped outside and looked both ways. No Kali. He turned. A figure huddled in a doorway to the right of the theatre entrance, arms around her knees, head down. "Kali?"

She looked up, her eyes wide. "Hey."

He held out a hand and pulled her up. Her knee was bloody, the skin torn. Her hands too. "What happened?"

She shrugged, clearly trying to laugh it off, to appear strong. But she was shaken. "You disappeared. There were so many people, and then the curb. The rest is pretty self-explanatory." She held up her hands.

"I'm sorry, I," Lincoln sighed. "A woman, she ... I was helping."

"Oh," Kali laughed, "well, that's what you're best at. Helping helpless women."

"You're not—"

Kali raised a hand. "Let's get back to the hotel."

"No dancing?"

Kali spiked an eyebrow. "Like this?"

Lincoln put a hand around her shoulder. She stiffened. He let his hand drop and held his arm out for her to grasp. She did, though tentatively.

They didn't speak the short walk to the train. Once in the car, Lincoln gestured for Kali to take the one seat nearby and stood in front of her. He wanted to say something, anything, but what? Did she enjoy the play? Of course she did. Did she blame him for getting lost, falling? And most importantly, the kiss. What did it mean?

He couldn't get the words out.

In the hotel lobby, Kali walked past Lincoln to the elevator. He lingered. "I'll be up in a minute."

She offered a tight-lipped smile and passed through the doors.

Several minutes later he entered their room, a first aid kit from reception in hand. The bathroom door was closed. He rapped gently. "Kali?" Nothing. "I got some alcohol swabs. Bandages. I thought—" The door opened.

She reached for the kit.

"I'll do it." Lincoln stepped toward her.

"I can tend my own wounds." Her voice was sharp. "I'm still a nurse."

"I know."

She held her hand out.

Lincoln passed her the kit and stepped away from the door. It closed, like a wall erected between them.

Lincoln plopped back on the bed. Something had shifted

... again. He closed his eyes, remembering the kiss. The feel of her lips by his ear, her fingers on his face, her mouth on his, and the tremble that shot through him, the way it echoed through her as his hand caressed the small of her back. It had to mean something.

The door opened and Lincoln pushed himself up from the bed with an inward groan. His mouth dropped. Kali stood before him in nothing but a red satin bra, panties, heels, and her bandaged knees. He swallowed. She walked toward him. "This is what you want, right?"

Lincoln couldn't speak. Couldn't move. She straddled him, her knees on either side of him, her arm wrapped around his shoulder, their chests almost touching.

"Isn't it? What you've always wanted?"

He nodded, but something seemed off. This wasn't the timid, expectant excitement of just an hour before.

She kissed him hard. Lincoln shuddered, his physical excitement rising as his mind shot warning signals. He held her away from him. "Kali?"

"Don't change your mind now." She leaned in, her kiss almost an assault. Lincoln met it, his arms clenching around her reflexively, his heart racing. She bit his lip and he pulled her away again.

"What? More gentle?" She approached slower this time. "This is what you've wanted. My hero. Protector. Well, here I am." She let her fingers drape behind his neck. "Take me."

Lincoln shifted Kali off of him and onto the bed. He slid himself away from her. "What's going on?"

"What you want. I've seen the way you look at me. Don't deny it."

"I'm not, but—"

"Come on." Her voice had an edge to it. "Isn't this what you hoped for when you saved me not once, but twice? And oh," her laugh was bitter, "what a perfect setup. Sex would have been much more tricky in one of those cramped cabins."

"I booked two."

"You knew I wouldn't let you just pay for—"

"Kali." He stood. "Stop. Not like this."

"Like what?" She stood. "I'm not all you imagined?"

He glanced down the length of her and rubbed a hand through his hair. "You're more beautiful than I ever could have imagined." He stepped into the bathroom, his mind reeling. She was right, this was what he had wanted, hoped for. But not expected. It wasn't why he helped her.

He reached for a robe and held it out.

Kali put her hands on her hips, daring him. He shook the robe and she grabbed it, slipping into its folds angrily. She stared at him, her face tense, then sunk to the bed, her head in her hands. She spoke so quietly her words were lost. Lincoln sat beside her. "What?"

"I'm sorry." She looked up at him. "You didn't deserve that."

"Kali."

"I just," she shook her head, all the anger and intensity gone from her features. "I don't know. I just wanted tonight to ... to feel like a woman. To feel desired. Normal."

"You're—"

"I wanted to be seen. Not like a charity case or a cancer patient, but like a woman. I just kept thinking, what if this is my last chance? What if the treatment doesn't work and my vision keeps going?" She put a hand to his chest, her fingers slightly grazing the thin fabric of his shirt, her eyes trained on the motion. "And I never get to *see* a man again, in this way. To see him seeing me." She turned her gaze to the floor as her hand fell. "And then I lost you and there were so many people and it was dark and I was on the ground and they just kept coming and coming. It was only seconds I'm sure until someone helped me up, but if felt like minutes." She looked up at him, her eyes moist. "I felt so weak. Like all the strength I've held around me all these years, just fighting to survive, was stripped away." She lowered her head again. "And I've let myself be weak. These past days, especially. Let you take control. I didn't know how to get back to the hotel. I didn't think to memorize what train or anything. I just trusted you'd be there, and you weren't."

Lincoln shifted closer.

"I sat there, huddled in that doorway like some homeless person. Terrified. Angry. Angrier and angrier as all these thoughts soared through my mind. So lost. What if you just assumed I went back to the hotel—which would be reasonable—what would I have done?"

"Kali."

"I knew in some part of my mind I'd be fine. I could ask for directions. I could figure it out. But I'm not who I was. That scared me. A year ago, months ago, being lost in New York wouldn't have scared me. It would have been a challenge, an experience. Nothing more."

Lincoln wrapped an arm around her shoulder, thankful she leaned into it. "You've gone through a lot these past months. It's normal you're a little," he hesitated, "fragile." He let out a nervous laugh. "I don't know if that's the right word."

"It felt like the tumour won, the blindness. Like it's stripped me."

"No. No way."

Her eyes were wide, scared.

He ran his thumbs across her cheeks, wiping away the tears. "You're the strongest woman I know."

She looked more exhausted than he'd ever seen her. "I'm so sorry." Her voice caught. "You didn't deserve that. You've been kind. You've never ... not like ..." Her words trailed off. "Which baffled me. Confused me. Men ... I mean, starting right from junior high all the way to this last year in the ER, men always made it clear what they wanted. From words to falsely accidental grazes, to ... more forceful attempts. Yet you, not ever, not really ... just that once ... the night of the firecrackers. But you didn't push. And you stuck around. Even though I could tell... even..." She closed her eyes, inhaling deeply. "It shouldn't have been like that. I shouldn't have been like that. I'm sorry."

Lincoln kissed her forehead softly then pulled back before it could go further. He brought her head to his chest, the scent of cinnamon and coconut swirled around him. "I don't want anything you don't want to give."

"I wanted to." She whispered. "Earlier. Before."

They sat that way for minutes before he brought her to her feet, pulled back the sheet, and directed her to slip into bed. She did, her body curling almost instantly. He covered her and walked around to his side of the bed.

Hands shaking, he undid his shirt buttons, slipped it off, then let his pants fall. He turned off the light and slid beneath the covers. He stared at the barely visible ceiling, hands behind his head.

A moment later Kali shifted. She found Lincoln's arm in the dark and pulled him toward her. He let her position his arm around her, his throat clenching as he felt the softness of her body sink against his. His legs fit naturally against hers.

"I'm sorry," she whispered. "And thank you."

Again, Lincoln breathed in the scent of her as he drifted to sleep with the soft rise and fall of her back against his chest.

CHAPTER THIRTY-SEVEN

Lincoln stretched and rubbed his hand over the bed sheet. He opened his eyes. Kali? Rumpled sheets covered the spot she'd laid. He pushed to a sitting position and scanned the room. The bathroom door was open. The space was empty.

He slid out of bed and rubbed a hand through his hair. Not once had she gotten up before him. Generally, he'd read for an hour or more before she roused.

He crossed to the terrace and pushed open the door. She turned from gazing at the river, a slightly embarrassed smile on her face. "Hi."

"Hi." Lincoln stepped forward.

"Sorry I was such a wreck last—"

"Don't." He stood beside her, his back against the railing so he could see her face. "You weren't a wreck."

She shrugged, looking exhausted. Lines from the pillow creased across her cheek.

"Couldn't sleep?"

"Couldn't go back to sleep."

"You look thirsty. I'll go get you some water." Lincoln took a step but Kali held him back.

"I look thirsty?"

He rubbed his thumb along the line on her cheek and she looked at him, questioning.

"Let me apologize for last night. Coming at you like that. Crossing that line."

Lincoln leaned back against the railing. He couldn't help the grin that crept onto his face. "You already apologized. Besides, it's a line I wanted crossed." He tilted his head, hoping for a smile. "Just not quite like that."

"No." She shook her head. "Nothing's changed. I just wanted to feel like a woman, desired. But the moment's passed. We're friends. Roommates. That's all."

Lincoln stared at her. "That's not all."

"It was a kiss." Her shoulders rose then fell. "People kiss. It was a wonderful, romantic night and—"

"Kali."

"I understand if you want more, but that more can't come from me. I understand if you want to move on." She turned back to the water. "It's all too complicated. It won't work."

"You don't know that. We can't know that unless we—"

She turned back. "And if we try and it fails? What then?"

"That's not—"

"We can't know. You just said that. And then what, are Theo and I back on the street?"

"No. That would never happen. I'd give you the apartment as long as you need it. And you're going to be getting sickness benefits soon, and you'll find another job."

"But what about Theo? This is a package deal. He's already so attached. He's—"

"If you haven't noticed, I'm pretty attached to him too."

"As a friend, a buddy, not a ..."

"A father?"

Kali nodded.

"I can be a father to him. You think I haven't thought about that? If you and I are together, if we decide to make it work, I'll stick by him as if he were my own."

She shook her head and stepped toward the room.

"Stop." He grabbed her arm. "Don't leave. Don't just walk away. What I felt last night, it wasn't one-sided."

Kali sighed, her brow furrowing.

"It wasn't. We need to figure this out. We can't just pretend it didn't happen. I can't."

"Lincoln," her voice rose as she yanked her arm away, "this isn't happening." She hesitated. "Maybe one of us should get another room for the last night."

"Kali," he stood his ground, "you don't get to just walk away. We're past that. If you're angry, be angry. Yell. If you're scared, explain why. Talk. Stay. Don't just leave."

"I did explain why. It's not going to—"

"No, you explained you were scared it wasn't going to work. But you didn't seem to listen to my side of it. If it doesn't, you'll be okay. We'll both be okay." He rested his hands on her arms, rubbing them slightly. "But I think maybe it can work. Maybe it will."

"I'm no good for you right now." She shrugged off his hands. "No good for anyone."

"Let me decide that."

Kali looked past Lincoln. "Every morning I look into the mirror and study my reflection. Some days I can see it better than others. On those days I look longer. Closer. I want to memorize it. To know it ... but no matter how clearly I imprint my own image in my brain, it's going to change ... and if the treatment doesn't work, if the tumour keeps growing, I won't know what that change is." She brought her gaze back to him. "I do it with Theo too. It's harder. Heartbreaking. With myself, it's just ... disconcerting. Who will I be if I can't see who I am? Maybe it shouldn't be, but my appearance, it's a part of my identity. Maybe it's stupid. It is stupid. But ..."

Lincoln stepped closer. "It's not stupid. But there's no reason to think it's going to happen, to think the tumour will keep growing."

"There's every reason to think it will ... or that it could. Maybe not now. But every year of my life until I die they'll bring me in to check it. They wouldn't do that if—"

"Kali."

"On the days my sight is worse, when the world blurs away, my hearing is so strong. Will it become stronger? Will it deafen?"

Lincoln oscillated between frustration and desire to take away her fears. "I don't think that's possible."

"And if we fall in love, if we realize it's going to work, and you're stuck with someone you have to take care of, someone who—"

"Kali."

"It's terrifying, okay?"

"I get the terror. I do."

"So how can I let you into that?"

"Love's always scary. There's never a guarantee. We both know that." Lincoln stopped, his smile growing. "So you think it's possible, huh? Us, in love."

Kali shook her head, but let out a close-lipped smile before biting her lip.

"I'll take that as a yes." Lincoln grinned. "You asked how you let me in? You just do. Like you have been." He stared at her, his grin growing. "You seriously need to meet some of these people at the CNIB. Their lives are so—"

"That's not living with them, Lincoln. That's sitting across from them for an hour and oohing and ahhing. That's not life. What if you can't handle real life?"

Lincoln held her again, firmer this time. "Kali. I'm here. I'm handling it. I see what you're going through. I'm not blind." He let his hands fall and rubbed a hand at the back of his neck as her brows raised. "You know what I mean." He let out a half groan, half laugh. "Bad choice of words."

She bit her lip again and shook her head. Instantly, his mind was drawn to that first kiss.

"What about me?" asked Lincoln. "Do I scare you? The potential time-bomb in me?"

Her brow furrowed then relaxed in understanding. "Your dad?"

"My dad. Is that part of it? Are you scared? My future could be far worse than yours."

Her brow furrowed again. "It is scary." She took a breath. "But I wouldn't let that stop me. Not if—"

"Not if what?"

"Not if—" She stepped away and wrapped her hands around the back of her neck. "Not if it was going to work now. Not if it was right." She dropped her arms. "I wasn't looking for anything, for anyone. Even before all this. I'd resigned myself to me and Theo. We were good. We were enough. We are enough. I appreciated your help but beyond that ..."

"We've already gone beyond that. Besides," Lincoln offered a half smile, "who wants to live with 'enough'?"

Kali stepped away and paced the terrace.

"This isn't just friendship, Kali. Not anymore."

"I told you, last night was about—"

"It doesn't matter what it was about, or what you thought it was about. This has been more than friendship for a while."

She stopped.

"Tell me it hasn't."

"I was scared and vulnerable. It was a mistake."

"What? All of it? Since we first walked into each other's lives?"

She shook her head.

He stepped toward her. "Okay. So we agree." He took another step. "This isn't all a mistake." One more step. "And it's more than friendship, or at least heading in that direction."

"I don't know."

A final step and he linked the fingers of his hand with hers. "We'll take it slow. No promises. No guarantees."

"My life is complicated." She hesitated. "More than you know."

"Whose isn't?"

"No, really." She tried to pull back. "More than you—"

He reached for her other hand. "A little more than friends. Exploring, without fear getting in the way. Being open. That's what we'll do." He squeezed her hands. "I messed up with that last time. I had all these ideas about what Lucy and my relationship was. About what it meant, thinking it was this settled thing and taking that for granted. I'm not going to do that with you. And I don't want you to do it with me. If you're angry, scared, uncertain, tell me. If you need space, tell me. We'll figure it out."

She swallowed, and he could see the blood pulse at her

neck. Her heart was racing, just like his.

"Okay?"

"I'm scared," she hesitated. "I'm uncertain."

"Okay. But are you willing to try to figure that out?"

She stared at him, and he could almost see her mind working, debating, deciding. She nodded. "But no promises. No guarantees."

"Just the promise to try." Lincoln stepped closer, their hands still linked. He smiled. "And to prove to you last night was more than just a mistake, to prove this has somewhere to go." He leaned in, slowly, giving her time to back away. She didn't.

CHAPTER THIRTY-EIGHT

K ali's heart raced. It felt wrong. But more than that, it
felt right. Before Lincoln's lips touched hers, her mind
flashed to last night, to the way passion had exploded
within her.

He was right. It wasn't just her desire for a man, any man.
It was desire for him. Lincoln, who'd saved her son, then
saved them both, again and again. Lincoln, who'd been
patient, understanding, and kind when she didn't deserve it,
when she'd been awful and standoffish, when her life was
falling apart and she didn't know what to do. Lincoln, who'd
stayed through it all.

Their lips met and everything she'd felt last night and
more flooded through her. The kiss was soft, closed-mouthed
but intimate. She raised her hand to wrap around him, draw
him closer, but he pulled away, smiling.

He stepped back. "Should we get breakfast?"

"Breakfast?" Kali stepped away, flustered. She didn't want
breakfast; she wanted him. But she'd asked him to take it
slow. He was listening.

It was all so new. She'd shunned men her whole life, her

plans and goals more important.

Until Derek. Derek hadn't really given her a choice. And in a different way, it seemed, neither was Lincoln. It scared her, but not enough to say no. Not anymore. She smiled. "Breakfast would be good."

And yet we hold on.

KALI ENTERED THE kitchen, her feet shuffling across the cool hardwood, her head feeling like it'd shrunk, or like her brain had expanded. Either way, there wasn't enough room in her skull and the pain was excruciating.

She slipped her glass under the tap, popped a pill in her mouth, and swallowed the cool liquid. She'd become a pill popper. She didn't like it.

They'd been back home for less than fifteen hours, and already the time away seemed like another life. As soon as she stepped in the door of their apartment ... Lincoln's apartment, the reality hit her. The trip was an escape, yes, but she couldn't escape what awaited her back home: a life sentence of doctor's appointments, medication, and the looming possibility of legal blindness. She may never get her job back, and though she felt certain she'd find some other work—there had to be rewarding work out there for someone like her—she couldn't imagine not being a nurse.

Nursing was hard. Exhausting. But it was what she loved. What she felt made for.

She thought of Theo, of the way he'd been waiting with Marilyn at the airport, how he leapt into her arms then reached for Lincoln right after. Lincoln said he could be a father, and he loved Theo, sure. He was good with him. But being good with your roommate's child wasn't the same as fathering him... not that Kali had any example of what a good father was.

She stepped to the window, her gaze following a flock of birds, and wrapped her arms around her middle. She'd given up the idea of Theo having a father years ago. Given up the idea of her marrying again, or even being with someone. There'd hardly been time to think of it—to hope. Certainly no time to date. She was with Theo or she was at work. It had been enough.

Kali paced the room, her eyes closed, turning the counts into a game. Nine steps from the window to the couch. Turn left. Three steps. Turn right. Four steps to the TV. She knew this was overkill, unnecessary, for now at least. But it calmed her, let her know she'd be at least somewhat prepared if the worst happened.

And she had time now. All the time in the world. Time for Lincoln. Time to explore what could be. It was easier, not being alone, having someone to rely on, to watch Theo if she had an appointment. But easy wasn't reason enough.

Did she want love? Kali brought her fingers to her lips, remembering the kiss. Kisses. But it was the last one that stuck with her, sent shocks of fear and hope through every vessel. The theatre had been passion. Lust. The kiss in the bedroom the next morning had been intimacy.

It hinted at an entirely different life than the one she'd been living or come to expect. It foreshadowed family dinners and soccer practice and mornings under the covers with Theo snuggling beside them. Another child, maybe. One day. If the tumour hadn't stolen that possibility away too.

She shook her head. Turn left. Five steps to the bookshelf.

Intimacy. A future

Her fear told her she wasn't ready, told her not to trust, told her it was selfish to intricately connect Lincoln to her problems. But he was connected anyway. And he had problems too. Plus, now didn't need to mean forever.

He said he'd take it slow, and he hadn't tried to kiss her again. She'd wanted him to … yearned for it at times. But she wasn't ready to push, to start something she wasn't sure she could finish. He touched her hand when passing her things, letting his fingers linger. He grazed the small of her back when she passed through open doorways. And it couldn't just be called chivalry or friendship. Not anymore. They couldn't go backwards. So it was living in this state of limbo, moving forward, or saying goodbye.

She couldn't say goodbye.

Kali let out an exasperated sigh and opened her eyes. She'd lost count and bumped into a door frame. She needed someone to talk to. Needed an outside perspective. She'd never been the girl to gab about her boy problems. She'd never had boy problems.

She'd shunned every man who showed interest until Derek. She'd tried to shun him too, but he wasn't having it. One day Derek wasn't in her life and the next he was. It'd been that simple. Any questioning had been washed away by his smiles and laughter and unflinching ability to make her believe he was exactly what she'd never known she always wanted.

But that's what friends were for, right? Helping you figure out the things you couldn't figure out for yourself or, rather, helping you see what you knew you wanted all along. Kali had been a sounding board for Shelley countless times before she met Jake. And several times after when he wasn't living up to her standards. And Kali had promised to call. Weeks ago.

Kali closed her eyes again. Right turn. Seven steps. Her hand grazed along the top of the bookshelf. She wasn't a good friend. She should have called when she said she would. She wanted to see Shelley; she just didn't want to talk about the tumour, which is all Shelley would want to talk about. Unless she talked about Lincoln. What was brain cancer when you could gab about a man?

Kali smiled, imagining the way she'd divert Shelley's medical questions by telling her about that kiss, about Lincoln's assertion that he wasn't going anywhere.

Kali tilted her head. A footstep? She stood still, waiting for more sound. Nothing. She turned and opened her eyes. Lincoln stood smiling.

"Morning."

"Hi." Kali put a hand to her chin.

"Practicing?"

She nodded. "I do it sometimes. The doctor suggested it." She stared at his topless chest. She'd seen him topless before, countless times. But it was different now. He wasn't just that odd man she roomed with out of necessity. She swallowed. "It's silly."

"Nah." He stepped forward and leaned against the wall separating the living room from the kitchen. "It makes sense. There's a lot you could learn to help with that. And to make the day to day things easier."

Kali nodded. It felt like a vice gripped around her chest. She'd been thinking about that the last days in New York. Thinking about it on the plane. If she'd had a cane that night after *Les Mis*, even just an identifier cane, would she have been trampled like that? Probably not. People would have given her a wide berth. And she could have felt the curb, felt the cobbles and ruts in the sidewalk. Navigated the city without her hand consistently linked in Lincoln's elbow.

"I'll think about it."

Lincoln smiled then caught Theo in his arm as he ran by. He scooped him up and tickled him. Theo laughed out loud then wrapped his arms around Lincoln's neck before squirming out of his grasp and over to Kali, where he flung his hands around her leg. She looked down at him, smiling, then up at Lincoln.

"How about pancakes for our first morning home?"

Theo clapped his hands. Lincoln laughed.

Was this what she'd never known she always wanted? Family. Someone to help with the little day to day things. Someone to make them laugh. A shiver ran through her. No, she'd wanted it long ago. Wanted it when Derek first rubbed her barely noticeable baby bump, when he'd promised her a future. It was a dream she'd hidden on a shelf.

"So? Pancakes?" Lincoln's grin was beautiful.

This thing they were trying out, it might not work. But no, she definitely couldn't say goodbye.

CHAPTER THIRTY-NINE

Kali clutched her satchel as she walked up the step and onto the porch at Alteregos Coffee House. She hesitated, then continued through the door. Shelley wouldn't be here first, but Kali checked the room anyway. It was bigger than she remembered and brighter. They'd renovated. She'd picked it partially for its past darkness, the ability to slip into a corner unnoticed. She ordered a tea and slipped into the corner anyway, though it wasn't as secluded as she'd hoped.

Which was fine. Absolutely fine. She sat straighter, trying to conjure up the woman she'd been before this diagnosis, before she became a person who was jumpy and nervous and insecure of all the life that existed just outside her periphery of awareness.

Several minutes later the door burst open and Shelley appeared. "Hiya!" She swooped into the chair across from Kali. "Let's head outside. It's like summer again out there."

"No." Kali fought to keep her smile, not wanting to explain.

"Girl, please, we have to enjoy the sun while it's here. The rains'll start soon."

"No." Kali took a sip of her tea. "I'd rather stay inside."

Shelley opened her mouth then closed it again, a question covering her brow. "If you insist."

Kali let out a breath of air. This was her life, she needed to be able to explain it. "People will walk by. But I won't be able to see them. They could be looking at me, waving at me, and I wouldn't—"

"Right." Shelley cut Kali off. "My bad. That makes sense." She shrugged off her jacket and slung her purse onto the far side of the table. "And this is your hood, too." She hesitated. "That happen a lot? People waving or signalling or ..."

Kali played with the strap of her satchel. "I don't always know."

"Right."

Shelley's face sobered further. "How are you feeling? I mean I know awful. I know this is all ... horrible. But how horrible? Are you in pain now?"

"I'm always in some pain," Kali bit her lip and shrugged, "but it could be worse. I've kept my looks ... for the most part."

"No," Shelley leaned back and crossed her legs, "you've kept them. Absolutely." She leaned closer. "No swelling. You look tired, doll, but no swelling. You on steroids?"

Kali nodded. "But a low dose. They've been weaning me off of it. Almost done now."

"Dexamethasone?"

"Uh huh."

Shelley tapped her fingers on the table, a nervous habit she'd had since childhood. "And your licence was taken away?"

Another nod.

"And your job ..."

"On leave. They'll reassess in a couple of months."

"Your dream job." Shelley sighed. "Me. I need the rush. The variety. I always get impatient with the cases who aren't giving me a shot of adrenaline. But not you."

"Not me."

Shelley pursed her lips, giving Kali a look of pity. "You'll get it back. You'll be fine. The body's an incredible thing, a few weeks and—"

"It's never going to be as it was, my vision."

Shelley's brow furrowed before she flashed a quick smile. "But you're so resilient. So amazing. You'll figure it out. You'll make adjustments."

Kali looked away. She wouldn't argue, there was no point. "How are you? How are the kids?"

"Same as always." Shelley waved a hand. "Jake Jr. is in soccer now. Desiree's a little Diva. But you're not getting out of this that easily. We're not done talking about you."

Kali took a breath. Second tactic. "I moved back in with Lincoln."

Shelley's brows shot up. "The homeless guy? I mean not homeless, but ... really?" She leaned in. "Out of need or ...?"

Kali let out an uncomfortable smile, knowing Shelley would gobble the words up. "It started out of need."

Shelley's eyes brightened. "Oh, girl, start talking. Let me live through you."

Kali laughed. "Go get yourself something to drink, then come back and I'll talk."

"You'll dish." Shelley grinned as she stood and grabbed her wallet out of her purse. "Dish is the word, my dear."

Several minutes later Shelley was sipping from her latte and pushing the plate of cookies she'd brought back over to Kali. She let out a long breath. "So you guys didn't," she raised an eyebrow, "just the kiss? Or kisses?"

Kali nodded.

"And they were ...?"

"Well, it's been a long time."

"You're a nun. I know." Shelley shook her head. "But—"

"Incredible." Kali's cheeks warmed as she remembered Lincoln's touch.

"Do you even realize what you just did?"

Kali returned her gaze to Shelley. "Hmm?"

"You just touched your fingers to your lips, like you were remembering, and the look on your face. You've got it bad."

"Or maybe it's just been a long time. Maybe any man could have—"

"He's not any man, Kali. He took you and your son in rent free after jumping in front of a car to save a boy he'd never laid eyes on. I saw at the party ... his gaze follows you around the room. And not in a creepy way, in," Shelley paused, "in this gentle, caring way. Like you're precious to him or something. I can hardly remember the last time Jake looked at me like that."

"Jake adores you."

"Yeah. He does. But it's different. Maybe it's the hope in Lincoln's eyes that you'd one day be his. Jake knows he's locked me down."

Kali nodded.

Shelley's face softened. "There's nothing wrong with letting yourself need someone, Kal. Nothing at all."

"I know but—"

"But nothing. It's admirable, you devoting your life to Theo like you have. But it's also not entirely healthy. You're a woman. You have needs, and even beyond that, it's just, having someone, knowing they're there for you, a partner. It's a pretty great thing."

"I know—"

"And Jake could tire of me one day. But I have him today, and I wouldn't change today."

Kali looked away, a shiver running through her.

"I know Derek—"

She snapped her gaze back to Shelley. "I don't want to talk about Derek."

Shelley raised her hands. "Okay. Fine. We won't talk about Derek." She inhaled and disapprovingly pushed the plate toward Kali. "Have a cookie. You're too thin."

Kali reached for a chocolate chip cookie that was half the size of her face and took a tiny bite. "It's the nausea."

"It bad?"

"Sometimes."

Shelley looked to the purple splotch on Kali's arm. "Bumping into things?"

"I'm getting better with the clumsiness. But it's like doors and shelves and railings jump out at me."

Shelley rested a hand on Kali's, sympathy behind her eyes.

"Don't." Kali pulled her hand away. "I don't need that."

"Okay." Shelley nodded, her lips pressed firmly. "Show me. Where's the vision gone? What can you see?"

Kali held her right hand to the side of her face and brought it in until she could see it. "On the left, it's almost all gone. So I have pretty much no peripheral. Just the hint of movement sometimes, or light or colour. If my right eye is closed, it's the same situation."

Shelley mimicked Kali's hand position and closed her left eye. She opened it quickly and dropped her arm, a look of pity coating her face. "That's bad, Kal."

Kali shrugged out a smile. "It's not good."

"Have you gone to the CNIB?" Shelley's voice cracked but she caught it quickly. "A cane could help or ..."

"I've been. Not that I wanted to. It seems like—"

"Admittance. Acceptance." Shelley nodded. "What would you tell a patient?"

A lump rose in Kali's throat. "This is your life. You can fight it or you can live it."

Shelley's mouth opened slightly and Kali could see her biting her tongue, a clear sign that her friend was trying to hold back tears. "Yeah. Live it, Kali. You can't go around with bruises all over you. What if you stepped out into the street again or—"

"I'm careful."

"Not enough. Clearly." Shelley calmed her voice. "You know I just care."

"I know."

Shelley pressed her lips again. She reached her hand forward but stopped the motion before gripping Kali's. "This sucks. Truly. You're going to get some of your vision back. I know that." She paused. "But don't fight the battles you can't win out of pride, babe. Go to the CNIB." She smiled and shook her head. "You probably won't like this, but I've talked around. Done some research. With your skills, your knowledge, there's a lot you can do in the field even if you don't get your own job back." Another pause. "And don't push this man away just because you're scared. We never have guarantees."

Shelley was right. On both counts.

"Oh," Shelley reached into her bag, "I almost forgot. Here." She passed an envelope to Kali.

Kali raised an eyebrow.

"Just open it."

She flipped up the seal and pulled out a picture. Theo, laughing, joyous, his face lit with the candles from his birthday cake; Kali beside him, her face equally full of joy.

"Figured I'd get it printed. More tangible."

Kali nodded. She traced a finger over her son's face.

"A little sliver of joy. To remind you."

Kali bit her lip and looked to Shelley. "Thank you. It's perfect." Kali had been so stressed that day, so in pain, she'd almost forgotten the joy, how good it was for Theo. Kali slipped the photo back into the envelope and slid it in her satchel. "Can you talk about you now? How's work? Are you still going for that promotion?"

Shelley grinned. "I got it."

CHAPTER FORTY

An elderly gentleman with a support cane held the door open for Kali. She closed her umbrella, shook it, and passed through. That made sense. He made sense. Or at least more sense than someone like Kali walking through these doors. He'd had a whole life of vision ... probably. A woman with a little girl, barely five and wielding a white cane, walked through the still open door. For all Kali knew, that man's vision had started going when he was this child's age or younger.

Kali hesitated in the lobby. She hadn't told anyone she was coming. Not Lincoln, not Shelley, not the CNIB staff. She'd gotten a notification about the Adjustment to Vision Loss meeting in her email but didn't want to confirm her attendance.

But here she was.

"Welcome!"

Kali turned to the voice. Alika stood smiling at her.

"It's good to see you back, Kali."

Kali's throat closed. Why did being here scare her so much? Why did she clam up?

Alika waited a moment then continued. "Are you here for the Vision Loss Group?"

Kali nodded. Talk. Just— "Yep. Thought I'd give it a try."

"Down the hall, third door on the left. I'll be there soon."

A different room than last time. Would it be different people? Kali nodded and turned down the hall. The old man and mother with her child had disappeared, so Kali walked the hall alone. She was early. But not too early. Enough time to find where she was going and get situated. Not enough for anyone to get friendly with her ... provided the meeting started on time. Let the meeting start on time.

It wasn't in her to ask for support, help, especially from strangers. But she needed it. Theo was getting better, way better with putting his toys away, with not running up behind Kali. But he was four. She'd yelled at him just last night when he'd pummelled her with a side hug. He'd thrown her off balance, causing her to fall against the bookshelf where a framed picture had toppled and broke. The fall also sent a shot of pain through Kali that showed itself with a hefty bruise.

He'd looked so sad. So sorry, and she'd regretted the angry words before they'd even fully left her mouth. But she'd said them. She needed to do better too.

Kali entered the room and sat on one of the chairs that filled the circle, keeping her gaze low. It was awkward, not knowing who could see and who couldn't. She didn't want to smile at someone in greeting and have them not smile back, or the reverse, have someone smile at her, expecting a response that she couldn't give. There were people on either side of her. She'd seen them when she sat down. But now she couldn't see either of them. It was why she'd walked here today, despite the rain. Sitting with Theo on the bus wasn't so bad. She'd take the window seat and wrap her hand in his, but having a stranger sit down beside her, having them so close while not able to see them unless she turned her head more than would seem normal ...

Kali took a deep breath, pushing the anxiety away, the feeling that her world was closing in on her, squeezing, until one day it'd be nothing. Blankness.

But that might never happen. It could be fine. It could be no worse than this. If the treatment had caused swelling, it could be better. Much better. Kali took two more calming breaths then raised her head as Alika walked into the room and welcomed everyone.

After a request for people to put their phones on silent and some cursory introductions about what the group was and what to expect from it, Alika passed the floor to a woman who looked to be in her mid-40s. She looked strong, but with a soft streak running through her. Heather.

"I wallowed when I first got the news. A degenerative disease. Hereditary, so I knew there was a chance it was coming." She paused and looked to the floor, a soft smile on her face, before straightening her back and letting her gaze travel around the group. "I was a lawyer. Sorry—" She glanced to Alika. "I am a lawyer. Just in a different capacity now. When I got the news my children were eight, twelve, and sixteen. At first, I pushed it to the side." She puffed out her chest. "This was my life. I was in charge. So I took care of the kids. I went to work and rocked it. I did my husband's laundry, just like always. But," the word came out clipped, sharp, "degeneration is degeneration."

Heather took a short breath as her voice wavered. "When I

couldn't keep up with work anymore, that's when it hit me, smashed into me." Another breath. "That's when I really wallowed. I still got up, got dressed, got the kids to school, kissed my husband goodbye. Then I'd go home, change into a comfy robe, and wallow the day away." She wiped a tear from under her eye. "Getting dressed, it was this seemingly insurmountable effort. But I ... surmounted it. Still though, keeping the clothes on, like my life was normal, like I was normal, I couldn't do it. As soon as I walked back in the door this weight pressed down on me and only by taking off the clothes that represented my real life, the one I'd never get back, could I breathe."

Heather shook her head then shrugged. "For weeks I lay on the couch feeling sorry for myself, feeling angry, furious, terrified my children would face the same fate. Feeling the victim, and like nobody in the world could possibly understand what I was going through. To have your life, your independence, torn from you. Not driving." She moved her head in a large sweep to take in the room. Kali, too, looked around at the nodding faces.

"A friend pushed me to come here. Said a friend of a friend of a friend had, and it transformed her. She was so independent. She was happy again." Heather's lips pursed. "Something had to change. So, very begrudgingly, I stepped through that door. And you, the staff ..." Heather paused and looked to the ceiling. "I wasn't alone. There were people who got it. My husband didn't. My kids didn't. How many times can you tell someone to put things back where they find them?" She gave a chuckle and wiped a hand under both cheeks this time. "Most importantly, I learned my life wasn't over. It was changing. But everyone's life changes.

Constantly. Ours is just a little more dramatic than the norm." Chuckles from the crowd this time. "Accepting that, it gives you the freedom to thrive."

Heather reached into her bag, pulled out a cane, and flicked it to its full length. "To accept this, what it means, what it says to the world, what it said to me ... I thought it would be admitting defeat. Thought it would take away my power. And it was life altering, no doubt about it."

Kali shifted in her seat. The woman's words cut through her. It felt like a set-up. But nobody knew Kali was coming.

"Is it easy? Any of this? Of course not. Do I still have days when I get angry or frustrated or wish I had a magic wand to take me back to the life I once lived?" Heather smiled wistfully. "Occasionally. But this isn't the end of life. There's so much I can do. Little and big. I'm not in the courtroom anymore, but I may be again one day. And the work I'm doing instead, it may take me longer than the average person, but I'm doing it. And it's good work.

"Outside of that, I get up, I shower, I prepare meals for my family. Better, healthier meals than I used to now that I don't have a sixty-hour a week job. I set an example for my children and my family. I listen to people. Really listen. Something I only now realize I rarely did before."

A shiver went through Kali. She felt Heather's words. Already she was more attentive with Theo ... when she wasn't angry or frustrated at least. And when people spoke she focused on their words. At first, it seemed like an annoyance, an effort. But she had noticed, sometimes, that it was an improvement.

"And then there's the larger scale things too. I set the tone for how people are going to respond to me by how I respond

to them. Both with my family and friends and with strangers."
Heather winked. "There's a world out there I can conquer
with the vision and skills I have now. I can help make it easier
for those who come after me. I need to remember that. We all
do. Live today as if the sight we have, or lack of it, as if the
breath we have, is a gift."

Heather looked around the room. She paused briefly while
her gaze was on Kali, her smile growing. "Obviously this is a
role I didn't sign up for. None of us did. But this is the life
we're living. This is the life we have." She shrugged. "It's
going to be as good or as bad as we make it."

Murmurs of agreement sounded throughout the room.
The conversation that followed was more natural, people
talking about little victories or frustrations they'd had in their
week, offering tips they'd employed or doctor's verdicts. Kali
barely heard any of it. A rumbling seemed to pass through
her. She'd thought she'd resolved so much of her pain and
anger and lack of acceptance before the New York trip.
That's what the trip was about, after all. Her taking control of
her life. Her showing herself she could still live. But the fear
on that street outside the Imperial Theatre had tainted all of
it, leaving her more fragile and ... handicapped than when
she'd left. Leaving her near hopeless that it would ever get
better.

She needed to talk to Heather. What kind of lawyering
was she doing now? What technology helped her? If she
could make it work, maybe Kali could too, even if she never
went back to Westwood. Her brain was still intact. Her
knowledge. And how much vision did Heather still have?

LINCOLN DIALED KALI'S number. He hung up just as the voicemail came on. It'd do no good for her to hear the worry in his voice without knowing the whole story. He didn't even know the whole story. Kidnapping. Assault. None of it made sense.

He paced the precinct, waited ten minutes, then called again. No answer.

An officer pushed through the door Lincoln wasn't allowed behind. Lincoln stepped toward her.

"Nothing yet, Mr. Fraser. Just take a seat."

"Is he okay?"

Her smile was tight, tired. "Take a seat, Mr. Fraser."

Lincoln dropped into one of the straight-backed chairs and pulled out his phone. Keep it light. Don't scare her—*Hey Kali,* he texted, *could you give me a call when you have a minute? Nothing big.*

He stared at the text then hit backspace until the last two words disappeared. It was big. He didn't know how big yet, but ... the door opened and another officer came out. The first waved her hand, dismissing Lincoln's eager look.

Lincoln pressed his head against the wall. This was ridiculous, not telling him anything. Was it even legal? He looked to the phone again, then dropped his head in his hands. All he could do was wait.

CHAPTER FORTY-ONE

After the meeting, Kali waited several feet from the door as Heather talked to a few people. Alika stepped toward Kali. "Anything I can help you with?"

"No, uh." Kali looked to Heather. "I was just—"

"She'll be a few minutes." Alika put a hand on Kali's shoulder. "If you ever do want to chat, my office is always open.

Kali nodded and walked toward Heather, who had turned from the people she'd been chatting with and was slinging a backpack through her arms. Kali angled herself so she'd approach Heather head-on. From the way she'd looked around the room, Kali suspected she didn't have strong peripherals either.

Heather looked up and gave a quick flinch. Clearly, she hadn't registered Kali's presence.

"Hi." Heather's smile was welcoming. "You're new, right? I don't think I've seen you around."

"First time." Kali tilted her head back and forth. "To this meeting, anyway. I went to a different one a few weeks ago."

"It takes time to acclimate." Heather's smile was genuine, peaceful.

"Yeah." *Get over this nervousness. There's nothing to be nervous about.*

"So, what's yours?"

"Pardon me?"

Heather laughed. "Your diagnosis. The reason you're here."

"Oh," Kali hesitated, "meningioma. Uh, junctional scotoma."

"That's a tumour, right? But the rest in layman's terms."

"The tumour's on my optic chiasm and my optic nerve. So it's affecting my full field of vision in my left eye and the peripheral on the right. It could eventually grow to—"

"Take it all away?"

"Yeah. That may never happen though."

"Treatment?"

"Radiation."

Heather nodded. "I hope it gives you a lot of time."

Kali let out a short laugh. "Me too."

"Mine's retinitis pigmentosa. So basically my vision just keeps closing in and closing in. Right now, it's like looking out of two straws. So straight ahead I can see, but up, down, side to side, nothing."

Kali nodded. Talk about the world closing in.

"Night vision's completely gone."

"And will it ... eventually?"

Heather nodded. "In time. How much time? Can't know for sure, so I try not to think about that."

"You're a lawyer? Still, I mean?"

Heather's smile was back. "Yeah. I work on Human

Right's laws. It's a lot of reading—or listening mostly now. Technology is great. And dictating. Research. Writing letters. It's slow-going for me. But, as I said, great work."

"That's awesome. I wa ... am a nurse."

"Good for you." Heather grinned. "You are. But you don't know how to be anymore. In practice."

Kali nodded.

"And now you're nauseated and dizzy and utterly fatigued from the treatment."

Kali raised an eyebrow.

"I have friends. Not your specific condition, but similar treatment." Heather looked to the door. "I have to go pick up my daughter. You want to take a walk with me?"

"Sure." Kali let Heather take the lead and followed her down the hall and around a corner. She walked without her cane. Was it just for the outside world? Kali imagined the halls here would be kept immaculately clear.

Heather paused outside a door with large windows. She pointed. "The older girl with the braided hair. She's mine."

"Is she—?"

"No," Heather turned around to look at Kali, "and hopefully never. She works with some of the children who are visually impaired or legally blind though. Helping them learn coping skills, teaching braille." She looked back through the window. "She's my youngest. She's thirteen now. It was the hardest for her, I think. She felt gypped, maybe." Kali thought of Lincoln, the way he had less years with his father than his siblings did. "It also meant she couldn't do as much at first because I couldn't drive her around. Now I have a support system though. People are amazing."

Heather looked to Kali again. "Do you have kids?"

"A boy. He's four."

"And how is he taking this?"

Kali let out a half sigh, half laugh. "I only recently worked up the courage to tell him. I don't know how much he understands."

"You should bring him here." Heather pointed to a young girl who was helping a little boy with some blocks. "That one there, she's a helper. And only five. It's really amazing how understanding the kids can be, how intuitive and patient. Kelly, my girl, started helping out three years ago and it transformed her—not just in how she related to me but in general. You should think about it. It might be good for ..."

"Theo," said Kali.

"Theo. I like that." Heather turned to Kali again. "Have you been to many of the seminars? Living skills?"

Kali shook her head, then realized Heather had turned back to the window. "No."

"You should. Falling a lot? Bumping into things?"

"Mmhmm."

"Cane training. It'll blow your mind." Heather's daughter caught sight of her and waved. Heather looked to Kali. "I've got to get going, but I hope to see you around again."

Kali opened her mouth to say maybe, closed it, then opened it again. "You will," she said. "You'll see me."

When she left Heather, Kali followed the path they'd taken back then searched out Alika's office.

Alika looked up with a smile. "Kali. What'd you think of the meeting?"

"It was nice." Kali stepped into the room. "Heather is," she searched for the right word, "inspiring."

"That she is." Alika pushed the papers she'd been working on to the side. "I think most people can be, given the right combination of circumstances." There was a pause. "What can I do for you?"

Kali stepped farther into the room and followed Alika's gesture to sit. "I'd like to learn more. About how to function better. I mean I'm not blind ... I may never be, but ..."

"But you've lost a lot of vision and it's difficult."

"Yes."

Alika turned to her computer. "We don't have another Independent Living Skills group meeting for a couple of weeks. The staff member who leads them is away, and she does the one-on-ones too. But—" Alika looked back to Kali. "One of our clients has been receiving training in that area. She wants to start helping others. I bet she'd be happy to let you be a guinea pig. I'd come too, just to lend a hand, some additional thoughts or tips."

"She's blind?" Kali asked.

"Almost completely."

Kali felt a tingle run through her. "I guess who better to learn from?"

"Wonderful." Alika turned back to her computer. "I'll contact her this afternoon and see if we can set something up in the next couple of days. Are you flexible?"

Kali stood. "Very."

KALI STEPPED OUTSIDE and searched for her phone to turn the volume back on. Three missed calls from Lincoln and a text. *Could you give me a call when you have a minute?*

Three missed calls. What could be important enough to warrant three calls?

Kali dialed Lincoln's number. He picked up on the first ring. "Hello?"

"Hi," Kali's voice was wary. Her gut twisted. "What is it? Is Theo—?"

"Theo's fine. I mean ... he's not with you?"

"I left him at Mrs. Martin's."

"Well, then I'm sure he's still there."

Kali's gut untwisted just slightly. "Okay, so, are you? What's—?"

"It's—" Lincoln sucked in a long draught of air, loud enough for Kali to hear through the line. "I don't even really know what it is yet. Can you come down to the police station?"

"The? What's going on?"

Another sigh. "Marvin. I don't know what exactly. They won't tell me much. I'm not family. I told them he doesn't really have family, but you're the closest thing, right?"

Kali hesitated. "I'm coming."

"Wait, where are—?"

Kali ended the call. Her chest tightened. Marvin in jail. Marvin trapped inside, in a cell, barred in. But she was jumping to conclusions. Maybe he was just in a room somewhere, waiting. But he'd be inside. He'd be without his cart. No matter the circumstance, he was trapped.

She ran in the direction of the police station, stumbled and screamed as she flew toward the pavement. She put her hands out in front of her and felt the thud of her body making contact with the ground. "Damn it!"

Tears sprang to her eyes as she lay on the pavement a moment, all the fear and frustration she'd felt while curled up on the street outside the Imperial Theatre coming back to her.

She pushed her hands against the ground and rose to her feet. Miraculously, beyond some surface scrapes on her hands and a knee that would probably be bruised tomorrow, she was fine.

Kali stood on the sidewalk, ignoring the buzzing in her bag and contemplating the best course of action. Lincoln knew she'd want to rush. And he knew what would happen if she did. She pulled out her phone just as the ringing ended. She swiped the screen open and debated calling him back. But if there was news, if Marvin was released, she wanted someone there for him.

Kali put in the number for Casino Taxi, hoping a driver was close. She texted Lincoln to say what she was doing and three minutes later was in the back seat of the cab, hands clenched, and on her way.

CHAPTER FORTY-TWO

A block from the station, Kali saw Marvin's cart toppled on the side of the road, its contents strewn onto the street. She bit her lip and willed the light they were approaching to turn green. When they pulled up in front of the large brick building housing the Halifax Regional Police Headquarters, she paid the cab driver and made her way up the police station steps, her hand firmly gripping the railings. When she opened the door, Lincoln was by her side almost instantly.

"Have you heard anything?" Kali asked before he could speak.

He shook his head and rubbed a hand through his hair. "Nothing. Nothing more anyway. I overheard two words. Assault and kidnapping. Neither makes sense. Did he assault someone? Did someone assault him? Why?"

Kali's brow furrowed. "The cart? He had a fight over someone who tried to steal his cart a couple of years ago. It wasn't pretty."

"But kidnapping?"

Kali shook her head. "No. Never." Unless ... could he have

snapped? He would never steal a child ... but if he thought it was his own? If he was confused, thinking it was Theo or Derek or Jason. If he'd lost sense of time ... or of reality?

Kali looked away. She couldn't even remember the last time she'd checked in on Marvin. It'd been weeks. She'd been so caught up in her own life, her own problems. It was before New York for sure ... Theo's birthday, perhaps? Almost a month ago. She'd abandoned him.

Lincoln's hand on her shoulder brought Kali back to focus. "Are you okay?"

Kali turned from him, she couldn't just stand there. "Yeah, I ... yes."

He gestured toward reception. "Maybe they'll tell you something."

She nodded and walked over to the desk, Lincoln one step behind her.

"Hi." An older woman looked up at Kali. "I'm Kali Johnson-Grant. I'm here to see about—"

"The homeless guy." The woman sent an annoyed glance at Lincoln.

"Marvin," said Kali. "His name is Mr. Marvin Grant, and I want to know where he is and what happened to him."

"You're his?"

"Daughter-in-law."

The woman shook her head. "We tried to contact your husband, but—" Kali put a hand up to stop the woman and turned to Lincoln. "I was supposed to be at Mrs. Martin's by now. I stayed late at my meeting and I meant to call her but ..." she hesitated and glanced at the woman, who didn't look impressed at Kali silencing her. "Could you go pick him up? Things have been so unstable. I don't want him worrying. Just pick him up and take him home and I'll call you if I need you or if I learn more or—"

"I can bring him here. You need—"

"No." Kali pushed out a smile. "I'm fine. I don't want to scare Theo. Just ... please."

Lincoln hesitated, looking like he wanted to fight her, wanted to stay. He took a step back. "You'll call me if—"

"I'll call you."

When he was out of earshot, Kali turned back to the woman. "I'm sorry. My son. He's four and—"

The woman sighed. "Do you have ID?"

Kali no longer had a driver's license, so she pulled out her health card. The woman looked at it then back at Kali.

"Picture ID?"

Kali dug in her wallet. She had her old student ID card, her credit card, her Video Difference membership.

"That's enough." The woman grabbed the credit card. Kali had been meaning to get her name changed for years. But it was one of those things that just always got forgotten. For once, procrastination seemed to help. The woman pushed the cards back to Kali. "He's a feisty one."

"Is he okay?"

"Let me call one of the arresting officers. They can do the explaining."

OFFICER GRAHAM TOOK Kali through a set of doors and down a hallway. She looked familiar. Kali had seen her around the neighbourhood—both in her uniform and out of it. The uniform made her look thirty pounds heavier, and her hair was pulled back in a tight bun, with wisps of curls only escaping at the nape of her neck.

She smiled at Kali, her face worn.

"Is he okay?" Kali asked as soon as they were seated.

Graham's brow furrowed. "What were you told?"

"Assault. Kidnapping. Neither of which makes any sense. But is Marvin okay? He's not ... he hates ... he can't be inside."

The officer nodded. "We figured that out the hard way. He's sedated now."

"But what—?"

"We're still trying to piece it together. The best we can figure, a toddler from a home day care over on Liverpool made her way out of the shoddily fenced back yard. Of course, when the day care worker realized the child was missing she searched and searched, then called us, crying that someone had kidnapped the kid—wanting to lay blame away from herself."

"But what—?" Kali shook her head and closed her mouth, letting the officer go on.

"The parents were called, a search began, and the father found Marvin walking down the street—to us, he said—with the child asleep in his cart."

Kali's brow furrowed. The officer, who seemed more exhausted as she spoke, continued. "It's always hard to get the stories straight. The father says when he took the child Marvin tried to stop him. They struggled. The mother showed up moments later and once the child was safely in her arms the father did what any father would—pulverized the man who'd stolen his kid. His words, not mine."

Kali put a hand to her mouth, her eyes filling. She could almost see it: Marvin confused, terrified, beaten.

"That's not right though, he wouldn't—" Unless he was confused ... but Officer Graham said he said he was heading to the station.

"Marvin's story is that when the man took the child she woke up and started screaming, the man didn't say anything about being the father—he looked rough, had just come from working on some sewer pipes or something—and Marvin thought he was stealing the child." She shook her head. "So he tried to get the child back from the man, to bring her here, to us."

Officer Graham leaned back in her seat. "The truth is usually somewhere in the middle. We checked out the fence. There was a loose spot where the child could have gotten out no problem. Should Marvin have picked her up? Maybe not. Especially considering his," she paused, "circumstances. But we think he was trying to do the right thing. And then the child got woken up suddenly, so she starts crying. Both parties are confused about what that means."

Kali nodded. "So now what?"

"We investigate further. The day care worker is adamant that the child was kidnapped. She says there's no way the child could have gotten out of that fence, and she only had her head turned for a moment, so even if the kid had she would have found her right away. Someone *had* to have stolen her away. She also says she's seen Marvin staring at the kids when she's taken them to the park or walked by him on the street, though she says she always crosses to the other side. Which may be true."

"No. He knows. I mean he loves kids but he never gets close. He makes a point not to go too near the parks. He knows what people think of him."

The Officer nodded. "Children are crafty and quick. My guess is the day care worker isn't as attentive as she claims.

The kid got out, and Marvin found her. My guess is he was trying to do good, just as he says." The Officer paused. "Look, I know Marvin. He does his best not to cause problems, and he's had a hard ..." she stopped again. "Beatrice was my teacher for a year. Jason was a year behind me in school. He's a sad man who's just trying his best to survive."

Kali pulled away from the Officer. "You knew Jason?"

"Not well, but yes. That whole situation with him and your husband ... and after Marvin had lost his wife the way he did and having to raise those boys alone." She shook her head. "Look, I think the best case scenario here would be for this all to be dropped. We convince the parents to drop any kidnapping charges, Marvin doesn't try to charge for assault. Chock it up as a misunderstanding."

Kali rubbed her forehead, trying to push away the pain building there. "Do you think that's possible? That they'll drop it?"

"I do. They're very on guard right now, but once they calm down, once we show them the fence ... and if they know the father isn't going to face assault charges." Officer Graham let out a breath. "Marvin wouldn't do well in court."

"No." Kali shook her head. "No."

"He was agitated when we brought him in. Crazy, almost."

"He can't be inside." Kali's voice shook. "It terrifies him. Especially if he can't leave."

"As I said, he's sedated now."

Kali stood and turned, paced a little, the Officer flashing in and out of her vision. "Can I see him? Is he here? Should he be in the hospital?"

"He refused. He's pretty badly beaten. We don't think

310

anything's broken, but a lot is bruised."

"I'm a nurse. I can—"

"You can see him. And if you can convince him to go to the hospital, that'd be great. We don't want a death from internal bleeding or brain damage on our hands."

Kali cringed as bile rose in her throat.

CHAPTER FORTY-THREE

fficer Graham led Kali down a hall. She stopped in front of a door that looked the same as the one they'd just left. Kali's hands shook as the officer pushed open the door. "Mr. Grant."

Kali stifled a gasp once inside. The room wasn't a cell, just a normal beige room with a table and chairs, but Kali knew to Marvin it might as well have been. One wrist was shackled to the table. He sat with his knees pulled up to his chest, the way a child would, hunched over, his arm resting on the table and his head on his arm.

"I've brought you a visitor." Officer Graham stepped farther into the room.

Kali followed.

"Mr. Grant."

Marvin's head stayed down. He sat motionless. If it weren't for the gentle rise and fall of his back beneath the layers of shaggy clothing, Kali would have been frightened he had left her too. She stepped closer. "Marvin?"

His head rose and there was no stifling Kali's gasp this time. She crouched beside him and rested a hand on his shoulder. He didn't flinch or jerk away like he usually would. He just stared at her as if trying to place her. "Sweetness?"

"Yeah, it's me." Kali bit her lip. She reached her hand up slowly and pushed the hood off of his face, revealing even more damage. His left eye was swollen and starting to discolour. Dried blood crusted below his nose, and his bottom lip was split and starting to swell. Kali took a deep breath, she had to stay calm, professional. She'd seen worse. Far worse. But not to her family. Not to Marvin.

"What did he do to you?"

She wanted to kill the man who'd done this. Show him what it was to be beaten. But she understood, too … if she'd found Theo in the cart of someone who looked like Marvin, thinking he'd been kidnapped … she may have done worse.

Marvin blinked twice before responding. "I was just trying to help the little girl. A sweet little girl like that, walking down the street on her own. It wasn't right." He shook his head multiple times. "I looked around for her people, but there was no one. I asked her where she came from but she just babbled. I was taking her here. I was trying to."

"I know. I know that's what you were trying to do. You wanted to protect her."

Marvin nodded. "She could have gotten hurt. Hit by a car or some bad man …" His voice started to shake. "I know I'm not pretty, but I'm not a bad man. I wouldn't hurt anyone."

"I know, Marvin." Kali wiped the tears from under his eyes, smudging dirt and blood across his cheek. She turned to Officer Graham and gestured to his cuffed wrist. "Is that really necessary?"

Officer Graham's brow furrowed. "It was." She stepped over and undid the shackle. Marvin pulled his arm into his centre like a turtle withdrawing into its shell. He rubbed his wrist.

"Are you hurting anywhere else, Marvin? Besides your face?"

He looked down like an ashamed child. "I'm okay, Sweetness."

"Marvin." Kali leaned closer. "Did he hit you anywhere else? Did you fall?" Silence. "Marvin?"

He nodded. "My ribs are a bit tender. My stomach doesn't feel so great." He glanced to Officer Graham. "But they gave me a shot of something. I don't like it. I don't like drugs."

"It was just a mild sedative," said Officer Graham.

Kali ignored her. "You could be hurt inside." She gave Marvin's shoulder a gentle rub. "We need to get you to the hospital, okay?"

He gave a side glance to the Officer. "They said I'm not allowed going." He whispered. "They arrested me. They made me leave my cart." He sat up straighter, as if suddenly realizing the enormity of the situation. "My cart. Sweetness, you need to go get my cart. Make sure no one steals it. Or all my things." He pushed her hand away. "Go do that now, Sweetness. Don't worry about me. Go get my cart."

Kali inhaled and made her voice firm. "You are more important than your cart. You need to get cleaned up. You need to go to the hospital."

Marvin shook his head.

"They will let you go to the hospital."

"With supervision," said Officer Graham.

Marvin shook his head. "No. No hospitals." He looked at Kali, pleading in his eyes. She knew he was thinking of Beatrice, of the way she begged to come home from the hospital, to spend her last days in her home with Marvin and the boys. Derek had told Kali this. Told her how, after Beatrice had passed, Marvin hated hospitals. When Jason got mono and Derek broke his leg he had stepped through those doors but acted like it was a step away from walking them into the morgue.

Kali shifted closer to Marvin. "I'm going to feel your torso, okay?"

He looked at her with slanted eyes.

She undid his bulky zipped sweater and trailed her fingers along his chest and over his ribs, noting where he winced. "Take a deep breath."

He gasped with the pain of it and Kali leaned back. "You need to go to the hospital. No fighting." She leaned in and spoke softly so Officer Graham couldn't hear. "I know I haven't been around, and I'm sorry for that." She paused. "But I need to know you're okay. With all that's going on, if I wake up tomorrow morning to learn you've died of internal bleeding I don't know how I'll cope." She held her hands on either side of Marvin's face, making him look at her. "Okay?"

He nodded.

Kali reached for his hand and helped him up. He seemed so small. Smaller than he'd ever seemed. He wrapped his arm around Kali's shoulder, resting his weight on her. Kali turned to the Officer. "We're ready now. Will you be escorting us?"

THREE HOURS LATER, Kali sat in an armchair in the ER employee lounge. She'd stayed with Marvin as a team of nurses cleaned him off. She'd waited outside as he was X-rayed. Three cracked ribs. Now he was in a drug-induced sleep as they waited for the results from the CT scan. The officer's sedation must have been wearing off and he'd flipped when they tried to get him on the scan machine. A second shot had calmed him, and now he was sleeping. Exactly what Kali wished she was doing. It was only nine-thirty at night, but she felt like it was three in the morning. Her whole body ached with the need to shut herself off from the world.

She'd called Lincoln shortly after arriving at the hospital and even that had drained her—telling him the whole story, right down to Marvin's cart on the side of the road, then the work of convincing him she was fine, of insisting she wanted him at home with Theo, not here with her. Now though, she wished she hadn't been so insistent. She longed for the feel of her hand wrapped in his or the weight of his arm draped across her shoulder.

The door creaked and Kali flicked her eyes open. Shelley stood before her, wearing a tired smile. "News?"

Shelley stepped forward. "No internal bleeding. Bruising. But no bleeding."

"Thank God." A lump of relief welled in Kali's throat. "How is he?"

"Still sleeping. With those ribs and the bruising he's going to be in pain for a while."

Kali nodded.

"You've got to convince him to come home with you, Kal. We'll keep him overnight but we'll have to discharge him in the morning."

Another nod. Could she convince him? Maybe if she kept him sedated. Not that she could do that ... Kali let her head fall into her hands. Her body seemed to weigh twice as much as usual. It ached.

"When it rains, it pours."

"Huh?" Kali looked to Shelley. She'd almost forgotten she was there.

Shelley made a non-specific gesture. "All you've been going through. And now this. You need to be taking care of yourself. Not an old man off his rocker."

"Shel—"

"I know. I know you love him. Heck, I love him too." She chuckled. "It's hard not to love such a sweet, harmless sad sack. But if his sad-sackness takes its toll on you, he's not so harmless anymore, is he?"

"He's family."

"Yeah." Shelley clenched her teeth. "About that. Family."

"No." Kali sat forward. "Just no."

"Kal—"

"I don't want to hear it." Kali stood. "How long will he be out for? I think I may go home. Try to get some sleep."

Shelley's expression softened. "Even after the drugs wear off, we're hoping he'll just sleep. Come back at nine."

Kali nodded and started to walk by Shelley but was pulled into her arms. She whispered against Kali's ear. "You don't have to be so strong all the time. If you need help, tell me." She pulled away. "Okay?"

Kali bit her lip, wishing she could understand why that came so hard. Why she didn't want to ask for help, why it just seemed easier to try to handle everything on her own? "I'm trying."

CHAPTER FORTY-FOUR

At eight-fifteen the next morning, Kali woke to the buzz of her phone. She reached for it, expecting the hospital. Instead, the CNIB number flashed on her screen. "Hello?"

"Oh, Kali!" Alika's voice sounded bright and alarmed. "I'm so sorry. Did I wake you? I know you've got a little guy so I thought ..." Her voice trailed off.

"Long night," said Kali. "Late night. But it's okay."

"Oh, okay. Good. Well, I just wanted to let you know that Madeleine is free this afternoon for a session from two to four."

"This afternoon?" Kali propped herself up in bed. "Is there another time? Maybe even the evening?"

"Oh, umm ..."

"It's just that my father-in-law, he, he's getting out of the hospital this morning and I'm not sure how much care he'll need."

"Ahh," Kali could almost hear Alika nodding, "well, I understand that then. Unfortunately, Madeleine is leaving to visit her sister tomorrow and will be gone for a few weeks. Of course, I can set you up with Casey—she's our Independent Living Skills staff member—when she gets back in two weeks. Will that work?"

It would. It was better than nothing. But uneasiness built in Kali's stomach. She wanted to do this now, to stop running from the life that was right in front of her. She held up her scraped palms and stared at them. She wanted a cane. No, she didn't *want* it, she needed it. And if she put it off, she didn't trust herself not to let fear and pride rule again. "I'll come today."

"Are you sure?"

"I'll figure it out. I'll come. Thank you for setting it up."

Silence travelled through the line. "Okay." Another pause. "If you can't, just let us know. That'll be no problem. Madeleine was planning to come in anyway so just ... by one-thirty. Let me know by one-thirty. You can just call this number."

They exchanged goodbyes and Kali swiped off the phone. She sat up fully, then thought she caught the wisp of a movement by the door. She turned. Theo's head was poking out. She waved her arm at him to come. He grinned and raced toward her, leaping onto the bed and into her arms. Kali wrapped her arms around him and nuzzled her face in his dreads. He pulled away and smiled at her. "You miss me?"

He nodded.

"I missed you more!" She squeezed him again. "Did you have fun with Lincoln last night?"

Another nod.

"Well, that's good." Kali smiled and caressed her hand along his chin. "Were you good?"

Theo gave a silent chuckle and put his hands palm down

under his chin, giving an angelic smile. Kali laughed. She wasn't sure where he'd picked this move up, but he'd been doing it ever since she and Lincoln came back from New York.

"That's my boy."

Theo leaned back, his face twisted in what looked like concern. He opened his mouth, closed it, then opened it again. "Grampie?"

"Oh," Kali shifted him in front of her, "what did Lincoln tell you?"

Theo tapped his chin. "Grampie need help." He paused. "So you help him."

Kali nodded. "That's right."

"He okay now?"

Kali tilted her head back and forth. "Not okay. Not yet. But better than yesterday." She took a breath. "We're going to see if we can get him to stay with us for a while, so we can take care of him."

Theo pointed to his chest.

"Yep. You too. We can all take care of him."

Theo puffed up his chest this time. He grinned. Kali slipped off of the bed and stood on the cold hardwood. She'd need to get a rug for this room. The mornings were getting chillier as the days sank deeper into fall. She stretched then turned back to Theo. "You know what, I have to go pick up Grampie at the hospital—"

Theo's eyes widened.

"And I bet if you came with me, you could help convince him to stay with us. Maybe you could even ask him or tell him you want him to, with your words."

Theo looked uncertain.

"He's never heard you speak before. I bet that would make him so excited and make him feel so special!"

Theo's brow furrowed then relaxed as he nodded.

"All right." Relief washed through Kali. If anyone had a chance of convincing Marvin to stay with them, it would be Theo. She shooed Theo out of the room so she could change and walked into the kitchen a few minutes later to the smell of eggs and toast.

"Hey." Lincoln turned to her. She could see the desire in his eyes to pull her into him, and the restraint. She stepped into his arms then looked up to see the surprise and pleasure on his face. He gave her a squeeze and she stepped away. "How are you? How's Marvin?"

Kali sat at the table and smiled her thanks when Lincoln set a plate down in front of her. "I'm pretty tired." She fought to keep her voice steady. "That man—" she glanced to Theo. "It wasn't pretty." She turned her gaze to Theo. "You eat already?"

He nodded.

"Go get dressed, please."

Theo looked between Lincoln and Kali. He was getting keener by the day. She could tell he knew the request had more to do with getting him out of the room than with the need for him to be clothed.

"Now, please."

He turned with a huff and slowly made his way down the hall. Lincoln slid into the seat across from Kali.

"Three cracked ribs. Internal bruising. No bleeding. His face looks like he's been in a fist fight. Though I don't think Marvin did much fighting back."

Lincoln swallowed. "He stayed in the hospital?"

"Just for the night. I'm heading over there shortly." She hesitated. "Can he—"

"Stay here? Absolutely." Lincoln took a swig of his coffee. "I'll take the couch and he can have my room."

"No." Kali reached an arm out. "I'll take the couch."

"Not happening." Lincoln stood and turned to the dishes in the sink. "You'll be taking care of him. You have your own issues. That fatigue. This isn't even a discussion."

Kali took several bites of egg on toast. It was good. Simple, but good. Her chest seemed to swell as she watched Lincoln wash the dishes. "Thank you."

He turned and smiled. "You're welcome."

She glanced at the clock over the oven. "Shouldn't you be at work?"

"Took the day off. I wasn't sure ... well, what the deal was."

Kali nodded. She hesitated as Lincoln turned back to the sink. Her plan was to call Mrs. Martin, see if she'd come over for two hours to watch Theo and Marvin, but at least Marvin knew Lincoln. At least ... "Can I ask something else?"

Lincoln turned, the drying towel in his hands.

"I have a meeting this afternoon. Two to four. I know it's asking a lot. But could you stay with Theo and Marvin? I'll reschedule it if I have to but—"

"What kind of meeting?"

More hesitation. Why? Lincoln would be happy. Thrilled. "CNIB." Kali gave a little chuckle. "I may just get my cane."

Lincoln's eyes widened.

"And learn some more skills. Work on acceptance."

He smiled. "You got it."

CHAPTER FORTY-FIVE

Lincoln leaned against the counter and watched Kali eat. She looked exhausted, but it didn't fade her beauty. If anything, she seemed more beautiful. After all she'd been through, all she was still going through, it amazed him she was still capable of giving so much to Marvin. She hadn't even hesitated at the task of taking him in.

And it would be a task. Lincoln recalled the night she'd gotten Marvin into her apartment to tell him about her tumour—the way he'd paced the room, beaten his head, how unhinged he seemed. It wasn't just the news of the tumour, he knew, it was being under a roof, contained.

She looked up and Lincoln turned back to the dishes. He finished washing and drying the last two then rinsed the sink. Now that things were progressing with him and Kali, he wanted them to progress faster, to know she was here because she wanted to be, not out of necessity. He had hardly thought about his tree house the past few days, he still wanted to finish, still would finish. But his life felt here. He turned again, but the kitchen was empty.

Kali was going to the CNIB. That was good. Of course it

was good. And he wanted that for her. Wanted her to stop living in fear, feeling like this diagnosis made her less. But if she regained her independence, if she went back to work or found a new job, if, once the inflammation from the treatment eased, she regained much of the vision she'd lost, would she still want him?

Lincoln crossed to the living room and sank into the couch, waiting. That's what it felt like his life was now. Waiting for Kali to make the next move. Waiting for her to give him some assurance that things had changed, that they weren't just roommates.

She entered the living room, Theo at her side. Lincoln stood. "You ready?" he asked.

She wore a question on her face, and it was like a stab to Lincoln's heart. She didn't expect he'd take her, that he'd see it as just as much his responsibility as hers. He wanted her to expect it.

"I'm driving you." Lincoln turned to the door before she could protest, but she did anyway.

"That's not necess—"

"Think you'll get Marvin on a bus? Or have him walk home with three cracked ribs? You could try a taxi, but he knows me, knows my truck."

She paused. "If it's no trouble."

"Nothing else I have to do today." He held the door and watched her pass through it, how she concentrated on each step, her hand tight on the railing. Once through the building's door, down the next set of steps, and onto the sidewalk, she turned to him. "You haven't been to the lot since we've been back, have you?"

"Nope."

"I don't want you to think you have to be here all the time. I can manage."

He took a breath. "I'll go when I want to go. Besides, I work most days."

"Most." She opened the truck door to let Theo inside. "Not all." Kali hesitated then stepped to the back of the truck. She stared at the tarp covering the bed. Lincoln watched her. She looked at him, her eyes widening then softening. "Is ..."

Lincoln nodded and stepped toward her. "Couldn't just leave it on the side of the road."

"But when?"

"Theo and I took a little outing after you called."

She exhaled. A hand rose to cover her mouth. She shook her head.

"Maybe it would have been better if I'd left it. Maybe it's enabling or—"

"No. Thank you. Knowing it's safe, that will make things better for him." Kali paused, staring at the tarp. "I can't believe you thought of it. I thought of it last night but knew I couldn't ..." Her voice trailed off.

"Well," Lincoln pointed to his watch, "we better get going." He walked to the driver's side. Of course he thought of the cart. How could he not think of the cart? Marvin lived and breathed for that thing. It'd be like forgetting a child's security blanket ... but worse.

He stepped into the seat. Why was it bothering him so much today, this fear that she wouldn't need him anymore? They had weeks still before she'd learn the result of the treatment. And he wanted it to be great news. Wonderful news. She climbed into the passenger seat, buckled her seatbelt, and smiled. He just didn't want her to leave him.

Kali crouched in front of Theo before they entered Marvin's hospital room. She smoothed a hand along the side of his face and whispered words Lincoln couldn't hear. Preparing him, he assumed. Letting him know they may not be walking in to see the grandfather he expected. Kali opened the door and when Lincoln stepped in behind her, he felt like he could have used some preparation too.

Without his layers of clothing, Marvin looked small in the bed. His face was wan—the parts of it that weren't swollen or bruised, anyway. His eyes seemed lacklustre. A nurse stepped to Kali. She spoke under her breath but loud enough for Lincoln to hear. "We had to sedate him again this morning. Less though. The doctor's prescribed some pills for you. Milder. He recommends you use them sparingly. Painkillers too. It's all written out."

Kali nodded her thanks and stepped toward Marvin, Theo in front of her.

"Hey, Sweetness." Marvin smiled up at her then looked to Theo. "Little man."

Theo put his hands up on the edge of the bed, trying to get closer. Marvin reached his hand down and Theo clasped it, his eyes wide and concerned.

"How you feeling this morning?" asked Kali.

Marvin gave his head a little shake. "They still won't let me leave."

"You can come home with me," said Kali as Marvin shook his head. "No choice, I'm afraid. It's either that or back to the police station. Under their custody."

Marvin's brows furrowed.

"They're hoping there won't be a trial. That this can be

326

figured out without any of that." She hesitated. "If you don't press charges ..."

"No. No." Marvin seemed to look to his feet. "It was the girl's father?" He turned to Kali who nodded. "All a misunderstanding then, wasn't it?"

"Seems so," said Kali.

"Well, then." Marvin looked away again. The room was silent except for the nurse slipping out. "So maybe we can just figure that out quick. I don't make problems for him, he and his wife don't make problems for me. And I can just—"

Kali nudged Theo forward.

"Come home."

Marvin turned his head.

"With us." Theo's voice was soft and sweet and gaining in confidence. "Come home with us, Grampie. We take care of you."

Marvin's lip trembled. He looked to Kali then Theo, his mouth open, then back to Theo.

"Okay?" The boy asked with a smile. He squeezed Marvin's hand. "We make you better."

Marvin stared at the boy, his eyes glistening, and nodded.

He turned to Kali, the tenderness vanishing from his eyes. "My cart, my—"

"Lincoln got it," said Kali. "He picked it up last night. It's safe in his truck. All covered up." She paused. "It'll be waiting for you when you're ready for it. When you're better."

Marvin let out a sigh. He smiled at Theo then turned his gaze back to Kali. "I need clothes. They took my clothes."

Kali laughed. "I'll get them back. I have to warn you though, they've been cleaned."

Marvin twisted his face then let out a little laugh before

gripping his ribs. "I guess that's all right." He winked at Theo. "It was probably time."

CHAPTER FORTY-SIX

Kali felt torn as she stood in front of the entrance to the CNIB. The morning had gone well. Marvin had walked the stairs to Lincoln's apartment with resistance but no fight. He'd protested about being set up in Lincoln's room, and eventually a compromise was made. He'd take the room during the night but be set up on one of the couches during the day so if Lincoln wanted privacy he could have it.

Kali tried to insist it wasn't practical. Marvin would need his sleep. If they were talking or cooking or Theo was playing it would disturb him. But he could sleep anywhere, he said, which, she imagined, must be true. Besides, he'd said with a smile. If he had to be there, under a roof, he wanted to see them and hear them. He didn't want to be stuck in a room alone.

He was a good patient. He took his meds when told. He ate when food was brought to him. He allowed Lincoln to help him to and from the bathroom. He passed his time watching Theo race cars around the make-shift track Lincoln had designed months ago. He called out suggestions and asked questions then slipped into sleep without warning.

So it was fine. He was fine. Kali needed to spend time on her. She looked at her palms again and noted the slight throb in her knee. She needed to accept that for now at least, and maybe forever, her life had changed.

"KALI, HELLO!" ALIKA greeted Kali with a warm smile as she stepped through the door. "I believe you and Madeleine have met once before? At your initial meeting?"

Kali nodded then remembered Madeleine wouldn't be able to see it. "Yes. Well, we didn't exactly meet, but she shared her story."

Madeleine shifted her head to the sound of Kali's voice and reached her hand out. Kali grasped it. "Morning, sweetheart." Madeleine's voice had a gentle lilt to it. "You ready to be my guinea pig?"

Kali chuckled back, hoping the hesitancy didn't sound in her voice. "Absolutely."

Alika held out her arm for Madeleine to grasp, and Kali watched as the two started down the hall. Alika glanced back to Kali. "This was meant to be a training session for Madeleine as well, so we'll go over some skills that may not be as applicable to you since you still have direct vision. But it won't hurt you to know these things."

Alika didn't say, 'In case,' but Kali could hear the words anyway. She dismissed them, but her chest still tightened. There may be an 'in case' for her, but hopefully not for years. Hopefully not ever.

The session started with Madeleine talking of practicalities. Some of which applied to Kali—wear reflective clothing at night to make others more aware of you. Buy strips to put on your jacket, or slip on a vest. Not necessarily fashionable, but your life is more important than fashion—and those that didn't, yet, such as familiarizing herself with the size and shapes of coins and bills. Apparently different coins had different edges, and all bills had braille on them.

She talked about placing raised beads on the stove for low, medium, and high heat, labelling cans and the various methods to do so. She continued with putting food in a cold oven and on a cold burner and turning both off before removing the food.

She gave Kali information on Canada Pension and Social assistance that would have made her earlier research and applications much easier and talked about another session she could take on career exploration and workplace accommodation assessments. Kali made a mental note to find out more about this.

"The most important thing," said Madeleine, "is to work with what you have today. Be thankful for what you have today."

Kali stared at Madeleine, at her smile. Overwhelm filled her. The tips were helpful. Wonderful. But they revealed so much of what Kali was still able to do, what may be taken from her one day. "How did you get through it?"

Madeleine turned to Kali's voice. "Through it?" That soft smile. "Darling, there's no getting through it. You just live it. Every day."

Kali swallowed. "Through the anger then? The fear?"

Madeleine sighed. "I cried for a few days." She paused. "Maybe more like a few weeks, and then I realized I couldn't cry anymore because I couldn't see the tears I was crying. It's just a physical thing. Sight. Tears." She was silent so long Kali wondered if she was going to speak again. "The fear. The anger. Those are things we can control; fight. The sight, we're powerless there. But how we view that loss, that's where strength matters. That's where we can fight each day."

Kali remembered Madeleine's words from the first meeting she'd went to, words she'd dismissed: *I can get up in the morning and have a day that's restful, peaceful, full of thanks and joy for what I still have, or I can have a day that's restless, agitated, bitter.*

Too many of Kali's days had been the latter.

Madeleine felt for a nearby chair, pulled it out, and settled herself down. Kali followed suit with a glance to Alika, who was already seated, observing the session. "The more we are grateful, the more we'll appreciate and begin to see the things we're given. The things we already have." Madeleine's laugh tinkled through the room. "It sounds cheesy, doesn't it? Like a made-for-TV holiday special." Her tone sobered. "But it's true."

"But how do you do that? Be grateful." Kali leaned forward. "This sucks. It's scary. It's infuriating. I'm not good at being helpless."

"But you're not helpless." Madeleine leaned back in her chair. "Not at all. Do you think I'm helpless?"

Kali opened her mouth. She hesitated. "No."

Another laugh. "I need help. More help than I used to, but no, I'm not helpless. And neither are you. As long as we can move and speak and think, we won't be." Madeleine folded her hands in front of her on the desk. "Peace is an inside job. No one can give you that. And no one can take it away. It's all on you."

Madeleine looked in the direction of Alika. "Should we

start some cane work? I'll definitely need your assistance with this section."

Alika stood. "You wanted an identification cane, is that right?"

Kali nodded then glanced to Madeleine. "Yes."

"We can get you started today. It takes time and practice for full proficiency and Casey is the best trainer we have, so we'll get you in for some sessions with her once she's back from vacation, but you should be able to learn enough for simple identification today and a little help with curbs and steps. The theory at least." Alika laughed. She reached into her bag and pulled out two folded up white canes. "First lesson," Alika flipped the cane out and Kali watched as it seemed to magically form into a long stick, "getting it open."

Kali mimicked the motion and laughed as the stick formed in front of her.

"Now hold on and position the cane with your hand centred in front of your body."

Kali did.

"With a gentle grasp, and keeping your arm still, tap it in an arc in front of you. When your right foot is forward, hold the stick to the left and vice versa."

Kali looked up with uncertainty.

"It'll feel simple soon enough," said Madeleine. She grinned. "Here, watch a pro." She moved around the room, shifting out of the way of a table and then a potted plant with one tap of the cane.

Kali knew what sight she had gave her a huge advantage, but when they left the room and moved to steps and curbs, nervousness tightened her limbs.

"It'll take time," said Alika, "and Casey does teach it better than any of us. For now, it will be a reminder not to rush ahead. To be cautious. And an identifier, to help others know you may need a little more time or consideration."

An identifier. Kali looked at the cane. A label.

After Kali practiced for ten to fifteen minutes, Madeleine turned to Kali's general direction. "Well, I think that's enough for today." She looked slightly past Kali. "I hope I did well. This was certainly more interesting, teaching a real student, rather than just Casey or Alika."

"You did great," said Kali. "It was so helpful."

Madeleine stepped forward and reached her arm out. Kali met it, and the woman slid her hand up to squeeze Kali's shoulder. It almost seemed like she was making eye contact with Kali this time. Almost. She was looking more at Kali's nose than her eyes. "It takes time. Be patient with yourself." She released Kali's arm. "Well, I'm off to the doctor." She grinned. "I'll see what tricks I can play on him today."

"Oh, give the man a break." Alika shook her head as Madeleine raised an arm in farewell and left the room.

Kali folded up her cane and held it out to Alika.

She raised her hands as if pushing it away. "That's yours now."

Kali looked at it. "Oh?"

Alika let several breaths pass. "You don't have to use it, but it would be good to practice."

"Sure, of course." Kali's gaze stayed on the cane. She flipped it open again and stared at it.

"You've been struggling with this, haven't you?"

Kali looked to Alika. "Well, you said it takes a while to get the hang of it."

"No, I mean with your diagnosis. Your fading vision."

Kali looked to the ceiling. Struggling? She stifled a laugh.

"Silly question. I know." Alika paused. "But you seem to be doing better."

Kali tapped the cane in front of her. She shrugged.

"You know," said Alika. "I learn a lot from the people I work with. It sounds cliché, but sometimes I think they give me more than I give them."

"Madeleine seems like she has some wisdom."

"That she does." Alika smiled more to herself than to Kali. "One day she told me, and I'll never forget it, that within her blindness was a gift. She said it took her a while to realize that, but once she did, it changed everything."

Kali's chest tightened.

"It taught her to be present. To live in the moment. You know how she used to do all that travelling, missionary work, always busy, always doing something?"

Kali nodded.

"Well, she told me one day that being present, living in the moment, is just as important to her now as all that busyness used to be. That it does more. And not just for herself, but for others. It taught her to slow down. To be present for and with other people." Alika paused and Kali turned to look at her. "Maybe you can't see your son as well as you used to. And that's gotta be hard. But maybe because of this, you'll always be able to see him better. You won't be allowed to be so busy. You're a single mom, working as a nurse?"

Kali rubbed her arm. "Was working."

Alika smiled. "You will be again. But you're going to be forced to slow down now. Maybe forever. Which will allow you to see him, hear him, be more present for him than perhaps you ever were before."

Kali bit her lip. Hear him? She tried to remember if she'd mentioned the mutism to Alika, the fact that, slowly, Theo was starting to talk. No, definitely not.

"That's a gift, Kali, being able to give your presence to someone." Alika raised her shoulders and offered another smile. "Easy for me to say, I know, when I'm not going through what you're going through. But I've worked with enough people going through similar situations to know. It's a gift. Or it can be, if you let it."

Kali tapped the cane again. A gift. She was just starting to accept, to let go of some of the raging anger, to climb out of the dark hole she'd been living in for the past months. It seemed a stretch to be thankful. But she had seen it already: the way she watched Theo more. The way she focused on everyone and everything more. She had to, when distractions were literally cut away from her vision.

Kali motioned to pass by Alika. "I should be getting home."

Alika rested a hand on Kali's shoulder. "Don't be a stranger."

CHAPTER FORTY-SEVEN

Kali hesitated outside the doors of the CNIB. She stared at the spot she'd face-planted the day before. She had folded up the cane after leaving Alika and slipped it into her satchel, but now she held it in her hand.

She didn't need it. Not right now. Not here. She could take it slow, keep an eye out for curbs and dips in the sidewalk. She knew this area—decently well, anyway. She knew the way home.

But she was tired of falling, and proficiency would take practice. Kali looked up and down the street, a hollow pressure rising in her throat. She released the cane and watched it form to its full length like magic. Theo would love that. She positioned it in her hand the way she'd learned and slowly walked forward, tapping side to side.

Her hand shook and her lip trembled. She bit it. She could see. She could still see. She squeezed her eyes shut, resisting the tear that fought to escape. She walked on. Tap, tap, tap, tap. *You just live it*, Madeleine had said. *Every day*. So that's what she was doing: Living it. Accepting that her life had changed, so she had better change with it.

She let out a ragged breath and looked side to side. She didn't want to live it. She wanted to hide.

What was worse? Scraped hands and bumped knees or this—feeling so exposed?

Kali walked on, her gaze averted from the people who approached then walked past her in a wide arc.

She stepped and tapped, stepped and tapped, resisting the urge to put the cane away.

She stood at a crosswalk, listening the way Madeleine had said, using her ears as well as her eyes, before turning to look each way. She stepped out. Tap, tap, tap.

She was walking faster; that was something. The curb had been less of a surprise than usual.

"Kali?"

Kali gulped. She heard the voice to her left, knew, just months ago, she would have seen the speaker. Kali turned and smiled.

"God, it's true."

The woman, a former co-worker from the ER, someone Kali was friendly with but wouldn't call a friend, stood with her hand over her mouth.

"I'd heard, but ..." She shook her head again. "Is there anything I can do to help?"

"I'm fine." Kali kept her smile on, though it tightened.

"You're not fine." The woman shook her head again. "My car's just up the road. I can drive you somewhere or—"

"I'm fine, really." That hollow feeling in Kali's throat intensified. "This is just ..." she stammered. "This is just to help. I can still see ... some."

"Right, of course. I didn't mean ..." The woman let out a high-pitched laughed. "We're thinking of you. All of us. And

I heard your father-in-law ..."

"He's doing fine." Kali swallowed.

"Well," the woman shifted, wearing her discomfort like a cloak. "Nice seeing you, I mean, running into, or," another laugh, "you know what I mean, right?"

"I know." Kali walked on, imagining the woman following her with her eyes. Pitying her.

But was that so wrong, when Kali pitied herself? Poor Kali. Poor, unfortunate Kali.

Tap, tap, tap.

But she wasn't helpless. She didn't need help getting home. *Peace is an inside job.*

Kali took a deep breath and walked on. Her mind travelled back to Madeleine. A teacher. A good teacher. Kali could teach, or counsel. She was a damn good nurse and if the assisted technology didn't help, she could still teach others. She would teach others—theory, bedside manner. She wasn't done. This wouldn't finish her.

She approached the next street. Stop. Listen. Turn, turn. Tap, tap, tap.

She upped her pace.

One lesson and she'd gone from shuffling along the street in fear to walking faster than she'd walked in weeks.

Could she view her blindness as a gift? Probably not. Not yet. Maybe not ever. But already she could see how good could come from it. Alika was right. She was seeing Theo more. Tuning-in in a way the hecticness of her life had never really allowed. And she could deepen that more, if she focused on it. She had the time.

And Marvin. Would she have taken the time off of work to care for if she was working at Westwood? Maybe, maybe not, but if she had she would have resented it, feared how it would affect her chances of staying on at the job.

Instead, she was there for him, present for him, and couldn't believe how well he was doing under a roof, how little he looked at the door. It had only been a day, but still, she was sure a part of it was him knowing he was wanted and not a burden. If she'd had to take time off from Westwood, he would have been a burden.

She couldn't deny it. She wanted her upcoming tests with the radiation oncologist and neuro-ophthalmologist to reveal improvement, to indicate a miracle … but if it didn't her life wouldn't be over. It'd just be a different life than the one she'd envisioned.

She could never have imagined this, any of it. Lincoln. The circumstances that brought them together.

Kali turned to cross another street. Her breath caught.

Derek?

It was his broad shoulders and massive arms, but bigger than she remembered. The curve of his shaved head, the rise of his nose. She only saw the man's profile before an oncoming bus blocked him from view. It slowed. Stopped. Her pulse raced. She stood, motionless. It wasn't him. It was just someone who looked like him. Exactly like him, who stood like him...

It couldn't be him.

Derek was gone and he wasn't coming back. He'd said as much. He'd promised. She could feel every beat of her heart, her gaze focused on the bus. Two and a half years without a word. Almost five years of abandonment. He wouldn't … he couldn't.

It was the stress, the overwhelm of the past weeks, the

mention of him at the police station the other night. Kali needed to get home, forget about this. Home to Theo and Marvin. Home to Lincoln, who hadn't abandoned her when things got rough.

But she couldn't move. What if it *was* him?

The bus pulled away, leaving an empty sidewalk. Kali's stomach flipped. This was nothing; her eyes playing tricks on her. It couldn't have been Derek. It was just a man who looked like him. Exactly like him.

THANK YOU!

Hello,

I hope you enjoyed *What We See*.

Lincoln and Kali's story isn't over. Book Three in the *Behind Our Lives Trilogy* will release in the winter of 2017/2018. While you're waiting for the rest of the story, I'd greatly appreciate it if you took the time to leave a review of *What We See*. Reviews are incredibly important, especially for independent authors like myself. They let other readers know whether or not it's worth taking a chance on an author and helps us get marketing deals, which can extend our reach and mean we're able to provide you stories for years to come! Head over to your favourite retailer and/or Goodreads to leave your review today.

To order your copy of Book Three in the *Behind Our Lives Trilogy* visit

http://www.charlenecarr.com/Book3Trilogy

Thank you for taking the time to read *What We See!*

All the best,

Charlene Carr

ACKNOWLEDGEMENTS

A huge thank you to my husband for constantly supporting my work. To my mother, for her keen eye on the many versions and revisions - this would be an entirely different process without you! To my beta readers, who read my works in their early form, with metaphorical bloomers showing - your feedback is invaluable.

I would also like to thank the clients and staff of the CNIB St. John's. Sylvia Staples, Jeana Bowen, Kelly Picco, and Kim Thistle-Murphy; thank you for sharing your experiences with vision loss and allowing me to draw from your words to create authenticity. You opened a window to a world I otherwise would have had to create from imagination. Kathleen May, Cindy Antle, and Lynsey Soper, thank you for opening the doors of the CNIB and educating me on the services your organization offers. I so appreciate your generosity with your time.

Thanks, as well, to Dr. Linda Magnusson and Dr. Teri Stuckless for your medical consultation and your enthusiasm for helping my work be as realistic as possible. If anything in the story does not make sense medically, that is wholly based on my lack of attention to detail or failure to ask the right questions. Your help and generosity have been a gift.

Finally, thank you to my readers. You're the reason I do this. You give me the motivation to keep on. I hope this story has given you hours of enjoyment.

ABOUT THE AUTHOR

Charlene Carr is a lover of words. Pursuing this life-long obsession, she studied literature in university, attaining both a BA and MA in English. Still craving more, she attained a degree in Journalism. After travelling the globe for several years and working as a freelance writer, editor, and facilitator she decided the time had come to focus on her true love - novel writing. She's loving every minute of it ... well, almost every minute. Some days her characters fight to have the story their way. (And they're almost always right!)

Charlene lives in St. John's, Newfoundland and loves exploring the amazing coastline of her harbour town, dancing up a storm, and using her husband as a guinea pig for the healthy, yummy recipes she creates!

Charlene's first series, *A New Start*, is Women's Fiction full of thought, heart, and hope.

If you would like the first two books in her Women's Fiction series for free, sign up for her mailing list at: www.charlenecarr.com/freebooks

44121539R00214

Made in the USA
Lexington, KY
07 July 2019